The Island

MIA SILVERTON

Published by 3 Powers Freedom, LLC
www.miasilverton.com
ISBN-13: 978-0-9991026-0-2 Ebook

ISBN-13: 978-0-9991026-1-9 Paperback
Printed in The United States Of America

To my children, Riley and Ian. You both are the best, brightest and most beautiful lights in my life.

PART 1
Resonance

"It's impossible," said pride.
"It's risky," said experience.
"It's pointless," said reason.
"Give it a try," whispered the heart.
- Unknown Artist

Chapter 1

"Until you can deliver yourself in an authentic way, *no one* will buy what you are trying to sell."

He couldn't say the seminar on branding was something he had been looking forward to, since he had a love/hate relationship with electronic devices—phones and communication gadgets in general—that were specifically designed to suck a human being away from actual eye-to-eye interaction. Brody Miller felt a little bit old-fashioned, but he thought that if you were going to spend time around other people, you should give them the honor of your full attention. In a crowd full of people, who were supposed to be listening, a quick glance around showed at least seventy percent of them were fiddling away on their phones.

Maybe they were taking notes…

At the studio's request, he was attending the seminar with many of the people he worked with on the show. The objective was to tap into what the "social media expert and branding ambassador" had to say in order to learn how to promote their show better. At least the powers that be had done their research well and brought in someone magnetic enough to hold their attention, which was a difficult thing to do in a large crowd.

The redheaded dynamo spoke with confidence, wit, and

enough well-placed humor that even Brody had to acknowl-edge some of her talking points—while angling his head to admire the length of leg showcased in powerhouse heels with wraparound ankle straps. For such a petite woman, that mile of leg was worth taking a moment to look at. The rest of her wasn't bad either. But her confidence was more at-tractive than anything, he thought, as she finished another point, referring to the example on the display, that left them laughing.

Chase leaned over. "What do you think?"

Chase was the head producer on his show, while Brody held the coveted position of head actor. He never thought of it that way though. Brody thought he was merely one part of an ensemble of highly talented people he was fortunate enough to work with. It took all of them together to make the show a success. An inflated ego only worked well in re-ality television.

"I think she's good. Seems to know what she's talking about," Brody answered.

"Good. Then maybe you can tweet or post something more than once a month."

A sound somewhere between a snort and a hmm was all Chase got in return. Just because he was attending a semi-nar didn't mean Brody was about to change his habits.

"The show is top-rated with or without me blasting out my thoughts every two seconds. No one cares what the hell I had for breakfast," Brody said, keeping his voice low.

Chase's muttered, "Bullshit," meant that their conversa-tion would continue once they were alone, and Brody didn't miss how the speaker paused briefly to look in their direc-tion even though she kept talking without a hitch. Feeling as though he was breaking his own code, Brody shut up and paid attention.

Ten minutes later, the talk ended to a standing ovation, and he stood to join in the applause.

"Come on. You can meet her at the cocktail hour. Maybe we can arrange private coaching for your stubborn ass," Chase joked.

Brody laughed good-naturedly as he followed his friend. "You'll be renegotiating my salary if you want that worked in."

Their easy ribbing had gone on for years, since they were boys, and was something only good friends or brothers got away with. They fought, joked, and laughed as much as they hung out. Although these days, they play-fought much, much less than when they were boys. As kids, they'd fought every enemy possible, from invading bandits to space aliens in Southern Texas. The slight bend in Chase's nose was from when they'd both taken exception to a middle school bully terrorizing a couple of girls. The two of them had won that battle and celebrated in detention afterward, broken nose and all.

Cassidy "Cassie" Rhone stepped off the stage, riding the thrill of another speech gone well, and was greeted by a stream of well-wishers offering congratulations and questions. The post-speech meet-and-greets were one of her favorite parts of speaking, since they gave her a chance to hear what had resonated with the attendees and how charged up they were to make changes in their businesses.

Forty minutes and many pictures later, the crowd thinned out, and she was almost knocked over by an enthusiastic greeting from Anna.

"You were so amazing. I can't wait to incorporate some of this into promoting my studio," Anna gushed.

Anna Drayon was a good friend, full time yoga master, and owner of one of the best studios in Atlanta, called Namaste. The two had met on a yoga retreat years earlier and stayed close ever since. This, however, was the first time Anna had ever attended one of Cassie's seminars. Arranging the extra ticket for her friend had been worth it when Cassie saw Anna's shining happy face in an audience of over one thousand. The fact that Cassie's seminars were steadily growing in demand was a point of personal pride. She and her partner, Nathan, were building something unique and incredible.

"I really appreciate you coming to listen. It's not often I have a friend in the crowd with all the traveling I do."

"Tell me about it. Sometimes I don't know why you even bother keeping an apartment. You could just room with Nathan and save the cash for the few days a month that you're home."

"Because three is a complete and utter crowd since you introduced him to Philip. Our happily married couple does not need a house guest to ruin their honeymoon bliss. Are you coming to the cocktail hour reception? My plus one tonight," Cassie asked on a laugh.

One of the networks in Hollywood had been the major sponsor for this particular seminar, primarily because they wanted access for the crew and cast of a few of their shows, which were produced here in Atlanta. In any event, the sponsor had the option to request her attendance at an after party, which was where Cassie was heading next.

"I'm in. Let's go see who's hot and who we can get you to meet," Anna said, slipping her arm around Cassie's.

"Must we always go there?" She sighed. "I don't have the time nor the desire to meet anyone. Besides this is a net-working event, not a happy hour. I'm working."

"All work and no play, Miss Cassidy Rhone. The motto you live and die by. So sad." Anna tsked-tsked on the way out the door.

One thing Cassie could say about the studio was that they had spared no expense for this particular event. By booking out a local popular restaurant for the after party, they had gone above and beyond. The food had been amazing and her conversations with the studio heads positive.

But now that tables had been cleared, the bar and dance area were lively with people and the band hired to keep the fun rolling. At this point, she'd spoken with more people than she could remember and wanted nothing more than to have Anna take her home so she could finally get out of the heels that were killing her feet. But when a company paid top dollar for your time, you smiled and gave it with style. Sleep could always be had at some point.

Anna was at the bar, refilling their drinks, while Cassie stood by a cocktail table, chatting with a young woman who had another question. One glance showed Cassie that Anna had also met someone, and Cassie knew from experience that the refill would now take a while. Anna always saw the best and brightest light in each person she met, and she loved to connect in that spirit of giving.

Cassie finished answering the woman's question, after a thank you and another picture, the admirer walked off. Since no one else was around at the moment, Cassie pulled out her phone to quickly check messages, her foot tapping along with the music. She wished she could step out and let go. She adored dancing, and years of lessons left her restless to move. If Nathan were here, they would own that dance floor.

"First I've seen you alone all night. You look like you could use a new drink?" a deep male voice offered, and Cassie looked up.

And up. Higher, to the man who had spoken. He had to be a handful of inches over six feet tall since, even in heels, the top of her head just met his shoulder. Sometimes she hated being only five foot two.

"I'm good actually. My friend is taking care of that, but thanks," she said automatically, offering a careful smile and going back to her phone.

"Would that be the one with the honey colored hair in the green dress at the bar?" he asked with a slow drawl Cassie couldn't place as he pointed with his glass toward Anna.

"It would be. Why?" Cassie said with a lift of her brow.

The guy only gave a low laugh and grinned. The lopsided kind that seemed to go well with his dark brown tousled hair and the mischief in his eyes. "She might be a while. That guy she's talking to is my buddy."

Glancing at Anna, she gave a short nod. "I acknowledge your point, but only because I know my friend well. She's chatty. Even so, I fail to see why that requires you to fix my drink? I'm capable of handling that myself."

He answered with another slow look of interest, eyes narrowing slightly as they traveled over her face. "I bet you're capable of handling just about anything that comes at you, Miss Rhone. You strike me as the independent type."

It was stated in a way that gave her the impression this man had studied her and knew all her secrets.

Cassie turned to face him and gave him her own study. She tried not to judge who someone really was, but the fact that this guy was wearing casual jeans and a black button-down with a faded black leather jacket that looked as though it had seen more than its fair share of years didn't indicate that he was one of the higher-up executives in the group. But then, she'd worked with many Fortune 500 companies out of Silicon Valley where the CEOs dressed in board shorts and flip-flops.

It was never a good idea to assume anything and always good to at least be civil.

"I'm sorry, do I know you? Beyond the fact that you sat in first row today chatting with your buddy at the end," she said.

Laughter vibrated from him. "I thought maybe you caught that. My apologies." His deep voice was strong and sure. Maybe he worked in radio or something. "No, we haven't met yet. I'm Brody. I enjoyed your talk today. You have an interesting and engaging speaking style. Kept my interest going even though I have less than zero interest in social media."

The way he said it made Cassie blink for a second. She was thrown off by his blunt dislike of her platform, but he didn't sound as though he handed out compliments freely and what he'd said was given honestly, without flattery. She'd learned to distinguish the fake praise from the real over the years.

"Thank you. I appreciate your comments and even your lack of appreciation for what social media can do. My team and I work hard to make learning a good experience."

"It was. I still don't know exactly how I'll use what I learned, but it was interesting." Brody took a sip of what looked like whiskey then nodded toward their friends. "Looks like they like each other."

Cassie followed his gaze and saw Anna standing so close to Brody's friend that she might as well have been inside the suit jacket the guy sported over tailored pants. The guy leaned into Anna's ear and said something that made her throw her head back on a laugh and slide her hand up his arm in a gesture that was anything but casual.

Warning bells went off in Cassie's head. Anna would follow her heart and whatever mystical vibe she was feeling at the time, even if it did occasionally land her in trouble. The infatuated sparkle in her eyes was obvious—even from this distance.

Turning back to Brody, Cassie offered an apology. "You'll have to excuse me. I'm going to go get that drink."

She gathered her clutch and walked toward the bar. Intent on rescuing Anna from her own friendly self, Cassie missed an inebriated partygoer stumbling out of the crowd until the last second when he crashed right into her. Her heels did nothing to stabilize her as she stumbled and started to fall, only to be caught at the last second by a strong arm that wrapped around her waist and brought her up against a long muscular frame and broad male chest. Letting out a gasp, Cassie looked up. Lights flashed brightly with the band's music, and for that second, she was caught in the most vivid green eyes she'd ever seen.

"Best be careful. Party's getting a little wild," Brody cautioned with warmth dancing across his handsome face. At least, he now seemed handsome, with those green eyes framed by thick dark brows, high cheekbones, and full lips twisted in a sensual look aimed only for her.

Reality slammed back in just as fast as it had flown away. She was being held by a virtual stranger, every single inch of them pressed intimately together. Cassie quickly disentangled herself from him, straightening her jacket as she moved. "Thank you for helping. I'm sure I would have fallen. Excuse me."

She hurried off, ignoring how strange she'd felt while being held by a man she didn't know. So close and firm against him that she could still feel the heat from his body.

"Anna, there you are."

Anna turned, absolutely beaming, while holding on to the arm of the man next to her, and she gave Cassie a smile as broad as the sun to match her golden hair. "Cassie, you'll never believe who I've met. This is Chase Bryant." She introduced him as if the strapping blond-haired man held all the answers in the known universe.

Chase greeted Cassie with a congratulatory smile and compliments about his impressions of the day. The guy seemed nice enough, but Cassie was there to be the reality check for her friend.

Brody joined them smoothly moments later.

Miss Rhone, it turned out, had a stand-off attitude in person and a body that felt like a slice of heaven. When she'd almost fallen, he'd thought for a moment that Cassie felt something too, as he stared down into the prettiest slanted hazel eyes. They went well with her equally delicate elfin features and chin-length bob of wavy hair. For a few seconds, those eyes had gone wide and curvy lips made for kissing had parted on a breath of hesitation. Then the professional demeanor had slipped back in place like a well-practiced mask before she thanked him and walked off as if nothing had happened.

Deciding Cassie was more than worth trying to talk to again, he'd followed, admiring once more the no-nonsense walk of long legs in shoes designed to make a man grateful for how they showcased a woman's athletic tone. Petite but dynamite. He didn't usually go for short women, but for this one, he'd make an exception. She was attractive way beyond the physical.

All night he'd been drawn to watching Cassidy Rhone off and on. She had a singular way of enjoying herself even though it seemed there was never a single second someone wasn't trying to talk to her. That kind of constant attention, after a while, usually made his skin itch. But Brody liked how whomever she was engaged with got her full interest and attention. More than one person had walked away thrilled to have met her. It was like watching a smaller version of a fan meet-and-greet. Eventually Brody had decided to meet Cassie himself if the chance presented itself. Now he was intrigued by the simple brush-off she'd given him. He didn't often get to actually chase a woman.

Chase was following up with his thoughts of how Cassie's tips could be used when he spotted Brody walking up. "Miss Rhone—"

"Please, it's Cassie," she interrupted smoothly.

"All right, Cassie then. Have you met Brody Mi—" A narrowed look from Brody and a slight shake of head behind

Cassie's back had Chase changing the introduction. "My good friend."

Brody didn't like to promote who he was and kept a low profile when out. Thankfully, he didn't get recognized that often. He hated seeing his face plastered all over for the latest Hollywood gossip sites. The only reason he'd come tonight was because Chase had assured him that all of the restaurant employees had signed confidentiality contracts — it was a given that everyone on the cast and crew of their show knew the rules. Anything posted without studio approval was met with automatic termination – no exceptions.

But Brody was now intrigued by the so-called "waste of a day" he could have spent relaxing. Cassie Rhone hadn't given the slightest indication she knew who he was, and for the time being, he preferred to keep it that way.

"We just met actually. Brody was giving me his kind thoughts on today as well. I've had a wonderful time getting to know your company this evening and working with you, Chase. But if you'll excuse me, my friend and I need to head home. The day is catching up with me," she said with a nod to Anna.

"Forgive me, sweet sister. Chase invited me to go for a drink somewhere a little more quiet and maybe another dessert later on," Anna replied with an adoring smile at Chase. She was draped on his arm like cling wrap.

Brody held back the snicker that wanted to escape. Chase always had been smooth as silk with women, but this time, he looked as if he'd found nirvana in Anna's big brown eyes as he grinned back at her. Brody wondered who had caught who first in their game of easy flirtation.

"That I did, and this beauty has graciously accepted. You'll have to excuse us. Once again, a pleasure to work with you today, Cassie. Enjoy your night."

He shook Cassie's hand, but before he could lead Cassie's friend off, she snagged Anna for a quick hug good-bye. Brody overheard Cassie's hurriedly whispered words trying to change Anna's mind to no avail. They were gone in a minute, leaving the two of them standing there. Cassie gaped in apparent disbelief mixed with a little disgust written all over her face at her friend's behavior.

Hoping to put her mind at ease, Brody spoke up. "Seriously, Chase is an okay guy. I've known him since we were practically in diapers. He's cool."

Cassie barely spared him a glance as she replied, dripping sarcasm, "That's so very reassuring. Thanks."

She stalked after the two heading toward the front exit, and Brody followed to enjoy the show more than anything else. Outside, a line of cabs waited. Chase had hailed one, and they were getting set to climb in. When Anna saw Cassie, she stopped Chase, ran back, and gave Cassie a set of keys and a look of sheer joy, then she kissed Cassie full on the lips.

"Talk to you tomorrow," she called, running back to Chase in a flurry of sandaled legs and a swirl of green.

The two were gone in a blink, leaving Cassie standing there.

She'd left her. Actually left her.

Cassie tried to be grateful she at least had the car keys to get home or she might be taking a cab as well. Clutching them tightly, she tried to calm down the worry snaking through her at the thought of Anna running off with a complete stranger. One glance at Brody standing next to her showed him rubbing his face and clearly trying to hold back a laugh.

He sobered up the second he caught her glare. "Cassie, I swear she's safe with him. You have my word."

"Seeing as I've only known you for a few brief minutes of socializing, forgive me if I don't really believe your 'word.'" Smiling with fake sweetness, she pulled out her phone and snapped a picture of him. "That's in case something does happen to her. I'll know where to send the police to start looking."

Brody laughed, this time not holding it back. She really didn't recognize him. Having someone treat him like everyone else was so damn refreshing, he could barely put words to it. He couldn't help but want to get the very cute Cassie to spend a bit more time with him.

"How about we solve that? Let's get out of here. Get to know each other. I'll meet you somewhere. Name the place," He said, holding up his own set of keys as proof.

It had been a while since Cassie had dipped her toe into the dating pool on purpose, but the look of interest on Brody's face hadn't changed her mind. There were specific reasons why she chose not to date.

"Unlike my friend, I'm not looking for a hook-up or drinks. It's late, I'm tired, so I'll just say good night," she replied, trying to keep her tone as nice as possible.

"Come on, breaking my heart here." Brody joked, leaning back and laying his hand over his chest in mock pain.

His dramatics made her snort out a laugh despite the irritation over the situation with him, Chase, and Anna.

"Another time, how about? This weekend? Can I get your number? Promise I won't be one of those losers who says he'll call and doesn't."

Cassie was sure more than one woman had fallen for that infectious laugh, good looks, and slow southern boy charm that left every word sounding like melted chocolate. Especially with that voice. She wasn't going to be one of them.

"Sorry, I'm not interested. It was nice to meet you and your friend. I'm glad you enjoyed the seminar." Cassie walked off and down the street to where Anna's car was parked.

"You sure? I'm a lot of fun once you get to know me," Brody called.

Cassie's only response was a backward wave in the air.

Chapter 2

Supporting and loving a friend sometimes went beyond the bounds of normal in Cassie's book. Call her a prude and, according to Anna, a bit uptight and married to her calendar, but she really liked to get to know a guy for a bit more than an hour or so before jumping into bed with him. That was, if ever came the day that hell managed to freeze solid. Of course, Anna wasn't like that at all. It was rare for her to make a connection with someone so fast, but when she did, she followed her emotions and heart, flinging herself into it with abandon. Sometimes they worked out and sometimes... well... devastation occurred.

Still, even with a long friendship of understanding between them, it was hard for Cassie to sit there on the phone and listen to Anna rhapsodizing on the magnificence of Chase, who was apparently "AH HA MAZING" in bed, out of bed, and just as sweet the morning after. Details swirled around Cassie like a slow-motion still of a hurricane. She heard all the incredible breakdown of the night, including the breakfast in bed Chase had brought Anna before asking if he could see her again. Little heart eyes were practically floating out of the phone.

Cassie chose to roll her own eyes at the situation and stay in equally supportive silence. At least Anna was safe, alive, and apparently more than well. Brody had been right about that at least.

"So did you go home with the delicious-looking friend?" Anna said, tossing Cassie a curve ball. "Knowing you, of course not, but I feel I have to ask."

"He was magnificent in bed and out of it. Honestly, I've never had better." Cassie listened to Anna's stunned silence, so deep Cassie could have heard crickets chirping before she burst out in laughter. "Of course I didn't take him home. You're nuts to even think to ask that, but I'm glad you had a fun time with Chase."

"Damn you, I thought for minute you'd actually had some out-of-the-box fun for a change. Brody was interested in you, by the way, for more than just your speaking ability, but knowing you, it would take a nuclear bomb going off for you to notice." Cassie sighed. She wasn't exactly known for breaking the rules or deviating from her carefully outlined schedule, and that included her moratorium on dating for professional reasons. "I don't have time to date, and even if I did, I wouldn't be interested in him."

"You don't have to date him, just use him. And by use, I mean let him get his—"

Cassie choked on her drink. "Oh God. I'm hanging up now. Goodbye."

Anna ended the call with the sage advice that using someone for something would be good for her. Cassie sighed as she cleaned up her tea and toast. The idea of fantastic sex may have been good for Anna, but the few years of marriage Cassie had suffered through had proven that sex wasn't her thing. Even if it was, she apparently didn't have what it took to keep a guy happy in that department, so she had long since set those failings aside. It simply wasn't one of her strengths. Everyone was excellent at a few things, and those few were what she focused on.

After packing her bag and grabbing a to-go Thermos of tea, Cassie headed out into the combined hell and joy of Atlanta's morning traffic. Normally she worked from home at her leisure, but this was the only time she had available to meet a part of her team and focus on the final details for launching the next leg of their business. As a marketing and social media brand expert, Cassie and her team specialized in online branding for companies and individuals. Their primary objective was always to get each client's message out — not only about their products but also about themselves or companies.

These days, people didn't just buy a product. The product was a side benefit. There were thousands of great products out there, after all. People wanted an experience and, if possible, to know what difference in the world they would be contributing to with their dollars. Customers were essentially buying the company or individual that went with the product. That was why branding was so essential.

Her company's move to Atlanta had come about as a result of needing to add to their staff when the company's growth had proven too much for Cassie and her partner to handle alone. Friends in Atlanta — Anna being one of them — had convinced her that there was a great environment to tap into in Georgia. Needing a fresh start after her divorce, Cassie had made the move with her business partner, inseparable cohort, and best friend, Nathan Jotte, about two years ago.

What had started as the two of them organizing a frantic and crazy move had turned into being surrounded by the fun team they'd hired. Every step of their growth had come right on schedule, according to Cassie's meticulously outlined business plan. She could not have dreamed up a better group to work with. They were the change-makers needed for the clients looking to contract their services.

Inside the small building she had bought to house Halcyon, Inc., Cassie dropped her bag off in her office space in the back corner and headed out into the conference area. It still gave her a thrill to look around at what she and Nathan had created. The open, informal concept was perfect. Couches and work stations, both standing and sitting, were scattered at seemingly random intervals. A large kitchen with conference tables was laid out on one side on the building.

She'd fallen in love with the old converted warehouse full of exposed brick walls, open ductwork, industrial lighting, and worn refinished wood floors. Everything in the building had been replaced with old or reclaimed parts and pieces, keeping the building's history intact. That supported conservation of resources and green living, which was one of Cassie's personal platforms.

Heading over to the conference table, she caught a ball tossed by Nathan after giving him a grin and a thumbs-up to his current look of retro fifties fashion. It went quite well with his natural blond looks and tall, elegant frame. If Cassie was the public face of Halcyon, then Nathan was the one who made everything behind the scenes run seamlessly. She'd said more than once that she'd be lost without him, both professionally and personally.

With a round of hellos, Cassie sat down to open the meeting with their team and plan the branding launch of a company from Utah they were coaching. Anna teased that Cassie was a workaholic, but Cassie believed that she was merely passionate about what she did. And when you had a passion for what you loved, it never felt like work.

Two days later, Cassie's daily checklist was finally complete and she was done packing for her trip out in the morning. It was time for another of her personal passions — fitness. Cassie shrugged off her work clothes and was suiting up for an early evening run when her phone rang. Not recognizing the number, she answered. Clients new and old sometimes referred people to her private number.

"Hi, this is Cassidy Rhone."

"Hey, Cassie. I was hoping to catch up with you. This is Brody. From the seminar the other night."

The deep voice coming through the line made Cassie pull back to stare at her phone as if it had just grown teeth. She was standing in her bedroom in nothing more than her underwear and sports bra, and suddenly felt completely naked.

"Hey… are you still there?"

She heard the faint words and slowly lifted the phone back to her ear. "I'm here." She waited, not sure what to say.

Brody had no problem carrying on. "Great. How are you doing?"

"I'm good. Listen… no offense… but how did you get this number?" she said slowly, having trouble forming words through the shock. She'd honestly forgotten about him. She forced herself to pull out her training pants and top to finish getting dressed.

"From Anna. I might have begged her after you blew me

off. You know she and Chase are seeing each other now? Go figure. Anyway, I won't keep you long. She said you work crazy hours. I haven't been able to stop thinking about you. Was wondering if you'd give me a second chance on taking you out for dinner?"

It was a slow south Texas drawl. Cassie finally placed the accent. "Look, I really don't mean to be rude—"

"Now why do people always say that?" Brody said, interrupting her.

Surprised that he'd thrown off her standard reply, Cassie almost dropped the phone as she yanked on running pants. "What?"

"About not being rude. When clearly you want to be rude to me. Go ahead. I can take it. I'm a big boy."

The comment left Cassie snickering for a minute as she remembered his size. "All right, being completely rude — and I'll add blunt — I'm not interested in going out with you or anyone. I really don't have the time."

"Yeah, Anna mentioned you work a lot. My schedule's a bit nutty too, so I'll take what I can get. Pick an activity. I'll meet you there. Lunch, dinner, dog walker, running buddy, coffee date. Just give me one hour to plead my case."

The reply Cassie had ready broke off as her mind ground to a halt. Her shirt was halfway stuck on her head for a few seconds before she got it untangled. "What did you say? That last bit?"

"What? An hour to plead my case. Yeah, basically, let's get to know each other some and see if you want to extend to date number two of a potentially longer time frame."

Cassie laughed in disbelief. "You know, my best friend and I used to say that when we started dating as teenagers. That most guys were worth an hour of your time to plead their case — if they met certain criteria." She giggled at the fond memory of her and Nathan's list of requirements. They had also come up with their own post-date evaluation list.

Brody laughed with her. "Well, how about that? What criteria do I need to fit?"

"Well back then, our criteria was pretty low since we were just starting to date, and you know how it goes when you're a teenager and mostly broke. So, a guy had to meet two things: he had to bathe on a regular basis and have a job."

More infectious laughter filtered through her phone. He really did have a great laugh along with that slow southern drawl.

"I swear I clean up most days. There's a rare one I might skip, and I do have a job."

"I know nothing about you," Cassie said, shaking her head. "What kind of work do you do?" God, she was thinking of saying yes! She put on running shoes, got them tied, and started to pace.

"I work in the film industry here in Atlanta. Coffee one morning? Text me a place and time, and I'll meet you there. Bring all the questions you want. One hour. You can even set a timer."

"It would have to be next Sunday morning. Early. It's the only time I have available." Dammit! The words were out before she could stop them. Miming hitting herself, Cassie continued pacing the kitchen.

"Perfect. Message me the when and where of it on this number. I'll see you then, Cassie."

And Brody hung up before she could change her mind,

leaving Cassie staring at the phone in horror over what she'd just agreed to.

An hour-long date with a guy she barely knew.

Chapter 3

Sunday morning workout complete, Cassie walked up to the outdoor area of the coffee place she'd picked out simply because it was close to where she lived and trained. Since she didn't really consider meeting a guy for coffee as a real date, she'd just paired her workout pants with a loose sweater she'd pulled on after finishing with Anna's Vinyasa yoga. Sheer vanity had Cassie at least adding on a coat of mascara and lip gloss, but she wasn't making a special effort for a guy she planned to blow off anyway. Cassie would keep her word for coffee and one hour, but anything beyond that was impossible.

Brody seemed to have the same thought, since he'd gone for the casual look as well. A black hoodie with jeans completed the look, only this time it was the jeans carrying the very worn and faded look. The chipped Texas Tech lettering on the hoodie confirmed her suspicions about where he was from. He'd thrown on a ball cap for added measure, looked tired and just as good looking. Still ridiculously tall too, Cassie noted when he stood to greet her. She barely came to his shoulder without the heels. They went inside to get in line.

"Thanks for meeting so early." She smiled. "I'm up at the crack of dawn usually."

"Morning person, huh?" Brody asked, handing her a menu.

"Irritatingly so, I'm afraid."

"I like mornings. Mornings in bed are even better."

Cassidy looked up from the menu to find Brody's eyes fixed on his menu. A sneaky twitch on his lips was trying to get out. She felt her own lips mimicking the response. His eyes flicked over to hers, and he winked.

Cassie rolled her eyes at him and the obvious innuendo.

"We agreed to coffee, but I haven't eaten yet, so I'm snagging breakfast while I'm here. Join me?" he asked.

"Why not?" Anna's class had left her drained and needing refueling.

"Look at that. Already we're past coffee and sharing a meal."

This time Cassie's smile flashed out. Damn, he was sneaky. In a fun, teasing kind of way.

Brody gestured her forward to go first.

"I'll have the Greek omelet and fruit. Mint Moroccan tea. Hot. Thanks."

When she handed over her card, Brody's hand came down over hers. He gave the guy his instead. "We're together and it's my treat. Veggie omelet, extra veggies, hash browns, and same with the fruit. Coffee black, extra shot of espresso."

The last item made Cassie's eyes almost water. "Need to wake up, do you?"

"Late shoot on set last night. Didn't go to bed until two a.m.," Brody said with a shrug, signing the check and taking the number for their table. "Eat outside?"

Mid-fall in the South meant it wasn't too cold out yet. Unlike the upper Midwest where her family was already pulling out cooler weather gear.

"Sure." Leading the way, Cassie walked out. "You didn't

have to pay, by the way. This is just a casual meet for coffee, not a date."

"Correction — it's coffee and food now, which hedges it almost toward being a date but not quite." Brody held out her chair.

The move surprised Cassie. Did guys actually do old-world chivalry anymore? Apparently one still did.

"And while I appreciate and admire your whole independent woman thing, call me old-fashioned, but I'm not going to bicker with you over who gets to pay for what when you're with me."

After a moment, Cassie acknowledged his gesture a bit grudgingly. She was so used to paying her own way, it was difficult sometimes to remember to just be gracious. "Fine. Thank you for breakfast."

Brody sat there staring at Cassie. His face might have looked tired, but the expression in his emerald eyes sparkled with deep interest, suppressed humor, and that quiet, steady, unrelenting assessment.

Cassie merely arched a brow at him. "So you wanted to plead your case, Mr. Brody No-Last-Name, who works in the film industry."

"It's Brody Miller." He studied her once more. "Tell me, did you come here with an open mind or just to pretend to listen and blow me off afterward? Cause if it's the latter, I'll just get my food to-go so we don't waste our time."

Cassie sat there a moment, flushing at the question. He'd jerked the rug out from under her feet. Such perception was rare in anyone. What was it with this guy, and how did he see through her?

Uncomfortable, she stared at one of the garden terrace

pots spilling late summer flowers and trailing ivy for a minute before looking back at him. "Okay, truth. I did come to do exactly that. I have no intention of going out with you or starting something I have no time to fully commit to."

"Least you're honest about it. Why are you here then? Why even show up?" Brody sat back with his arms crossed as their drinks came out.

"You caught me in a sentimental weak moment with something you said, so I said yes. I don't break my word once I give it." Stirring the tea leaves carefully in her teapot, Cassie judged by the smell that it had steeped long enough. She poured a cup while remembering a simpler time in life with Nathan.

There was something more there than she was ready to say. Honor and integrity were important to Cassie, it seemed, like she'd been betrayed before. Brody took a drink of his coffee and closed his eyes in gratitude of finally having some caffeine to latch on to. He loved what he did for a living, but sometimes the hours sucked, especially coming off of three days of sixteen-hour shoots.

"No one's making you stay," he offered, leaning forward again. "But I'd appreciate the chance to try. Might be I could change your mind."

Something close to a wry smile drifted across her face. "I doubt that. But you're right. I didn't walk into this with an open mind or even remotely open ears, so I'll apologize for that. It was rude and unfair of me. So tell me, Brody Miller, what exactly do you do in the film industry? I understand it's a booming piece of business in Atlanta."

Confident that he at least had Cassie listening openly now,

Brody decided on being open and honest himself. "I'm an actor. I work right now on a series that they produce and film here on location."

"Really?" Cassie said, intrigued despite her intentions to not take things any further. "I've never known an actor before. What's it like? Do you enjoy it?"

People and the professions they chose always fascinated her. It was what made social media branding and marketing so fascinating.

"I do. It's fun to learn new things all the time for the different characters I play, get to meet new people, and learn about the different time periods I get to represent. Then there're the places I get to travel to."

"Where are some good ones you've been to?" Cassidy asked and was duly impressed with some of the locations Brody named off. She had dreamed of traveling to most of them when her business reached a higher level of success. "How long have you been acting? That's a fair bit of travel."

"Pretty much since college. Chase and I went to Juilliard on scholarships and never looked back. I fell in love with film and stage. He went into the producing and directing end of things."

"I don't recognize you, but then I don't really follow the whole Hollywood scene. What show is it you're here to do?"

Brody named the series. It was one that her staff had raved about and she told him so. Cassidy had never so much as peeked at the show herself, since it was considered serious drama.

"Glad they like it," Brody said just as their meals were served. "It's been a really great experience working here, and the character I play is a complicated guy. Sometimes I wonder if I'll ever get him totally figured out all the way."

"I don't really watch a lot of TV, and when I do, it's pretty limited. I stick to comedy since I like to laugh," Cassie said. The genre helped to ease the constant stress she put herself under with her tight schedule.

"I'll make you laugh a lot if you agree to date number two." Brody grinned at her.

"Which brings up an interesting point, given what you do." She pointed at him with her fork. "Why are you so interested in me? Surely you must have other ladies in your path. Not to stroke your ego or anything, but you're a good-looking guy."

"Thanks, and you can stroke anything you want anytime." Tossing her another wink as he forked up a bite.

Damn him, Cassie thought trying not to smile. He did make her want to laugh. No one she'd ever known had flirted so outrageously with her before. He went from fun and teasing to serious and thoughtful as he responded.

"To answer your question, it's harder than you think to meet someone, much less get serious with them. I meet women all the time, but finding someone who doesn't want to go out with me just because of who I am, or worse, some character they're in love with that I played— that makes for an interesting hurdle. I like that you have no clue who I am. Right now, you're only seeing me. Which is a really nice change."

The look on his face was charming and softened Cassie's heart. It seemed Brody was lonely even if he was completely happy with his life the way it was. As if to prove the whole popularity thing, one of the waitresses came over at that moment, stammering, and asked for an autograph and picture. Brody chatted with the girl for a few minutes and posed for pictures before she left, walking about two feet higher off the ground because he'd spent a few brief minutes asking the woman about herself and her family.

"That was cute. Does it get old?" Cassie asked.

"No. Well, sometimes. The press can be a pain in the ass when they want, and I avoid them like the plague. But since I never do anything interesting, like have sex affairs with my costars or do the party scene, they got bored years ago and stopped following me. I don't get recognized that much. Thank God. Most films I do, I look like someone else entirely, so that keeps it easy when I'm out. Personally, I think I look pretty boring in person."

"Well, she didn't think so, and I'm sure she'd much rather you be taking her out. I'd like to also point out that she's more in line with your direct height ratio than I am."

Brody choked out a laugh. "Is that why you're saying no? My height?" Leaning back with his hands behind his head, he gave her another cocky grin. "I'll make sure you have a box to stand on when we get around to kissing. Works on set."

"Ha ha ha. Funny. You have to admit there's a huge difference."

And double-damn Brody Miller and his cocky confidence — now Cassie was thinking about kissing those really sexy full lips he had. It had been a long time since she'd allowed herself to think about anything physical with a man, and the memory of why sneaked in. Cassie ruthlessly buried the pain back where it belonged — in the past.

"You didn't seem to mind my height the other night. And I liked holding you when you almost fell. I admit, I think you're a pretty sexy package wrapped up in all those boundaries and the back-off wall you have around you. The fact that your mind is as sharp as your tongue doesn't make you any less attractive. I don't care about the difference in our vertical statuses. It's not really an issue to me. I want to get to know you better. Both our schedules are crazy, but I bet we can find an hour or so, here and there, to see what the potential is." Taking a sip of his coffee, Brody waited for her response.

The fact that Brody had been so blunt about what he wanted threw Cassie off. Her self-imposed moratorium on dating left her on rocky ground as to how to deal with him. She'd gotten used to handling her life, along with most of the people in it, just the way she wanted. She'd easily shoot down any other man, but Brody was a different story. He didn't seem at all put off by her schedule, nor the boundaries Cassie guarded so carefully. And how easily Brody could read her was unnerving. Only one other person in her life had that ability, and that was Nathan. To some extent Anna at times, as well.

"Does anyone ever turn you down?" she asked.

"Of course. All the time. Rejection is part of my life given what I do. I have thick skin."

"Persistence, I imagine, is another quality you have in spades."

The answering look in his eyes said it all. Going out on a limb, Cassie might classify him as slightly pushy along with his extreme bluntness. She'd bet money those qualities saved Brody a lot of time wasted on people's bullshit — something she fervently wished she could get away with sometimes in her own line of work.

Cassie thought it over, all of her crazy schedule and life as it was right now. In addition to his physical attraction, Brody was actually interesting. Their semi-coffee date had turned out to be one of the most enjoyable times she'd spent with a man in a long time. For the first time in a long while, part of her was curious beyond belief. The other, more familiar part of her was sure there was no possible way it could work out. Especially the part of her wounded by the past. Cassie squelched that like the bug it was. The past wasn't part of this decision.

She had learned, through the years, that the number one priority in a professional career was that distractions didn't make for success. There was no doubt in her mind that Brody Miller would be a very big distraction.

She eyed him over her cup. "I'm pretty sure things would never work out between us."

"One way to find out. Is that a yes or a no?" Brody asked, cocking his head.

"It's sadly a no. I'm tempted to say yes, but reality is that I'm selfish with my spare time. Dating just isn't something I want to do right now while I'm building this next phase of our business."

Brody shook his head. The corner of his mouth lifted in a wry half smile. "Can't say I'm not disappointed. What do you say to keeping me in mind if things change or lighten up?"

Cassie gave a sincere smile. "I can do that."

He took the let-down well, making her almost wish she had said yes. For the first time in a long time, she had actually wanted to say yes. To take a hesitant step in that direction again.

"Good. Now that we're all casual-friends-like, tell me more about this business of yours and what you're building. I still have a good twenty minutes of our hour left," Brody said.

Cassie found herself sharing with him the what and why she was dreaming big, and if their hour turned into twenty minutes past the limit, it was only because she forgot to keep a sharp eye on her watch. At least, that was what she told herself when they said good-bye and parted ways.

Chapter 4

"You did what?" Anna choked in disbelief after yoga class the next weekend. Weekly yoga was one of the few relaxations Cassie allowed herself. "Did you even look at him? He's Brody Miller. He's gorgeous! Are you out of your mind?"

Upside-down in a complicated headstand, Anna watched Cassie while she held her own. Cassie was sure Anna wished she was standing on her feet with her hands on hips in exasperation, yelling at Cassie instead.

"Please, how can you even say that? You know how swamped I am right now with this new launch. The only times I get to see or talk to you lately is when I take your class," Cassie said in frustration. This conversation could not be happening again. Nathan had given her the same feedback.

In a move like a ballet dancer, full of grace, Anna lowered down and came smoothly to her feet. "I find those facts irrelevant, and you are a certified idiot. He's hung out with Chase and me a couple of times. I like him. He's really nice. And fun. The easiest, loveliest vibes to be around. He's centered and relaxing. You could use some of that, not to mention a distraction from all the stress."

Letting herself down, Cassie moved to final stretching. "I can assure you, adding in a man would not decrease my stress. It would only make things worse."

"Well, it sure would make you less bitchy. You need some good old-fashioned fun for a change. When's the last time you did anything except work or work out?"

Cassie stood abruptly and went to the wall to crouch and pack up her bag. Her movements were jerky from Anna's comment. "Just because you need a man to function and feel good about your life doesn't mean I do." Tossing in her water bottle, she stood.

Anna stopped dead. The comment had been a slap in the face, and her hurt matched Cassie's own when Cassie turned back around. One that spoke volumes. Only love for her good friend kept Anna from lashing out. Cassie was brilliant and success-focused, but she also had a head like a brick when it came to men. And that brick was part of the wagon full she'd used to build a wall — permanently — around her heart.

Cassie swore quietly and fervently, eyes full of regret. "I'm sorry. That was out of line and not true. I'm happy for you and Chase. He seems wonderful from all you've said. You're lucky to have found each other."

"Not all men are Daniel," Anna said, reaching for her. "They don't all cheat and make you feel horrible about yourself. It's been almost a year since you signed the divorce papers. Two and a half since you left him. One date with someone won't kill you."

Throwing Anna a glare, Cassie took a deep breath. "Daniel has *nothing* to do with any decision related to Brody."

"Are you sure? Cassie, you're a rock star in everything you do, but I haven't seen you so much as glance at another man since that ass ran over you with a Mac truck and left you bleeding in the dirt."

"He left me bleeding a long time before that." Defeat slumping her shoulders, Cassie lifted her bag and, looking close to tears, stepped back from the hug Anna tried to offer. "We both know I don't have what it takes to hold a man. What makes you think that dating some hot actor would be any different? My own husband wasn't even faithful."

Anna cursed, which she rarely did as she tried to live a life of harmony and peace. "Daniel was a self-centered asshole and got off on making you feel like shit. Nothing you did or didn't do changes that. Not all men are like that. Brody isn't like that."

"It's still not worth the hassle or the emotional roller coaster of trying again." Cassie headed out the door.

Anna sighed and sent up a prayer to any entity in the universe listening that Cassie would one day find it in her heart to trust again.

After stalking to her car and tossing her bag inside, Cassie sat in the driver's seat and laid her head against the steering wheel in an effort to calm down. The fact that she'd had basically the same conversation with Nathan right after her "pseudo date" with Brody was irritating as hell.

"Darling, I'm just saying, it's okay to give someone a chance to take you out, have a drink and a little food with you. You did say he was interesting to talk to," Nathan had said.

Cassie's stunned amazement had flown right over his head. "You of all people… how can you say that to me?"

Nathan crossed his arms, his blue eyes nailing her in place. "Don't look at me like that. I lived every minute of that shit time with you and that bastard, so stop acting like I don't have a clue what you went through. All I'm saying is that it's okay to try again. With someone who's decent. And Brody certainly seems decent from everything I've read about him over the years."

"Fine, why don't you go hook up with him then? Tell me all about it when you're done."

Nathan had looked absolutely wistful for a moment before coming back to the topic with the laser focus that made him so great as a business partner. "You know I would, in a heartbeat. Brody Miller is as hot as they come, but I have Philip now, so I don't have to. I can live vicariously through you. Just promise me, sweetie, the next time you happen to trip and he catches you — make sure you land on his lips."

The suggestion had made Cassie shake her head as she walked out of Nathan's office. Heaven save her from well-meaning friends. As far as reality went, her chances of seeing Brody Miller, much less tripping into him again, were slim to almost none. Even if she did, she doubted that dating him would ever be an issue. After all, most guys didn't appreciate being rejected.

Cassie worked about as hard as she ever had as fall headed into the holiday season. Business was perfect and grew at exactly the pace she had wanted, if not a little faster than anticipated. And if Brody Miller crept in to her thoughts, every now and then, it was only because the man kept a friendly and casual sort of association going between them.

Once every couple weeks or so, he'd send Cassie a funny text or picture, shared from somewhere that he was working at the moment, and she would trade a couple of lines with him before caution slipped back in and shut it down. The one time he asked her to send a selfie, Cassie gave in during a weak moment while stuck in Chicago with weather delays. Brody had responded with a single word of "GORGEOUS," leaving her feeling pretty for the first time in forever. Strangely, in those moments when he reached out to her, Cassie found herself start to give a little bit with each smile he brought to her.

When she brought it up to the only person she trusted beyond life itself, Nathan theorized that Brody was courting her. Subtle and smooth, he termed it. She might have Googled Brody once out of professional curiosity, but Cassie told herself it was only that and nothing more.

Brody Miller, it seemed, was an oddity in Hollywood, in that he managed to be a huge success while flying completely under the radar and keeping his private life just that — viciously private. There were no random pictures of coffee meet-ups with friends or late-night dates with dreamy starlets, but the list of awards, accolades, and major projects he'd been a part of was more than impressive. Brody shunned social media like the plague and had a fan base that was equally protective of him. His current show had gotten its fair share of Emmy and Golden Globe awards. In a world of people who preferred to flaunt themselves to the extreme, Brody was a rare breed and walked his own course. Cassie couldn't help but admire that he seemed to know exactly who he was and what he was about. Boundaries and all.

The end of November drew near, and Cassie flew back home to celebrate Thanksgiving with her family. Over the holiday, she enjoyed seeing her nephews in person instead of via video calls and pictures, but she had to sidestep the Spanish Inquisition and concerned looks from family members who didn't understand what she did. Cassie tried in vain to use the four days to rest instead of work while her mom let her know in great detail how Cassie failed at that particular goal. With it being the height of the marketing season, Halcyon was in an impossible position. There was always something a client needed taken care of.

Chapter 5

Surviving December seemed a lesson in endurance and stamina during the busiest year she had ever had. Cassie just needed to make it through the next three weeks, then things would lighten up for the Christmas season. After that, she could sail through the new year and into the January launches for the businesses they worked with. Her new seminar series would kick off, and the first few months of next year were laid out with endless travel for her. Receiving an invitation to speak in London was a small jewel in Cassie's crown. International expansion was the next step for Halcyon, and it was happening earlier than expected.

Back in her office on a rare Friday evening in town, she sat browsing through travel sites. Cassie sighed dreamily at the idea of a four-day getaway. A cruise maybe, or she could rent a condo somewhere on the beach. It had been an exhausting few months, and her business trip to New York over the past few days had left her dragging. She was trying to decide if taking time away over New Year's would be worth it or just add more to her to-do list.

Technically, Halcyon was mobile and could be worked anywhere, even at the beach. She would still have to work, but at least she would be surrounded by sun, sand, and beautiful sunsets. Atlanta to Hawaii was quite a jump of time zones.

Atlanta to Costa Rica or Mexico was a better option. All-inclusive, full spa setup… definitely a massage on the beach. Facial mask, mani, pedi… Her dream of time off, the sparkling fantasy of blue waters and sandy beaches, went up in a happy little pop when Cassie's phone rang.

"Hi, you're still coming tonight, right?" Anna launched without preamble.

"Yes, I have it down. Eight p.m." Confirming her calendar at a glance, Cassie added a sincere threat. "Anna, no more setups with would-be suitors. You and Nathan promised me you were done after the last guy. The architect."

The one who had made dry toast look appealing. Anna had surprised Cassie with him at a quick lunch catch-up a couple of weeks back. The move had been completely obvious when the architect had just "happened" to stop by their table.

"Whatever. I admitted he was a mistake and apologized. Move on." Anna flicked it away unconcerned. "You'll wear what we agreed on, right? The cocktail dress, black tunic style, sleeveless with the cute little decorative chains on the sleeveless edges."

"Yes, yes. The length of which is barely past legal. I know."

Cassie had lost a bet and per their deal, Anna got to pick Cassie's clothes for tonight's party. While Anna typically had the better and bolder style sense of the two of them, Cassie hated short dresses. This particular one would ensure she froze her ass off. At least she wasn't back home, where it was even colder. On the plus side, maybe the dress would be perfect since holiday parties were typically hotter than hell with all the people that came cramming themselves into one or two rooms. After being gone all week, she didn't want to deal with a room full of people. Her dream right now was a bubble bath and a bottle of wine, but she'd given her word that she'd be there.

"And don't forget the heels. They make your legs look amazing."

"Of course," Cassie ground out, practically feeling Anna grinning in delight. Cassie was a professional woman – heels were part of her job. However, according to Anna, the sparkly Jimmy Choos *simply made* the dress.

"It's the holidays. What would we be without a little sparkle? Don't forget the jewelry. See you later."

Cassie found herself at home later, taking in her new look in the bedroom mirror. The dress fell to mid-thigh. Barely. Bending over would take some care. A bet was a bet, Cassie reasoned as she slicked on lipstick and double-checked her hair before putting on the tourmaline crystal pendant Anna had given Cassie for her birthday over the summer. Anna had sworn the crystal would combat stress and channel amazing energy. Cassie had to admit she felt amazing when wearing it, as though the crystal held a little extra confidence booster. She would need that tonight.

Anna and Chase were throwing the holiday party together, and Cassie would know very few people there, if any. Nathan and his partner, Philip, were also going, but they wouldn't arrive until much later in the evening due to a prior engagement. Who would have thought a relationship born in the middle of a seminar would have blossomed so crazily? Even Cassie had to admit that Chase and Anna were perfect for each other.

Giving herself an extra smile, Cassie set her intention to enjoy the night and meet new people. She might even make some new connections, and connections were always good for business.

Chapter 6

Walking into Chase's house was enough to make anyone's eyes pop. Located in one of the poshest neighborhoods in Atlanta, the ten-thousand-square-foot estate, plus additional acreage, boasted just about every convenience a person could ask for, including wide, open designer-decorated rooms, both indoor and outdoor pools, tennis courts, putting range, and indoor theatre. Not too shabby for some studio executive.

Cassie smiled, taking in the gorgeous holiday décor, which hit the line between whimsical and lush with the overall theme colors of gold and green. She could definitely see Anna's influence there.

Anna spotted Cassie from across the room and gave a wave and a squeal before she dragged Cassie in. Anna's golden hair was twisted up in a festive tie, and she wore a dress that seemed to be made of multiple colored scarves stitched together. It was a risky look that only Anna could wear perfectly. Even Nathan took more fashion risks than Cassie.

Soon settled with champagne in hand and introductions being made all around, Cassie almost bobbled her drink when she spotted Brody Miller across the room — the last person she had expected to see tonight. He gave her a slow, bright smile and a wink, raising his drink in her direction.

Cassie returned the gesture, minus the wink and nerves rose high inside to settle like butterflies in her stomach causing her to look away. She'd have to talk to him at some point, but she hoped, if she was lucky, to avoid him altogether. There had to be at least a hundred people here.

"Come on, there's someone I want you to meet." Anna was pulling Cassie forward. "He's in finance, CPA, amazingly sweet. Works in Chase's company. Of course I thought of you."

"Anna, you promised." Glaring at her friend's back, Cassie was pulled unceremoniously along while trying to drag her feet as much as humanly possible.

Too late.

Anna pulled a man out of the crowd as if she'd conjured him up by magic. "Dennis, this is Cassie, who I told you all about."

Cassie stared at Dennis then back at Anna, trying to keep her face carefully blank. Her friend could not be serious?

"You two have so much in common." Anna was plowing on, keeping one hand latched onto Cassie, probably in case she decided to bolt.

There was a good chance of that happening. Dennis was of average height and bald. Cassie might have been able to get past both of those traits, but within ten seconds, she instinctively knew it was headed toward disaster. Dennis had the conversational skills of an overeager puppy and, unfortunately, not the cute puppy breath to go with it. An obvious misunderstanding about personal space allowed him to prove that last detail in spades, making Cassie want to gag every time he opened his mouth to speak. She was left alone with him, cornered at the side of the room, when Anna slipped away, saying she needed to find Chase.

Anna sauntered off on mile-high stilettos. Chase's idea to get Cassie and Brody together was brilliant. Like something out of a screenplay he might have helped write, Chase had laid out the concept and tagged someone from a local actor's guild to be every definition of horrible while he hit on Cassie. Anna was pretty sure the man had chewed raw garlic before he met Cassie, and the look on her friend's face had been indescribable. Phase two was up next — bring in the hero. If all worked out according to plan, it would play out like a perfect romance story. Cassie deserved a happy ending for a change. Her ex had conditioned her to expect nothing but misery in a relationship, but Anna had recognized the look of interest in Brody's eye every time Cassie's name came up in conversation over the past few months. He was the one man, in a very long time, who wasn't put off, at all, by her friend's "back off" policy.

Cassie didn't know what Anna had told Dennis, but apparently she needed to track her soon-to-be-ex-best friend down and kill her with a dull kitchen spoon. The duller, the better to ensure more pain. She would look up appropriate killing methods with dull spoons just as soon as she escaped. Research was one thing Cassie absolutely excelled at. By tomorrow, she would know enough to perform open heart surgery with a spoon.

Right now, however, she was caught in the depths of hell. Even with all her social skills and years of navigating events, Cassie still hadn't managed to extricate herself from "Mr. Stinky" as she was mentally referring to Dennis.

God, who didn't understand basic oral hygiene this day

and age?

When she caught Brody Miller watching her, Cassie threw her pride under the proverbial bus and put as much of a plea as she could into her eyes that she prayed said "Please, come save me." How could she not know a single other person at this event was beyond her, but it was Chase's party. Cassie almost got down on her knees in thanks when Brody walked toward her, his tall manly form easily cutting through the crowd. He was cleaned up in a tailored jacket, black pants, and midnight blue button-down shirt with his hair combed in place for a change. He might as well have been wearing a shining suit of armor, he looked so wonderful to Cassie.

Like the class-A actor he was, Brody never batted an eyelash; he just walked right up. "Hey, darling, so sorry I'm late." Slipping an arm around her, Brody dropped a kiss on Cassie's cheek and whispered in her ear, "Need a rescue, gorgeous?"

"I'm so *glad* you made it. I was starting to worry something might have happened with traffic." Knowing her eyes were swimming with gratitude, Cassie laid a hand on his chest as though they were the best of friends and a whole lot more.

Her heels brought her to a little above his shoulder. Brody held her snugly against him so that Cassie felt the party drift away for a few seconds as eyes green as the holiday decor smiled down at her.

"It's all right now. I'm here, baby." Shifting, Brody extended a hand to Dennis, dropped his voice a few octaves, and added a threatening edge. "Nice to meet you. Hope you don't mind. Cassie's with me."

Dennis took one look up at Brody, stuttered, and disappeared into the crowd so fast, Cassie thought he might have teleported.

Dropping her head on Brody's chest, Cassie gave a heart-felt sigh and breathed in just about the manliest scent in the universe. Maybe it was because Dennis had had such bad breath, but Brody smelled incredible — like fresh mountain air and deep earth combined.

Raising her head to look at him, she said, "Thank you so much. You'll never know how awful that was."

"Didn't look too fun from where I was standing. More like you were trying to wrestle an octopus," Brody said, grinning down at her. "I was hoping someday I'd get to run into you again, Cassidy, or you might give me a call. I meant it by the way. You do look gorgeous." Angling his head down for another appreciative look at her.

He still hadn't let go of her and Cassie tried to shift away, but his arm stayed firm around her. "Thanks. I lost a bet with Anna. This outfit is my punishment. You can let go of me now."

"Now why would I want to do that when I've been wondering if I'd ever get you in my arms again? Must have been some bet. I look forward to hearing about it. How've you been?"

He did let go of her though, only to take her hand instead, and he guided Cassie through the crowd toward the bar, where he got them a couple more drinks. She had to give Brody credit — he owned confident self-assurance. No ego or arrogance, just a male completely sure of himself and who he was.

"I've been good. Insanely busy, but thankfully it should be slowing down soon. What about you? Season wrap up yet? I liked your last picture from San Francisco." Why on earth was she walking with him, holding hands no less? Because she didn't have to be rude, Cassie thought, chiding herself. The guy had just helped her out, after all.

"It's good, almost done. A couple more weeks. Some re-shoots here and there of extra stuff, but we're almost wrapped until after the holidays. Anna tells me you work nonstop, but business launched well."

Cassie listened while he talked. His zest and love of life was still very much apparent. When a partygoer, a bit drunk, tried to pull her in for an embrace, Brody stepped in, blocking the guy easily. Wrapping an arm again around Cassie, Brody steered her toward where the buffet was spread out with enough food to feed a small army. The offerings included tastes and samples of every famous dish the South was known for cooking around the holidays.

"You eat yet?" Brody asked, holding up a plate.

"No, actually. Ran out of time and didn't get to. Thanks," Cassie replied, trying to take the plate from him.

Brody merely handed her his scotch and grabbed an extra plate to balance in his broad hand. "Tell me what you want. I'll load us up, and we can find a place to eat."

Thinking they would be eating with the crowd where they were, Cassie directed him with the foods she wanted and watched while Brody filled both their plates and loaded a third with some dessert options. He balanced the load easily enough to make her think at one point Brody had to have been a waiter.

"Follow me." He grinned at her before walking back to the bar.

There, he had a brief conversation with the bartender and gestured for Cassie to follow him. Curious, she went along and soon realized that they weren't going to eat anywhere close to the main party crowd. Winding through the house, Brody led them into an enclosed sunroom filled with lush tropical plants, patio furniture, lounge chairs, and a fire pit. Potted poinsettias had been added in to the space in honor of the holidays.

Cassie.

It was a lucky thing that he'd decided to come tonight, since for a majority of the day, he'd thought about blowing off the party. The past couple of months, he had kept track of Cassie in a casual sort of way through Anna. Brody hadn't met anyone as remotely interesting as the delectable Cassidy since she had turned him down, and now here she was, wrapped up like an early Christmas present in some sexy dress that left miles of leg exposed.

And she'd needed a rescue, which he'd been only too happy to provide after Anna had come over and mentioned Cassie had an overeager admirer. Better yet, Cassie hadn't turned him down after Brody played the hero. The evening was looking up, all of a sudden. Less time in a crowd of people — most of whom he didn't know or care for, since many of them were kissing his ass and hoping for favors — and now he had a chance to get to know Cassie a little better.

"How's this?" Brody said, putting their plates on the table before laying out the napkins and utensils he'd grabbed.

Walking over to the fire pit, he flipped it on to cast a cheery glow, then he went to the opposite wall panel and dimmed the lights. Brody turned back to look at Cassie over his shoulder, admiring, once again, the toned figure and noted her wary expression, probably over being alone with him. Sending her a smile and a wink, Brody pressed another button.

White Christmas lights came on, scattered across the ceiling, and Cassie gasped in surprise. He pressed a few more buttons on the wall and music started to flow, low and sweet. The effect was instantly intimate and romantic. After all, it was all about setting the scene when a beautiful woman was involved.

"Um... Brody, I don't know what exactly you're going for here..." Cassie said clearly uneasy with the changes.

Thinking how fun it was to keep her off guard, Brody held out his hand and gave a smile he'd been told was infectious. "Come on. Fate threw us together tonight. Date number two?"

Chapter 7

Cassie found herself blinking in surprise before taking the offered hand and letting him pull her into his arms. Brody moved her in a waltz around the room. Of course he would have to be an excellent dancer. Another point making him so hard to resist. Cassie loved to dance.

"Now where did you learn to dance so well, gorgeous?"

"Years of dance lessons and competitions." Cassie enjoyed how well he moved. It was so hard to find anyone who knew how to dance, especially men, and Brody moved almost as well as Nathan. "I must be losing my mind." She said looking up at him.

"Makes two of us." He drew Cassie a bit closer to him. "I swore I'd leave you alone like you wanted. To hell with it. Let's be crazy together."

Giving her a spin, Brody swept Cassie into a dip at the end of a turn, leaving her laughing and clinging to him, lost once more in those incredible green eyes. Heavens, she loved how he made her laugh, and being held in his arms again felt better than she was ready to admit.

Just then, she heard someone clear their throat, and Cassie look over to see the bartender Brody had spoken with. He walked in with a couple of bottles of wine and two glasses. Brody let her go so he could go exchange a few words with the man. She saw them shake hands and what she thought might have been a discreet exchange of money before Brody walked the guy out and locked the door.

He came back over to the table and held out a chair. After helping Cassie sit, Brody grabbed one of the new bottles and uncorked it with a skill that only came from years of practice. He poured them each a glass, saying this wine was way better than the stuff they had at the party.

"To third chances," he toasted, saluting her with the glass.

"To third chances," Cassie agreed on a sigh. "And being crazy." She clinked her glass against his. "How did you know this was out here?"

"I'm over here a fair bit. Chase is one of the producers for the show and the aforementioned friends forever thing." Brody explained, digging into his food. "How've you been, Cassidy? Tell me what all you've been up to and where you've been traveling. And most important — I want to hear about that bet."

And so she did, sharing about Halcyon's expansion, and Brody shared what he'd been up to over the past few months. The bet she'd lost to Anna was over who could beat who in their annual fitness challenge. Cassie's highly competitive nature had served her well over the years, but Anna had outstripped her in the crane hold during the yoga portion of the challenge. At the two-minute mark, Cassie's balance had failed. Until then, they had been dead even in their timed mile-long run and pull-ups challenge.

The two of them talked until the meal was done and long after, enjoying the atmosphere and wine until she found herself holding his hand, slightly giddy from the wine, and feeling attractive for the first time in forever it seemed. Cassie was enjoying herself immensely. That was, until Brody asked her if she'd ever been serious with anyone and Cassie felt the night come to a screeching halt of reality crashing in like a freight train.

"Once. Married for a few years. It didn't work out." Taking the bottle to refill her glass, she thought desperately of just heading for the locked door and leaving.

Brody watched Cassie's face go blank and knew he had screwed up big time. Her delicate, fine-boned hand actually shook when she reached for her wine glass. From such a rock-solid woman, that said a lot. Somehow, here was a line he'd unknowingly crossed.

No, it was more like a chasm the size of the Grand Canyon. There was getting to know someone, and there was getting to know the real someone. She clearly didn't want to talk about it, but he could take a wild leap knowing he'd probably uncovered one of the reasons she was such a workaholic with all those boundaries. Brody had wondered since he'd met her what made Cassie that standoffish. Was it men in general or just him?

Cassie watched him warily over her glass. "You're going to ask me what happened, aren't you?"

"I am. And you sure as hell don't want to talk about it." Leaning back, Brody nodded at their impasse. She needed the fun and humor of their evening back, and he was willing to give it to her. "Guess that leaves nothing more to do than change the subject or get naked and enjoy the hell out of each other."

Cassie stared at him a moment then broke into laughter, shaking her head. "I don't know why I like you, Brody Miller, but I do."

"You like me because you need some fun in your life. I'm your guy."

"We are *not* getting naked any time soon," she said, bringing those boundaries clearly back into play.

"But we will," he stated with confidence. "Took me a while, but here we are at date number two. I should have you naked, in my bed, by the time we turn fifty."

The idea had Cassie cracking up despite the lines she so obviously wanted to keep.

He took her hand again. "Tell me what happened?"

When Brody Miller was being fun, he was sexy and seductive. When that humor was gone, replaced by a look of caring — it was devastating. He offered no patronizing, condescending gaze, only support and a willing ear to listen. He'd amazed her all night by how good a listener he was.

Cassie swirled the wine in her glass, watching the flicker of the lights above them in the deep red, and took a deep breath to steady herself. Sharing your deepest hurt took guts.

"Nothing much." She shrugged. "Typical story, I suppose. Thought we were right for each other. Got married. Turned out, we weren't right after all. We grew apart. Nothing I did in any area ever seemed good enough. In the end, he felt our marriage included having sex with other women in our bed. I strongly disagreed. I divorced him. End of story."

Daniel had paid her back by dragging her name through the mud and trying to take everything she had ever built. The legal battle had been almost worse than his pithy and cutting evaluations of her bedroom talents. And he'd managed to insinuate that lacking into every level of her life, from simple domestic skills to even the way they socialized while out with friends.

"I'm sorry. I can't imagine what you went through. To trust someone with everything you had, enough to marry them, and to be betrayed like that. I had someone cheat on me years ago. When I was just starting to make a name for myself. We were working on the same show together, and I fell head over heels for her. Now I'm old and wise enough to look back and see it as just lust. Found out she was sleeping with the lead actor to try to get a good word in for her career. Crushed my poor twenty-something heart. I'd never do that to anyone— in any situation."

Cassie looked at him and saw the truth in his eyes. Honor was clearly something Brody held sacred, and what he had said was comforting instead of full of pity, like she got from most people. He had an understanding and insight that most missed. At the core of it all, Brody got it.

"Thank you. I try to look at the whole thing as a positive. We never had kids, at least, so it was only the two of us that fell apart. Could have been a lot worse." She saluted him with her glass. "Your turn. Worst tragedy of dating? Anyone ever serious?"

"Sadly, no, outside of the one who stomped all over my young heart. A lot of weird fan obsession stuff over the years, but mostly everyone is respectful. I've come to what I thought might be close to a good relationship, maybe love a couple times, but reality is that the life of an actor can sometimes suck. The travel and time apart are hard to bear if you aren't both strong people who are happy and content to be on your own a lot of the time. I can sometimes be gone for weeks or months. Takes trust. Especially living in the weird world of Hollywood where everyone lives for the next hottest rumor."

"You don't seem to play into any of it though," Cassie said. "I was curious and Googled you. Brody Miller is a vague mystery of sorts. Social status 'unconfirmed.' Lots of rumors though. Interesting that they think you swing the other way a lot of the time."

Brody laughed it off before turning serious. "I think people think that about everyone in acting at one point or another. I've never cared what they think of me. I act because it's all I ever wanted to do, and I pick the roles that are the most intriguing and challenging. My private life is exactly that — private. So you were curious about me, huh?" A grin stretched from ear to ear. "What else did you find out?"

"You aren't on any social platforms that I can tell, other than Twitter, which makes you a dinosaur. You generously give a shout-out on about once a month, or even longer than that, which your fans go into raptures over. You're a rare guy who isn't plugged in. Impressive in an age that's all about self-promotion."

"And that's what you do for a living. Aren't we quite the pair? I hate phones and devices with a passion. Give me wild country and no service any day. A backpack and sleeping bag is where it's at. These days, I only work when I need to and on exactly what I want to do. I give a lot of my time when I can to causes I feel are worthwhile, like conservation. But I like to keep busy, so it's a fair bit of work in between the play."

"I still haven't watched anything you've been in," Cassie said sheepishly. "It's a pretty big list you have."

Brody shook his head. "I don't care if you've watched a

single thing or ever do." Leaning back in his seat, he still held her hand. "I know you're not here because of what I do for a living."

And therein lay the question. What the hell was she still doing here with Brody Miller, going on close to eleven o'clock? Talking the night away, holding hands, and being charmed right out of her shoes. By Nathan's definition, she would have been having fun. On. A. Date.

Tugging on her hand, Brody brought her attention back to him. "Come here, Cassie."

"What?"

"Come over here. I want you to sit on my lap so I can kiss you."

All teasing aside, Brody seemed ready for more than talking. Cassie's mouth hung open in disbelief. "You can't be serious."

Pulling harder, Brody helped her up.

"I'm serious as hell." Drawing her down onto his lap, he rested her on thighs made of pure steel and slid an arm around her waist to bring her closer. "I've been watching those sexy lips of yours all night, wondering what they taste like." He searched her face, threading his hand into her hair and tilting her face into his.

Cassie's nerves were dancing again as her hands came up to rest on the deep blue of his shirt and curled in tight fists at the anxiety that threatened. She tried to hold him off, but his arms only stayed gentle and soothing around her. Waiting.

"I'm not really all that good at this," she said softly knowing she couldn't possibly measure up for someone like him. A man who probably had women throwing themselves at him on a regular basis.

"I bet you are," Brody murmured at her lips. "Maybe just out of practice a bit."

Cassie saw eyes like emeralds, then Brody laid his lips on hers and she forgot everything.

Every. Single. Thing. In the world.

Except the feel of his lips. Full, soft, and warm. Kissing her. Teasing and gentle, they played across hers in a thoroughness that started slow then switched to something deeper. They built a heat that only went hotter and pulsed inside her.

When she pulled back to try to slow the spinning in her head, Brody groaned and nipped at her bottom lip, showing he wasn't ready to let her go. Cassie gasped against his mouth in surprise, and that was all the invitation Brody needed. His tongue swept in to tangle with hers, and Cassie was caught in the storm that flashed like lightning around them.

Wrapping herself around him and burying her hands in his dark hair, she gave everything she had and fought to get more. Never had anyone kissed her so deeply and passionately. Never had she so acutely wanted to give the same.

Wave after wave of color rolled through, so bright and intense, Cassie feared she might drown in it. Brody's hands were moving up and down her body, and she moaned from the flood of sensations sweeping over and through, leaving her aching from head to toe.

When Brody finally let go, her hair was a mess as she looked down at him in unrealized wonder. Both of them were breathless, and Cassie was sure her heart was about to explode right out of her chest, it was hammering so hard.

"Holy God! What was that?" Laying her head against his, she clutched at him madly, trying to steady her raging body and spinning head. To anchor herself somehow on something.

His incredibly strong, wide shoulders.

Brody's arms were wrapped around her, and one hand was splayed out on her bare thigh and inching its way up toward her ass. Cassie could honestly say she was fighting to find the ability to care.

"Chemistry. God Almighty! Chemistry."

Working his way down her neck, Brody absolutely loved the fact that her hair was short and sassy so he didn't have to take his hands off her to move it out of the way. Cassie tasted like magic, pure and simple.

She was sweet, hot, and wrapped around him, and Brody wanted nothing more than to drown in her.

"Please, Cassie, don't ask me to stop. You feel amazing." He would beg on hands and knees, if need be, to touch her.

Every single inch of him was hot and hard and dying to flip her onto the table and bury himself deep. Taking her lips again, Brody felt her moan echo in his head, and he knew that time would be sooner than later if he didn't let her go.

Dragging away and framing her face in his hands, Brody looked at her. Pure, elemental, and male, Brody held nothing back. It was devastating for Cassie. He wanted her, and for the first time in her life, Cassie rode nothing but the whip of emotion. Logic flew out the door as she was pulled into the storm swirling inside those devastating eyes.

She nodded breathlessly. "Yes! God! Put your hands on me!"

A smile of pure male power lit up Brody's face in a way that said she had just handed him the world, and Cassie knew without a doubt hers was about to be set on fire.

Lips captured hers, and Cassie was swept under. Brody lifted her and she protested the lack of contact, then somehow she was straddled across his lap and he was molding every inch of them together. Never in her life had she been with someone so big, strong, and powerful. It was thrilling and mind-bending all at same time — the thought of just being completely taken and knowing instinctively she could trust Brody to take care with her. He whispered across her face and neck exactly how beautiful he thought she was and what he was going to do to her. The promises made Cassie go weak, like rain flowing into him.

When his hands slid up her legs to cup her backside and ease her forward to press against full arousal, Cassie gasped in surprise, looking down at him.

"Is nothing about you average?" A hand flew to her mouth in utter mortification of what she'd just said.

With a look of supreme smug ego, Brody pulled her back to whisper at her lips, "I promise it will fit."

His hands moved her hips against him until Cassie caught the rhythm, and her head fell back on a groan from the blatant heat pulsing between them. Those same strong hands came up to cup her breasts while his mouth worked its way down her neck. The explorations continued until his hands moved to the back of her dress. Easing down the zipper, Brody let his hands play across her skin like fire, stroking across her back and sliding the dress forward over her shoulders to pool in her lap.

Creamy skin that felt like silk was showcased in nothing more than sheer black lace. Brody gave some thought to tearing it off then did just that, enjoying the shock that played across Cassie's face. Stroking a hand down the front, he cupped one now-bare sexy curve and arched her back to draw it into his mouth. He felt something between a moan and a scream from her as he gave and gave to that one perfect peak before taking equal care of the other. About mindless himself, he jerked her against him harder and captured Cassie's mouth again just to taste her sweetness.

Deciding he wasn't nearly as comfortable as he wanted to be, Brody stood and carried Cassie over to one of the double chaise lounges in front of the fire. Kicked it sideways so it was behind a bunch of tall potted palms. Satisfied he had ensured as much privacy as possible, he gave in to the madness boiling inside him and sat down with Cassie wrapped around him like a dream.

Her dress was bunched around her hips and she was bare in front of him. Brody's hands and mouth were doing things Cassie had never experienced before or during her marriage. Things she hadn't known were possible to make her body feel this good. Fighting to get his shirt off, her fingers fumbled and the buttons snapped, making her laugh at the craziness of it all. Then there was a stunning naked chest the likes of which Cassie had never seen in person — and she was pressed against it. Every curve and plane of them molded together. Flying high on the heat searing through, she shuddered as her panties were tugged off on another snap of fabric. Then Brody was touching her. His fingers teased and drove her mad before taking her over the edge in a whiplash that left her choking and clinging to him in wide-eyed amazement that she even could.

Still buried in her, Brody smiled and bit her neck before

those talented fingers drove her up again. Not willing to wait any longer, they both fought to open his pants, and Cassie slid her hands inside on a moan. Her eyes widened when she felt his size, stroking the thick length, hot and pulsing against her hands, before Brody pulled away to protect her with a condom.

She watched and waited, the realities of the past trickling in and bringing old fears with them.

Everything between them had been so wonderful up until now. Knowing she was about to disappoint him, Cassie bit her lip, wanting somehow to please this one man who had gone out of his way to charm her in a way no one else had ever done.

Brody caught the look on Cassie's face and stopped what he was about to do, which was flip her under him and drive them both insane. All of a sudden, she didn't look like the woman she had been, the one who had been completely lost in pleasure. Cassie was now tense and tight instead.

Figuring he could take a little more time to make sure she was with him all the way, Brody gathered her close again and took his time stroking Cassie back up, nipping, nibbling, kissing, and touching. Finally she was on the edge and mindless again, his name falling like music from her lips.

Cassie was beyond awareness. Brody had stopped to kiss her and just kept on kissing her. Long, slow, and so deep, until the taste of him was imprinted on her soul. His hands had taken over her body. Lost in nothing but him, she barely felt the change until he was easing her down onto him, stretching her, filling her. Her eyes flew open and locked with his, pinned by that magnetic stare. His steady hands guiding her, Brody helped her move, inch by inch, until her eyes closed. He was buried inside her, and Cassie was lost to nothing but this one man.

All there was was pleasure and more pleasure as she rocked against him. It built higher and higher, tighter and hotter, like a spiraling storm, then the world burst around her again, leaving her weak and shaking in his arms.

Even then, Brody never let go. Taking her lips again, he coaxed and teased her to reality again. Cassie's eyes flew open to look down at him. When she realized that Brody was still rock-hard inside her, doubt slipped back in. This wasn't what men liked, and she struggled to make it what it was supposed to be — hot and fast.

"You… you haven't… stop… you need to… please… let me…"

Brody, it seemed, had other ideas about how the night was going. Breath short and hot against her neck, he wrapped Cassie's arms back around his shoulders and held her there. "In a minute. I've waited a long time to have you." Taking her lips in a searing kiss, he smiled wickedly against them. "I'm enjoying myself."

Sweat broke out over both of them as he built the fire once more. Cassie struggled now to keep up with a man who wanted everything she had to give and more. Demanded it all in his slow, seductive voice and the eyes she all but drowned in.

"I can't… I can't…"

Brody knew on some level that her bastard of an ex had something to do with her struggle. But he refused to let Cassie go there. When he was done, she'd only see the future with him in it and never doubt herself again.

"Yes, you can. Look at me." Holding her close, Brody locked eyes with her pretty hazel ones, gone almost midnight in passion. "Yes, you can. I'm gonna help you get there."

Good as his word, with Brody's help, Cassie let go and flew high once more. The look on her face when she did almost sent him over the edge, right then and there. Reaching back, Brody pulled the lever for the chaise, and it flattened out. Rolling them both in one smooth move, he pulled Cassie under him and slid into that vivid heat once more, feeling her arch up like a bow toward him. Groaning and unable to hold back anymore, his mouth roamed wherever it wished and he took her in a surge of hips. Guiding her legs around him, Brody watched her face and strained to hold himself back, wanting to see her come apart just one more time for him. Then suddenly Cassie was calling his name over and over, her body locking around his like a vise. Swallowing her cries, he delved deep and took her, hips pistoning madly, and with a guttural cry, he jumped off the ledge and poured himself into her.

Chapter 8

Starlight danced overhead. Glittering and glowing, it shifted and coalesced in and out of focus while Cassie drifted back and she wondered why she was outside with a fire crackling merrily nearby.

When had she left to go camping in December?

Then her brain clicked back in and focused on the fire pit next to them and the Christmas lights draped across the ceiling. She was sprawled on a chaise lounge with a heavy male still passed out on top of her. Raising her head, Cassie peered down at the length of stunning, half-naked man that was Brody Miller. His pants were still half on, her dress was a wrinkled bunch of fabric around her waist, and Cassie noted one shoe still glittered on her foot. With no idea where or even when the other one had flown off, she dropped her head.

Reality snapped back in, and a war of ping-ponging emotions rocketed through, leaving her a bit giddy with happiness and shock over what she'd just done. Anxiety bloomed next at what had happened between them and she waited for the aftermath of criticism she knew would be coming. Brody had well and truly turned her world inside out and blown it apart all in one fell swoop. She prayed that at least this one time a man would be kind with her. Raising a hand to her mouth, she bit down — hard — trying to hold back the maelstrom circling inside.

Brody shifted, pressing his lips lazily up Cassie's neck. His post-sex coma was being disturbed by her going tense underneath him for some reason.

"What are you thinking about so loudly?"

Giving a slow roll of his hips, he heard Cassie's groan of response and relished still being buried inside her warmth. She felt fucking phenomenal. Like nothing else he'd ever experienced.

"I must not have done a good enough job helping you relax." He took her lips until Cassie gave a low hum of pleasure. "Give me a few minutes, gorgeous. I'll get back to work."

He teased himself by running a hand down her body, over a hip, and down the length of leg still draped over his own and found himself utterly infatuated with the softness of her skin. The scent of her was something floral and sweet. A man could get dizzy off that sweetness alone. Then there was the rest of her. A naked goddess. Just enough curves packed into a sweet little body that boasted a good balance of athleticism and tone to make every inch something he couldn't wait to explore better next time around. Cassie took fitness seriously, it seemed.

"I'm sorry," she said on a deep, hitching breath.

Confused, Brody braced himself above her, peering down in amazement. "What on earth are you apologizing for?"

Cassie focused somewhere over his shoulder and alternated with his chest. "It was all really wonderful. I'm sorry, though. I... I... know I didn't keep up my end of things. Like I should have..." She sounded as if she was waiting for a lecture.

Brody studied her beautiful face, wanting nothing more than to smash his fist into her ex's face. He'd had the brief suspicion from the way she talked about her marriage earlier that it had bordered on abuse, but now it was more than obvious. His heart went out to Cassie, laid bare in this vulnerable moment between them.

"Hmmm… afraid I won't be able to accept that, gorgeous. That sounds like a bunch of bullshit. Your ex tell you that stuff?" He saw the truth in Cassie's face as soon as he said it. The low vicious oath that followed made her pretty hazel eyes go wide. After taking Cassie in a blistering, soul-searing kiss that left her breathless and clinging to him, Brody swore again. "You're a more than satisfying woman. Don't you ever doubt it again. It's a wonder the two of us didn't blow the roof off this house."

His comment made Cassie blink, smile, and finally giggle. She sobered on another hitch of breath, and her teeth tugged at her bottom lip. "I don't do things like this — have sex with guys I hardly know. God, it sounds so cliché to say that, but what did we just do?"

Flipping over and taking Cassie with him, Brody settled back to hold her, wishing only that they were in a more comfortable bed. A quick glance around assured him that they were still shielded from potential prying eyes, and he offered thanks for not having lost his mind entirely while getting her naked. He'd kept Cassie safe from the front page.

"I'd say we both enjoyed Christmas a little bit early this year." He cupped her ass to bring her up to kiss again. "I plan on enjoying it again soon."

Her teeth tugged on her lip again, which Brody was coming to learn meant she was worried or unsure about something. It was fascinating to know she was so confident in the public eye and so different when entirely stripped raw with emotion, lying naked next to him.

"At the risk of sounding crazy, it's been a while and I'm not really sure what to do next here," she said.

A shiver hit her, so Brody felt around and grabbed his shirt to keep the chill off of her. She brought out every bit of the protective side of him that wanted to play hero as he laid down with her again.

"Thanks. Are you always like that in bed?" she asked and charmed the hell out of him by turning bright red and burying her head in embarrassment.

Brody rolled on his side and tucked her close. He couldn't think of the last woman who had been shy enough to blush in front of him. Most were too brazen and bold, which was always a complete turn-off. They never wanted him for himself. It was always the extras of what he came with that made him appealing to them.

"Like what in bed?" he teased between kisses. Cassie seemed more at ease when she forgot to think, and it was no chore to keep kissing those beautiful lips to distract her.

"I don't even know. Insanely intense. I might need a new hashtag."

Playing his tongue across her lower lip, Brody got a sweet little hum of pleasure from her. "I'd say the intense factor had to do with both of us. Takes two to make it happen, and, baby, you sure do inspire a man. How about hashtag 'cosmic'?"

"Cosmic." She giggled. "What a perfect word. You ripped my underwear clean off. I've never had anyone do that before." She sighed with a dreamy smile that had Brody grinning right back at her.

"I could apologize, but I think I'll buy you bags of lingerie instead so I can tear them all off you again."

The statement left Cassie with vivid visions of next time, and she felt heat creep up from her toes all the way to her face. Judging by Brody's face, he was thinking exactly the same thing, since he was smiling ear to ear.

"Thank you by the way. I can't believe I came three times," she said.

"Uh uh, gorgeous. Four."

"Hmmm?"

"Four times." Brody was smiling against her lips. "I kept count. You needed it. How long has it been?"

"Since I had sex or since I faked it last?"

The comment was out before she realized it. Flushing, again, a red she was sure matched her hair by now, Cassie buried her face against Brody. God, how much more could she let slip on how bad this part of her married life had been?

His fingers cupped her chin, tilting her head up to look at him. "Seems the same thing to me."

"Well over two years, give or take."

Brody's green eyes sparkled with a promise that was nothing but pleasure and mischief all rolled together. "Sounds like we need to make up for all that lost time. I loved watching you come apart for me. As soon as my legs work right again, we're going to go find us a proper bed upstairs in one of the twelve bedrooms this house has and enjoy it all night long."

When he lowered his mouth back to hers, Cassie was so

tempted to give in. "I really can't stay. I have to work tomorrow."

"It's Friday. What can you possibly have to work on this weekend?"

Tracing Brody's face and down over handsome shoulders, she stopped only to return to play in the edges of thick dark hair. Cassie took a breath and let it out. The reality of her life wasn't for the faint of heart. "Contracts to do, preparing the team for the entire week I'll be gone. A conference call with Nathan. Presentations to finalize for Monday, Tuesday, and Thursday, depending on which company I'm at in which state. Washing clothes and packing to leave Sunday evening to be in New York bright and early Monday morning."

"That sure is a whole lot for one woman. Any time for me in there?"

"I don't know. This is why I said no to you in the first place. Around Christmas, things will slow down for three blessed weeks, which just means no travel, before it all picks up again after the holidays. This weekend would be very hard to make work."

"Just gonna use me and leave me begging for more?"

Cassie knew he meant to tease, but his words only triggered the anxiety once again. Her ex had always had a problem with her business and how much time it took away. "I'm sorry."

"I thought we already talked about you not needing to apologize. I'll take whatever time you want to share with me, all right? We can make this work if we both want it badly enough, and I do want that with you. I didn't stop thinking about you, even after you told me no at our coffee date."

She saw nothing but complete honesty in him, and she

closed her eyes a moment as sadness drifted in and brought the past with it. All the doubt and insecurities. "It won't work. You won't be happy with me. I'm not cut out for this — being with someone."

"Cassie?" His kiss was sharp and swift with an edge of anger that startled her. "I'm not him. Don't ever compare us like that again. I would never treat you like that. Whatever you're building and making — it's special and worth it. Don't apologize for being strong enough to go after it. My life, my schedule, and being in the public eye won't be any easier for you to deal with. We choose to make it work, or we don't. Simple as that. Say yes, gorgeous? Let's give this a chance. See what we can have together."

Looking into Brody's handsome face, Cassie felt the lock inside her open a little and knew she couldn't deny she wanted to spend time with him. Even knowing that it would be short-lived, for however long he put up with her limited life, it had to be worth it. He had been so wonderful and caring, and he'd helped heal part of her bruised heart already.

"All right." She nodded.

Brody pulled her tight to him, his green eyes flashing. "No way. You don't go into this thinking it will fail and only giving half of yourself. I'm asking you to be more with me. No more of those walls, and no holding back."

Shocked and wide-eyed, she could only stare, amazed once again at Brody's ability to see through all the barriers she tried to throw up.

"I want you to fight for us just like you do everything else. You don't hold back with me. It's that or don't even bother. You're just wasting both our time if you do," Brody challenged, throwing the proverbial gauntlet at her feet.

The truth was there in everything he'd said — it wasn't fair to either of them if she carried an expectation to fail. Something inside her bloomed at his words. That he wanted so much more with her and was ready to step up fully, if she was willing on hers, made her want to take the leap.

"All right, dammit. All the way. Don't complain when you hate it," she warned.

"No complaints. You have my word." Brody lowered his lips to hers again.

Clothing hitched back in place, the two of them sneaked up the back stairwell like thieves in the night, carrying the as-yet-untouched dessert plate and spare bottle of wine. The party in the other part of the house was still thumping wildly along. Brody escorted Cassie inside the bedroom he used when he stayed over and said he'd be right back. Back a minute later with a box of condoms lifted from the master bedroom, he locked the door with a flourish and shoved a chair under it to ensure privacy. He couldn't be happier to have won the woman and a chance to have more with her.

Undoing the couple of buttons on his shirt and pulling it slowly off, Brody walked to the bed where his gorgeous Cassie sat waiting for him. She looked nervous as a cat again.

There was no doubt what Brody Miller had in mind. He was moving like a panther stalking prey, but Cassie still squealed like a girl when he snagged her foot and playfully dragged her across the bed to him then flipped her over. Peeling down the zipper on her dress again, he set his teeth on her neck in a move that lanced heat straight to her core, then his hands slid under and around pulling her back up to kneel in front of him. The dress went up and off in a slither of fabric. Brody wrapped around her from behind while his fingers moved up between her legs again. Cassie was sure her eyes rolled back in sheer bliss as her head fell back on his shoulder.

"Now, back to this whole 'leaving early' thing. I don't really like arguing, but I think we need to talk that little detail out between us." He turned Cassie's face to catch her lips with his. "I want you to stay, baby, and sleep in my arms tonight."

When Brody got done with his unique form of persuasion, Cassie couldn't help but agree that his viewpoint had many merits worth considering.

Chapter 9

Waking up after a night of sexual bliss was brilliant, in Cassie's opinion. Sun peeked into the room as she gave a languid stretch, every bit of her feeling wonderful and completely used.

She'd finally passed out in Brody's sexy strong arms in the early morning hours, but not before he'd taken her through round two of fun; thought they might be a bit sticky after sampling dessert with round three; and carried Cassie to the shower, where he'd proven just as adept during round four of water sports. Pinning her to the shower wall with the water coursing over both of them, Brody demonstrated the benefits of having a tall, strong man in her life. Limp, exhausted, and grateful to the bottom of her soul from discovering that her sexual drive was alive and well, Cassie had drifted off to dream world, utterly content.

Enjoying the sun's sparkling brilliance lasted a full three minutes before a glance at the bedside clock had her eyes popping. It was just after six thirty, and a to-do list a mile long was waiting for her and then some. Usually Cassie was up well before the birds started their morning song.

Inching out of the bed like a secret ninja, she'd almost made it to the edge before those same sexy strong arms caught hold and dragged her back into bed.

"You weren't kidding about being a morning person." The sleepy timbre of Brody's low voice wrapped around her as his arms tucked her backside against him.

"I am. Sorry, I woke you up." Cassie silently swore she'd enjoy one more blissful minute of sensual warmth, then she absolutely *had* to go.

"That's all right. I can adjust, baby," Brody said, shifting against her and proving that he was already up and ready to go.

Cassie's breath caught, and she giggled. "Let me go. I don't have time to play with you again."

She shoved and grasped at the sneaky hands traveling expertly over her after a night of learning just what made her come alive. Exactly how her body was responding yet again. She couldn't stop the moan that escaped when his fingers went lower to discover the proof of that response.

Still half asleep, Brody rolled her under him and slid inside in one smooth move, leaving Cassie's breath lodged in her throat and her nails digging into his back.

"That's all right. I'll be quick," he murmured, working his lips on her neck.

Then Brody started to move and Cassie forgot all about her schedule.

Cassie dragged the black dress over her head and threw Brody a fuming glare. The man blew her a kiss and sauntered naked into the bathroom. Damn, now she really was behind and the worst of it was she couldn't really be mad because she felt so damn good.

When he came out, Cassie was trying to get her hair back into some semblance of normal. Going to sleep with it wet had left it looking like she'd stepped out of a Guns N' Roses video. Red snarls stuck every which way, and worse than that, she had not a single stitch of underwear to put on. Cassie prayed to heaven she would meet no one she knew or get pulled over by the Atlanta police on the way home. How on earth was a woman supposed to maintain any dignity when she didn't even have her panties left?

After slipping into her heels, Cassie turned and bumped into a naked chest and pants half undone. Brody, she noted, still had his briefs.

"Sorry. Next time we sleep over together, let me know what time you want to be gone by." He dropped a kiss on her cheek. "You did tell me not to stop..." Nipping at her neck again sent warm little shivers of heat streaking across her skin.

"Duly noted for next time, and stop right now."

She shoved him away, and Brody pretended to fall away, laughing with her. "Come on." He tugged his shirt on and tossed Cassie his jacket. "Let's see if we can sneak out and not get caught."

Anna stood in the kitchen, though she had to acknowledge it was more swaying and stumbling on unsteady legs than actual standing. She offered up a personal gratitude for not having to handle any classes today, since she had no sense of balance at the moment and would probably wind up in the ER if she tried to do yoga. She felt half dead, half dressed, and blurry-eyed. Her head ached like an anvil with an army of Tolkien's dwarves beating on it with their massive hammers. She swore that their sharp axes were also on the offensive with the rest of her body. Whatever she had drunk last night must have been the equivalent of Klingon Blood wine. Cassie would have gotten all those pop culture references. She loved that stuff in spades. It was one of the reasons they were such good friends — few people really got sci-fi humor.

Hoping she wouldn't die before the coffee was done, Anna figured she was hallucinating when Brody Miller stepped out of the back stairwell, holding hands with Cassie. It was a toss-up as to who was more shocked — Cassie or Anna — as they stopped and stared at each other.

Cassie, her friend who never had a strand of hair out of place, was a current giggling and rumpled mess.

Brody just pulled Cassie along in his wake and out the front door. The only words Anna heard were said in Brody's slow Texas drawl, which uncannily matched Chase's.

"Morning, helluva party last night, wasn't it?"

The vision and commentary assured Anna that the world had indeed come to an end and hell was frozen solid with everyone ice skating inside it.

Chapter 10

Only a few short hours of sleep should have left Cassie dragging. Instead, she stayed charged up and powered through her to-do list with the single-focused intention of getting as much done as possible so she could spend some time, any time at all, with Brody again before she left Sunday. If she caught herself drifting off and staring at absolutely nothing during periods of the day, Cassie figured she had a good reason.

And that reason was Brody Miller.

Salt-N-Pepa's "Whatta Man" hummed in and out of her head all morning after she'd heard it on the 90's flash back hour on the radio during the drive home. It was the perfect song to wrap up and summarize her crazy, perfect, wonderful night.

She'd fielded Anna's phone call, caught up on laundry, nailed her final presentations, and completed a good chunk of her list before the scheduled online meeting with Nathan to talk shop and outline the week.

Cassie had been Nathan's best friend since all the way back in their high school days. They met while shopping at the mall, bonded over the latest fashions, and a discovered mutual crush on the same boy — one who never acknowledged either of them. They'd been close to inseparable since sophomore year, and he loved her as much as he loved the man he was partnered with.

For Nathan, life would have been empty without Cassie Rhone. They'd gone to the same college since they shared a love of business and taken separate career paths for a while before taking the dive to start Halcyon together. They had also been through the hell of various relationships, including when Cassie's marriage had fallen apart with that bastard she'd been married to.

Nathan had been one of the few to support her during her divorce, when even her family looked down at her because of it, and to this day, he suspected her family had bought some of the lies Daniel spewed out like the cockroach he was. Only her brother, Christopher, had stood strong by Cassie and Nathan's side.

So when she'd asked him to follow her to Atlanta to start over, Nathan hadn't batted an eye. The move and her need to grow something amazing, which was what they were doing, were yet more things her family didn't understand.

They'd met new friends in the area, plus they'd reconnected with Anna. Most importantly, because of Cassie's determined drive, Nathan had met the love of his life a few weeks after their move to a different zip code. It was fitting in the universal circle of love that Anna had been the one to play matchmaker when she referred Philip to Nathan to build some customized shelving in their new office space. Nathan fell in love at first sight with Philip's combination of southern manners, a low-slung tool belt and worn white work pants that fit just right and went perfectly with Philip's All-Star golden boy looks.

But none of it would have been possible without Cassie leading the charge.

"I've got it all covered, Cassie. It's not the first time you've left town," he said over their video call while stirring his third cup of coffee for the day.

"I know that. Humor me and let's just go through it again. There's a lot riding right now, and I don't want anything missed with the holidays. This is the most critical sales time for most companies."

"Which is why we, with you as our leader, are one of the best," Nathan pointed out. "Rock stars, remember?"

He let Cassie take them through all of the items on her checklist, knowing it was the only way she would feel comfortable leaving town. More often than not, they discovered something to improve upon, so the review was always worth it in the long run. Becoming complacent and in a rut was a sure thing to ensure a company's failure.

"How was the party last night?" he asked when they were through. "We had another get-together to go to first, and I missed you when we did finally get there. Where were you? What a dress Anna picked out for you! You looked amazing. Thanks for sending the picture. You're glowing by the way, today."

Dead silence tipped him off that something was up —plus the fact that all of a sudden, Cassie wouldn't meet his eyes.

"It was fantastic. I got to meet some great people. Chase's place is outstanding, isn't it? The first I've ever been there. The decorations were off the hook. Anna looked deliriously happy with him, didn't she? Did you see her dress?" Cassie hedged and rambled like she did only when nervous.

"Yeah, yeah, quit babbling. Get to the interesting part.

Who did you meet?"

"God!" Cassie blew out a breath. "How do you always do that?"

"Hmmm… because I've known you *for* — and I do mean *for* — ever. Because you're glowing. And you haven't met anyone for a veeeery long time. And more stalling only means he's a really big something."

Cassie blushed like a virgin schoolgirl on a first date. Even through the computer, it was completely obvious.

He couldn't help but stare at her open-mouthed in shock. "Oh my heavens. You didn't!" Disbelief rolled over him like a steam engine when she refused to meet his eye. "You *slept* with the really big something?"

If possible, Cassie went even redder. Nathan raised a single eyebrow, much like Cassie did when surprised or irritated.

"Just how big *was* the really big something? Spill, or I'll call Anna and find out anyway."

Cassie bit her lip and offered sheepishly. "About six five, dark-haired, green eyes, handsome."

It took Nathan about six point five seconds to connect the dots. "Brody! Brody Miller! Your really big something was Brody Miller!"

Cassie's continue redness confirmed it.

"Well…" He blew out a breath. Cassie had slept with a man out of the blue? And not just any man! "Holy Jesus. I'm so jealous of you right now I can't stand it. And so damn proud!" He mimed wiping a tear from his eye. He'd been in on Anna's plan but doubted the success. Now he owed the crafty blonde fifty bucks. "Please, please tell me how this happened. Anna mentioned she was thinking of trying to set you two up again. I didn't think she meant for it to be, like, now though. Did he take care with you? 'Cause if he didn't, I'll bury him so far underground the ants won't find his carcass. I don't care how damn hot he is."

"He was wonderful. All of it was just wonderful. And he wants to keep seeing me."

She sounded as though she still didn't believe that request could be real. Nathan knew why only Cassie would think that about herself and he damned Daniel to hell all over again.

"Of course he does, sweetheart. You're amazing! Only if Brody were an idiot would he not want to get to know you better and that man has never struck me as an idiot."

He was a huge fan of Brody's, after all. Loved his show and all his other work. Pleased and impressed that the famous Brody Miller had taken such care with his best friend, Nathan gave her a smile. Cassie had been bleeding far too long from the wounds left by Daniel. If it took a famous movie star to make her smile again, Cassie had his utter blessing. Telling her exactly that, he watched Cassie's smile bloom in return.

"Thanks. I was hoping you would be happy for me."

"Of course, Cassie Bear. Always. Now, details and don't spare a single thing, especially how he looks naked. Start with the kissing scale — one to ten. Where is he?"

Chapter 11

Cassie sailed through the rest of the day in a flurry of checklists and product outlines and contract finalizations. She had told Brody that they could possibly do dinner that evening, so she was happy to catch up to where she needed to be for the day.

She hadn't shared all the night's details with Nathan, wanting to keep some of it all to herself like a beautiful secret she could hug close when no one was looking and wondered if tonight would be just as wonderful. It had been so long since she had had another person in her life to worry about that Cassie, feeling a little lost, stood in her kitchen before he was due to come over. What should they do? What was right to serve? Brody had said he would take care of dinner for the two of them, but Cassie didn't know if that meant eating in or out, since he valued his privacy. Was she supposed to do drinks or something first at her place? Or appetizers? She hadn't had time to go to the store for anything.

What should she wear or expect, especially with him being who he was? They were starting at the opposite end of the dating spectrum, since they'd already slept together, so Cassie thought she was okay to feel a little bit weird about it all. Settling on black casual pants and a nice sweater, she added heeled boots and hoped she looked all right.

Nervous and jittery, Cassie opened her door that evening to one of the handsomest men in the world. "Hi! Come in."

"Hey there, gorgeous. Nice place," Brody said, looking around with interest before setting the bag he'd brought on the kitchen counter.

"It is. I like it. I know it's more normal at my age to have a house — a better investment — but an apartment makes more sense right now. It's small enough to take care of easily, and the location is amazing. I can walk to almost everything I need, like the market or gym. I don't have to worry about house maintenance and upkeep."

He liked her apartment. The place suited her even though it had a typical apartment layout, with the living room and kitchen opening into one another. He assumed the bedrooms and bath were in the back, down the hallway. Every inch of it was colorful and neat as a pin, just like the woman who lived there. The plush furniture looked comfortable and was covered in a cream fabric that set off the handmade cushions scattered across them. A deep jewel tone blanket in blue was draped across the back of the sofa.

Bookshelves lined the few walls that weren't taken up with wide planes of windows. In and amongst the books on every subject possible — organized by specific genre, he could tell at a glance — were crystals and whimsical statues. Brody hadn't expected to see them, since Cassie always struck him as serious. It seemed she had a sweet side that liked to dream.

Right now, however, Cassie was fidgeting and biting her lip, making him wonder what was up. It hit Brody that she was a bit nervous again.

"I didn't know if we were staying in or what," she said moving to tuck her phone into her purse. "Should I change into something nicer?"

Brody caught her hand and pulled her to him. "Thought we could stay in. I brought dinner to make for you." Smiling at her, Brody watched the words sink in.

Beautiful hazel eyes stared up at him. "I'm sorry. Did you say you were making dinner for me?"

Brody smiled and laid his lips softly on hers, enjoying her sigh and how she wrapped her arms around. "I did. How does lamb chops with mint sauce, salad, and bread sound?"

"That sounds incredible. Like, *wow* incredible. I didn't know you could cook."

"I can do lots of amazing things. Most of which I usually do up front when courting a beautiful lady. Seems I have some catching up to do."

Reaching into the bag, Brody pulled out a surprise and had the pleasure of watching Cassie's eyes go almost misty when he handed her the bouquet of Christmas greenery and calla lilies. "These are for you."

"Oh, Brody, they're stunning." Beaming, Cassie buried her face in the flowers.

Knowing he would be giving her a lot of flowers in the future just to see her light up like the sun, Brody pulled her back to him. "I'm glad you like them. They reminded me of you and last night. Your hair in the firelight."

"I'm not used to this. I don't know what to do with all this romance. Making me dinner… flowers…" Cassie said, looking as though she was off balance again.

Brody's answer was a slow smile as he lowered his head to hers for a kiss. "How about just enjoy it? I plan to romance the hell out of you."

As if to prove it, he told her to go get some more stuff knocked off her list while he cooked. That way, he said while wagging his eyebrows at her, the two of them could enjoy the night more. Cassie chose to split the difference and brought her computer in to work at the counter once Brody assured her that he didn't mind Cassie ignoring him until the food was ready.

Content that they were able to spend an evening together, Brody got to work on date number three. He pulled out the lamb he'd marinated earlier, hoping plans with Cassie would work out, and the makings for salad. He spent a minute locating a cutting board and the knives in Cassie's small kitchen, of which, he almost tossed the latter in the trash. Her kitchen knives barely qualified to a home-grown Texas boy who believed a blade of any size, shape, or origin should be able to kill invading enemies, shave with, and if needed, help in the kitchen.

Her knives were almost as pitiful as the contents of her refrigerator, which boasted a few eggs, a small container of spinach, a jug of almond milk, and a bag of blackberries. She either didn't cook much or have the time to cook. He was betting it was a little bit of both, which supported his theory that she could use someone to help her here and there and give her a bit of pampering.

The only question was how much support would the very independent Cassie be willing to accept.

When he slid a glass of wine next to her, she thanked him with a distracted smile and a kiss on his cheek before her eyes slid back to the screen.

Th"That" night, Cassie did something completely out of character. She let someone else — a male who wasn't Nathan — take care of the evening while she got one more item done on her checklist. Since it was a big item, it freed up more of her Sunday. She might even be able to relax for a bit before she hopped on a plane to New York. Trying to work with Brody in her kitchen hadn't been too bad. She'd only sneaked the occasional glance at him over her laptop.

He looked way more competent than she did in this area of domestic skills. Cooking had never been her strength, which was another thing Daniel had always criticized her for. The constant cut-downs hadn't made her eager to try to learn how to get better since every effort failed anyway. She'd finally just accepted that cooking wasn't her thing. But she was a master at ordering in and dining out.

Vegetables were chopped up, pans and utensils found and put to use. Soon the kitchen smelled incredible, reminding Cassie that she had skipped lunch again. Giving up, she closed the computer and enjoyed the show.

Cassie got lost for a few minutes admiring the view of Brody's tall, muscular body wearing faded jeans that clung faithfully to him, along with a button-down shirt under a deep green sweater that complimented his dark looks perfectly. Visions of what all he'd done to her last night drifted in.

"What are you sitting there smiling about?" Brody broke into her thoughts.

"Hmmm… what?"

He leaned down to her. "I asked what you were thinking about that brought such a smile on?"

Fighting not to look embarrassed, Cassie meticulously

stacked up papers and the computer. "I was admiring the way you cook. You're a lot better at it than I am," she said, trying to keep things innocent.

As he arched an eyebrow at her, his lips twitched. "Really? Cause for a moment there, I could have sworn I caught you watching my ass."

This time, Cassie felt herself blush.

Grinning, Brody went back to the stove to flip the meat. "You can look at my ass all you want."

"Your backside is pretty fantastic." Cassie acknowledged the point, getting down to put the computer back in her office and came back to get out plates and flatware to set the table.

Brody wrapped an arm around her when she came back trying to refill their glasses. "All done with work?"

"Yes. I shut it down for tonight."

"Good." Switching off the burner on the stove, he pulled Cassie into a kiss. His hands drifted lower, cupping and molding her to him. Grabbing hold, Brody boosted her up on the counter. "These need a few minutes to rest before we eat. How about we practice kissing some more, and you can whisper in my ear what you like about my ass. For the record, I believe your ass is especially superior, and I love having my hands on it."

He demonstrated exactly that, sending Cassie into hysterical giggles. Brody was left with no choice but to work his way down her neck until she dragged his head back to hers for a more intimate connection.

"Gonna ask me to stay the night, baby?" Brody whispered at her lips.

"I was thinking about it."

Brody pulled her closer. "Thank God."

They sank into each other again, leaving them both turned on until the oven timer went off breaking them apart.

Brody laid his forehead against hers in an attempt to calm down, but the hands under her shirt made that almost impossible. "We better eat. This isn't one of those meals that will taste fine cold. A fact which I will take into account next time we have dinner together."

"Good plan. I love the way you think."

Since she was starving, Cassie was only too happy to dive into the fantastic meal Brody had put together. Taking her first bite of lamb, she closed her eyes in euphoria and let out a groan. "Where did you learn to cook like this? It's incredible. Like something at a high-end restaurant."

Cassie knew the difference since she had spent years of being wined and dined by clients in some of the best restaurants around the country. The mint yogurt sauce was perfectly prepared for meat so tender it all but melted in her mouth.

Enjoying the praise, Brody speared another bite and lifted it to her lips just so she could close her eyes again in happiness. "Well, we're big into cooking in my family. Mom is the best. Dad is too, although he'll tell you he's more of the grill master. They made sure my three brothers and I learned our way around the kitchen. Then while on location in India for this one film — it was a smaller production film, so most of the cast shared a house. Anyway, we were lucky enough to have a chef who came in to cook for us in the mornings and evenings. This delightful older lady who decided that since I asked so many questions all the time, I might as well learn something at the same time. So I learned a whole new way of looking at spices and flavors."

Registering Indian cooking was part of the explanation, Cassie's mind had still gotten stuck on the fact that there might be three others just like Brody out there and his mom had raised that many boys. What a woman she must be. And his dad. How had she not learned about his family last night? Brody was good at keeping the conversation focused on others and learning more about them than he let on about himself. Still, she could wheedle out information with the best of them. Tonight, she intended to learn more about Brody — at least what he was willing to share at this point in their relationship.

"Well, I send out my blessings to each and every one of them. You have a gift to be able to create like this. I can do a couple of dishes okay, maybe. Manage breakfast a little, but other than that, you're taking your life in your hands. I'm great at picking up things at the prepared section of the grocery store for get-togethers though."

"We'll see how bad you are. Bet I can help you learn to cook a few things."

She grinned. "Doubtful. Many have tried and failed. Tell me about your brothers. What do they do?"

Brody eyed her for a moment as if making a big decision, crossing his arms. "You know, I kinda hate talking about my family and personal crap."

"I've gotten that impression. Why don't you like talking about family and personal crap?"

"Guess that's part of my own baggage. I never know if the things I tell people are going to stay between just us. There's been a few times some acquaintance thought it was better to make a quick buck with a bit of gossip. Gets old, never feeling like you can trust people."

"And yet you're the one who insisted on pursuing this thing between us," Cassie observed dryly, but she understood his hesitation of being the center of people's gossip. After her marriage fell apart, supposed "friends" had had a field day with speculation. "Guess we both have to decide what we're willing to share."

Brody took a sip of wine and set the glass down slowly while he eyed Cassie with a laser focus before offering a nod. "Okay. Fair's fair. So far, you seem like keeping your word means the same thing it does to me, and I like that part of you a lot. You want to know about my brothers? Strangely enough, most of them enjoy traveling and being outdoors as much as I do. Cooper is an environmental explorer. Takes to the wilderness to find new and rare specimens of animals all over the world. Think he has a woman in every part of the world too. Mom calls him a rake. Simon's the odd one, being that he prefers a desk job. He's a lawyer, which comes in handy since he handles all my contracts. Can't say enough about how much it means to have a family member I can trust in that area."

He laid down his fork to rub a hand over his face. Up until that moment, Cassie had never seen Brody looking so sad and lost.

"The baby, Jake — if you consider twenty-nine a baby — he's starting over, you might say. Lost his wife over a year ago to a drunk driver. He and Maddie were high school sweethearts. I can't remember a time it wasn't the two of them together. Losing her hit all of us really hard. Jake and Sarah, his daughter, moved back home and are living on my parents' farm. Since they're getting older, he's playing farmer and helping out while he gets settled. I think he's just lost right now without Maddie, although he hides it pretty well most of the time, for Sarah's sake."

Hearing of such a tragedy and thinking about what Brody's brother and niece must have gone through broke Cassie's heart. It broke again when she saw the pain Brody was obviously still feeling after having lost a family member.

"I'm so sorry. It's horrible to have something happen for such a senseless reason," she said, touching his hand.

"What about your family? You mentioned a sister last night?" Brody asked, picking up his fork to eat again.

Cassie shifted uncomfortably with the quick change of subject. She wanted to throw up her own wall but felt that would make her a hypocrite. "One. Claire's a homemaker. We don't really get along right now. And I have a brother who works in finance. He's a blessing and a curse all in one since he's a bit overprotective and handles all our accounting stuff for our firm. He's always bugging me for every last receipt and invoice, but I adore him for taking care of it for me. You two would probably like each other. He detests his phone too."

"Brothers should be protective of their sisters. It's a rule."

"I've never seen that rule written anywhere."

"That's 'cause it's part of our DNA coding." Taking a careful sip of his wine, Brody watched her eat. "What about you and your sister? Why aren't you getting along right now?"

Cassie sighed and picked at her food. "That's a hard one to explain. Claire's married. First to her religion, her husband and kids second. I have no problem with Christianity or the Bible and any of its teachings, but for her, one's husband is the personification of God on Earth. All love, obedience, etc, should be given forth or some such nonsense. She's kind of a zealot about it, and everything that's wrong in my life is because I apparently don't pray enough or something like that. I really can't win. She didn't understand my divorce or take it well. Seems I was abandoning my marriage even though I'd already tried going to counseling for a couple of years and we were still failing miserably. I apparently needed to just tolerate and indulge his 'habits,' as she referred to his cheating. Being an independent thinker, I had a few choice things to say back about those 'habits.' Hence, the not getting along for the past couple of years. We dance around each other in person and agree certain topics are off-limits. She's happily married, and my nephews are a joy that make up for it when I go home." Since talk of Claire always brought her down, Cassie switched gears. "Does your family like you being here in Atlanta when they're in Texas?"

"Well, they feel it's closer to them than some places I get to work. Except for Jake, most of us are scattered anyway. They're happy and supportive wherever I am. I've kinda been on my own since I left for college. They love me, always make the premiers if they can. I go home when my schedule allows. I'm excited about Christmas coming up. Which I still need to finish shopping for."

"That's nice. My family supports me." Cassie laughed, taking her wine glass with her as she sat back. "With a whole lot of eye rolling and wondering when I'm going to pack it in and come home to work a normal job. Chris is the only one who doesn't make fun of my business." She rolled her own eyes at the thought. There was nothing on Earth that would have bored her to tears more at this point than working for someone else.

"Let me guess. They don't get what you're making here?

What it will be when you're done?"

"Exactly. How did you know?"

"Takes a different mindset to be someone with vision. Visions like you want to build are the kind that scare most people."

Once again, Brody had made Cassie smile with his perception and insight. Saluting him with her glass, she said, "And how is it you get that when very few people do?"

"I've never settled in going after what I want. Guess I'm always surrounded by big dreamers in show business. People who live their everyday lives working nine to five have a hard time dreaming big. They go to work, make a check, and are happy with that. There's nothing wrong with that. Others, like you, want more."

"I would have never been happy doing that. I tried. It was sheer misery. I love that you get that the hunger to dream big is okay."

"He didn't, did he? Your ex?" Brody asked, taking Cassie's hand.

Memories and regret swamped through leaving her staring into the now-empty wine glass. "No, he never did. In the end, he blamed me for it. Tried to destroy and take everything from me with every made-up lawsuit he could think of."

She had celebrated last month with Nathan and the hugest bottle of champagne possible when Daniel's last lawsuit was thrown out by the judge. The courts could tie things up forever, and finally being free of her ex was liberating.

"Why'd you marry him?"

The wall came down again and she shut Brody out. "I wish to God I knew." Getting up, she started stacking plates.

"Dinner was fantastic. I'll have to get your recipe so Nathan can try it."

Taking them into the kitchen, she tried not to slam the dishes in the sink. Cassie took a deep breath before she went back to wrap up the leftovers — only to be pulled onto Brody's lap.

"I hate it just as much when you shut me out like that. You do it really well, you know. The whole 'fuck off' polite wall of ice thing when you don't want to talk about something."

"I hate when you manhandle me just because you're bigger." Cassie shoved at him, knowing she had no way to win in a show of strength and feeling like an idiot for even trying. She was more pissed than anything, because she hated to talk about her past.

To her surprise, Brody let go, leaving Cassie just sitting there. "Okay. I won't manhandle you. Except when I'm carting you off to bed." He winked, probably to try and lighten the mood, then became serious again. "I'm sorry. For dragging up the past. I've never been married before. Just trying to understand what happened so I don't screw things up with you."

She could only stare at him. The look of caring and need to understand filled his handsome features, and she tried to find some understanding of her own for his point of view.

"I'm sorry for shutting you out," she said and realized she actually meant it. Doing that had been unfair to the both of them. Getting up, Cassie went to the sink to start the dishes. When Brody got up to help, she stopped him. "No, I have this part. You cooked after all. Besides, I need something to do with my hands right now."

Opening the dishwasher, she started to rinse and stack.

He'd asked that she try to be together with him. Part of being with someone was opening up. At least, that was what she'd thought a relationship should be once upon a time, before Daniel had proved otherwise.

"We met a few years after college. Daniel was on the business fast track, and so was I. For a long time, we seemed to have a lot of things in common. We both had jobs with great companies. Got married. Were busy. He was happy in his work. I grew steadily not. I tried a couple of other companies and finally decided I wanted to branch out and start my own thing since marketing and social media were my specialty. I wanted to be my own boss, so Nathan and I started Halcyon Connections. Our business grew, and Daniel and I grew steadily apart, changed, or became different people. I'm not really sure exactly what happened. All of a sudden, there was just nothing I could do right in any area of our life together. The long hours I needed to work and the travel just added to it. I'd be a full-on powerhouse rock star, as Nathan is fond of saying, when I was away and a folded up miserable mess when I was home. I was always trying to please him, walking on eggshells, waiting to hear what next I wasn't good enough at. We tried therapy — at least, I tried. To this day, I don't know why I put myself through that part of it."

She'd hated the therapy sessions, hated opening herself up to a complete stranger pretending to be a specialist who only smiled and nodded and offered the occasional suggestion that Daniel would ignore. Cassie added more to her wine glass. Brody was a good listener, just sitting there, his legs and arms crossed as he waited for her to go on when she was ready.

"Nathan thought Daniel was okay in the beginning, but

that illusion faded after we got married. Nathan would tell you these days that the rat just finally showed his true colors, like a copperhead shedding his skin. I was checking our credit card statement one day and found something suspicious — a dinner out on a night when I wasn't in town. At first, I thought he had been out with friends. Not a big deal. We each had our circle of friends, after all. Then I realized it was a night that Daniel had told me he was home sick. Other things started cropping up, and I thought he might be cheating on me. I came home one afternoon. Caught an early flight back, deliriously happy to be home, one day early even. I remember thinking I could surprise him and have a special night in or something. We'd had a terrible fight over money before I'd left.

"I'll never forget it. I walked into the house with my bags, and there on the kitchen floor was a woman's shirt and a bright red bra." Leaning against the counter, Cassie almost started laughing or crying. She was too close to both to realize which would come out. Never talking about her ex and the emotional hell she'd been through was a conscious choice she'd made for a long time. "I'm sure you've seen enough movies to know what happened next. Husband and lover — who I was told later, in explicit detail, was everything I wasn't in bed — going at it when I walked in." It still hurt to say it out loud, how she wasn't enough.

"What happened then?"

Cassie threw him a twisted smile. "I have a nasty temper. I think I broke everything I could get my hands on while throwing them both out. Happy to say that I hit the bastard in the head more than once. I have a wicked arm. Baseball." She shrugged as an explanation.

Taking a damp cloth, she turned and wiped down the counters. "The sad thing was, I didn't love him at that point. I don't think I'd loved him for a long time even before that. He'd destroyed everything I ever felt for him. But I was blaming myself for all the problems, wrapping it up in a fine bow of guilt and trying to fix it. It was basically a relief to be able to have a reason to divorce his ass. I knew we were heading there. Things just got there quicker because of it. I guess that doesn't say much about me as a person... to say I was glad it was over."

His hand closed over hers, stopping the cleaning. His arms encircled her and held her back against him. Cassie closed her eyes, savoring the strength at her back.

"I'm so sorry, Cassie." Brody said softly, resting his chin on her head and holding her tightly.

Turning toward him, Cassie wrapped her arms around his neck and just held on. She wasn't exactly sure why, but being held by Brody helped. It was an anchoring and support freely offered.

Sliding his hand into her hair, Brody tilted her face up to him. "Thank you for sharing with me. It helps to understand the past sometimes."

"You too — for listening and sharing as well. It's hard to figure out how to be with someone again."

"Whatever he said to you over the years, he was wrong. It takes a weak person to blame someone else for their problems and choices." Laying his lips on hers, Brody offered the comfort and healing of physical touch. His lips were twisted in a half grin full of trouble when he let her go. "I'll tell you one thing — if I ever meet him, I might just shake his hand." At Cassie's incredulous look, the grin widened. "His being a pure jackass is what brought you here to me. I can only be grateful for that. You're a helluva woman. For the record though, after I shake his hand, I will knock his teeth out for you, gorgeous. You bring out my overprotective hero side too."

Cassie found herself laughing despite it all. Brody made everything better somehow. "Chris already beat you to it. He broke his nose when he found out."

"You know, I believe I will like your brother quite a lot." He pulled her close again. "How about we go for a walk? Clear our heads and walk off dinner before dessert?"

"There's dessert too?"

Taking her hand, Brody walked to the door to pick up his coat and ball cap. He grabbed Cassie's coat as well to help her into it. "Course there's dessert. Now, I don't actually bake or anything, since I'm more of a chef, which is why I leave it to the experts and pick something up at the bakery."

He pulled Cassie out the door, laughing with him.

Chapter 12

The week passed in a whirlwind of travel, wining, dining, and presentations followed by Q and A through three different cities in five days. To say Cassie was exhausted would have been an understatement. She was exhausted and felt like a dried out shell at times, but she was also exhilarated since all three clients were thrilled with their work and signed contracts inked for more. The next year coming up would be amazing for Halcyon.

On late Friday afternoon, Cassie went straight from the airport to catch up on updates with Nathan and their team. Practically doing the foxtrot into the office, Cassie stopped dead at the looks of amusement and interest that followed her. She caught Nathan's grin and watched his smile bloom.

"Change of plan, fearless leader. We're going to celebrate all your stunning success with this amazing champagne I bought," Nathan said. "A stellar week needs to be recognized."

He tore off the foil and gave the wire a twist. There was a huge pop, then glasses of bubbly were passed around.

Stunned with the impromptu party, Cassie took one glass and turned to her team, saluting them as she looked at every last face that she adored. As a leader, sometimes you had to adjust on the fly – even from your own perfectly outlined agenda for the day. Nathan was right. Recognition was important. Especially when your team worked their asses off.

"We are *all* celebrating this amazing week. None of it would be possible without every last one of you guys. I'm so proud to work with all of you. It makes every day a pleasure and an adventure. Now let's freaking celebrate!"

The party exploded with cheers, food, and music. Halcyon was pumping with energy as they ended the successful week.

Nathan had just finished giving Cassie the short version about a potential new client when, in the middle of their celebration, a delivery guy walked in bearing a vase of flowers. Surprise overtook his partner when the guy said he had a delivery for Miss Cassidy Rhone. Ignoring Nathan's interest, Cassie signed and accepted the container before taking it over to her desk. Nathan followed her, already more than a little suspicious of who had sent them. Cassie removed the card carefully, as if it were a snake about to bite her. She looked at the inscription and didn't say a word.

Ever nosy and a true friend, Nathan peered over her shoulder to read it himself. "'Welcome home, gorgeous. I missed you. Looking forward to seeing you tonight. Brody.' Well then, nicely done. About time someone in this city took notice of what an amazing woman you are." He kissed her cheek.

Cassie lifted stormy eyes filled with hopelessness. "I don't know if I can do this."

"And why exactly not?" Leaning on the desk, he cocked his head at her as he'd done since they were young. The look that said Cassie was capable of anything.

"I'm worn out, exhausted, physically and mentally drained. I want a bottle of wine, a bubble bath, and my bed. Why did I tell Brody I'd see him tonight?"

"Maybe cause you missed him a little bit too?" Seeing the misery in her eyes, Nathan pulled her into a hug and kept holding her. Since he had lived through her divorce with her and picked up the broken pieces along the way, Nathan knew the signs and could see Cassie falling right back into that rabbit hole of not being good enough now that she was home. Brushing his knuckles on her cheek, he used his other hand to fix her hair by tucking a stray lock behind her ear. "He's not that asshole, sweetie. This is Brody Miller, some-one who's man enough to hear you say you're tired and give you a hot meal and put you to bed instead."

"And what if he's not and expects more?"

"You want my advice? Let him take the lead on that to-night. He had no problem with anything last weekend. When you worked most of it anyway, right?"

"No, he didn't. But maybe it was just a fluke, you know… because of the sex?"

God, Nathan hated seeing her like this, beating herself up over nothing but the past. Nathan had never forgiven himself for not seeing how bad things were in her marriage. Cassie had learned to hide things well until she hadn't been able to any longer and broke down in their office one day, crying her heart out. The fact that she'd lived for two more years in that hell while she and Daniel tried therapy hadn't made things any easier.

That she had even allowed Brody to get close to her at all said a lot about how much she did actually like the man, even if she had no idea on how to handle it yet. Tears filled her eyes, but Cassie held herself tight, furiously blinking them back. She hated to cry, and Nathan wished — not for the first and probably not the last time — that he could beat Daniel's head in with a shovel for destroying someone so wonderful.

Nathan let her go only to hold her arms and make her look at him. "Cassidy Leanne Rhone, do I need to be ashamed of you? If it was just sex, I doubt Brody would have come over to make you dinner the evening after. He'd have just left it at a one-night stand. Now, stop listening to that bullshit from that asshole and go enjoy yourself."

Chapter 13

With Nathan's sage advice ringing in her ears, Cassie drove to Brody's house that evening. He'd said he was more than happy to pick her up, but she figured having her car was safer — in case she needed to leave if the evening went badly, as she expected.

Trying not to hit her head on the steering wheel at a stoplight, Cassie reminded herself yet again that Brody was not like Daniel. In every way, so far, he had proven to be different. They had traded a handful of flirty, fun texts during the week, but their longest actual conversation had been a whole eight minutes long. Cassie had been between meetings and Brody was just getting off set. He hadn't been kidding about his schedule being crazy too.

Telling herself that unlike Daniel, Brody had never once seemed upset by her schedule and that everything would be okay, she drove on, following the directions she'd been given. No matter how many times she went through the pep talk though, Cassie was still a bucket of nerves when she arrived at the gated road and pressed the security button. After being buzzed up, she tried once again to convince herself that everything was fine and the week had only left her a little tired.

Pulling up the driveway, Cassie got her first look at Brody's house. She wouldn't call it the lavish estate that Chase's house was, but it was definitely high end and exclusive, judging by the few other scattered houses on the road up. His house was located in a mostly still forested area in the bluffs outside of the city proper. Beautiful, she imagined, when the sun set down off the cliffs and rolling Georgia countryside.

Lit up and perfectly accented in the dark evening sky, the tumbled stone and huge wood beams of the house suited the property. Seemingly at one with nature rather than trying to fight it as most new construction did. When she turned off her car, the front door opened and there was Brody, walking toward her with a huge smile.

He looked... amazing! That was the only word Cassie could think of. Really amazing. He gave new inspiration to the phrase tall, dark, and handsome. How could jeans and a loose sweater look so good on any one man?

That only made her feel more awkward knowing how worn out she must look, and her last-minute phone consult with a client had run way longer than anticipated, making her later than she'd said she'd be. Cassie had barely had time to freshen up.

"Hey there, gorgeous. Thought you would never get here." Brody opened the car door to help her.

"I know. Sorry. Last-minute phone call. I hope I didn't hold up dinner too long." Ratcheting up a smile, she handed him a bottle of wine. "For tonight. This is really beautiful out here. I've never seen this part of the county yet. Didn't even know this area was here. How long have you had it? Is the property very big?"

She knew the babbling came with nerves, so it was almost a relief when Brody only smiled and solved the matter by drawing her in, wrapping an arm around to lift her off her toes for a slow, soft and devastating kiss, right there in the driveway, until Cassie was clinging and her brains were half leaking out of her ears.

"Three years, give or take. About four and a half acres total. Thanks for the wine, you didn't need to bother. I don't really give a damn that you're late — you're here now." He grinned before taking her lips again in another sinful caress. "I missed you, baby."

"Hmmm… wow… when I can think straight again, I'll tell you how much I missed you too."

"Yeah? You missed me, huh?" Bending, Brody swept her up in his arms, and Cassie gave a cry of surprise.

"I can walk, you know. Put me down," she said, laughing.

"I know you can, but you look a bit tired and here I am, all big and strong and wanting to play the hero again." Grinning at her, Brody carried her into the house. It was a move that left a woman feeling like a princess.

If the outside was a showstopper, then it was only rivaled by the inside. Made to impress, the house was built on levels that went steadily downward on a curve of staircase that married the dynamic atrium style with carved pieces of wood that intertwined to create a banister on the wide stairwell. Oceans of gleaming reclaimed wood floors flowed on all levels, and wide walls of windows opened to the outdoors, letting in the starry night sky.

Still carrying Cassie, Brody went down the stairs to the main level.

"Is that a tree growing in the middle of the house?" She angled her head to see better. Cassie had never seen the likes of the house outside of HGTV.

"It is. Cool, isn't it?"

"It really is." His house connected with Cassie on some level deeper than she wanted to admit. It was soothing and relaxing at the same time to have the outdoors growing inside.

Landscaping was layered over the same tumbled stone that clothed the outside of the house, and it perfectly showcased a variety of native plants and seasonal colors. Pretty pansies in eye-popping red and white for the holidays were scattered throughout. Cassie wondered if Brody took care of all the plants himself and decided yes, he was too private a person to see an army of caretakers coming in and out of his home.

At the base of the stairs, the lower level spread out into a large space that included the kitchen, eating area, and living room. The back wall boasted a huge TV and wall-to-wall bookshelves. A huge tumbled stone fireplace stood between the kitchen and living room, red and gold flames already crackling in the hearth.

"This is incredible." After Brody set her down, she turned in a circle to take it all in. "Can I just say super *wow!* How did you find this place?"

"Studio exec wanted to off-load it before he filed for divorce so his wife wouldn't get the property. He swore she would cut down every last tree and probably burn the place out of spite. Since it needed a special buyer and knowing my love of nature, he came to me first. I came out and fell for it the second I saw it. Knew from the outside, without even seeing the rest, I'd buy it. Worked out perfectly since I was tired of apartment living. The series had taken off, so it seemed like I would be here for a while. For when I'm in

Atlanta filming, it's perfect. I keep a place in New York and LA for when I'm there too."

"You keep a place?" Cassie slanted him a look. "That's cute. I keep a couple of plants in my home."

"They're good investments, that's all. I enjoy dabbling in real estate. It's been a fun venture and profitable. I'm not invincible enough to think acting will always be there. Pays to have alternative avenues of income. Drink?" He held up her bottle.

"Yes, please. Forgive me, I'm just going to wander around."

The place was really too fantastic not to wander, and exploring might help settle her nerves. God, she felt way out of her league all of a sudden with Brody and his really amazing home.

Huge beams ran through the open ceiling spaces. Sky lights opened at random, and through the patio doors, she saw a tumble of stairs and landscaping that was cannily lit up to show a low sloping hillside and the glimmer of a pool below, shaped to look like a natural pond. She imagined in the summer there would be lush plants around it and probably the flow of a waterfall somewhere close.

Wandering into the living room, Cassie took notice of the space and Brody's apparent love for reading. Books on every single subject possible were messily jumbled together along the shelves. Some were piled at random, stacked three and four deep in places. Fiction and non-fiction, biographies, science, philosophy. The list was endless, and her fingers itched to properly organize them.

"I like to read and learn new things," Brody said from behind her, handing over a glass of wine. "Fortunately, both of those passions combine for every new character I play, and I get to do lots of research."

"It's just… I had no idea what to expect… but this?" She gestured around. "This certainly wasn't it. I love it."

"Glad you like it." He took her hand to kiss it. "I was hoping you might spend the night with me. The view in the morning is even better."

Her nerves bounced higher with a vengeance. "I'm sure it is." She said carefully, walking over to admire some pictures on the mantel.

They had to be of family. His brothers for sure, she thought, taking in one photo that had the four of them and an older man who had to be his dad — judging by the same sparkling green eyes full of fun — all standing together, covered in mud, wearing sweaty clothes, and laughing.

"The annual Turkey Day football challenge," Brody explained as he watched Cassie checking everything out.

Still dressed up for business in a dark blue and white-trimmed pantsuit that showed every cute curve, she looked incredible but damn tired. It showed in the shadows under her eyes that makeup didn't quite cover up. Cassie was also a massive bundle of nerves for some reason. Practically vibrating with anxiety, she'd barely met his eyes since he'd met her on the front step.

Brody took a seat on the couch and stretched out his long legs, crossed at the ankles, to settle in and figure out what was wrong. With Cassie, he'd learned that nervousness usually meant the past and the easiest way to deal with it was to just ask. "You want to tell me what's bothering you?"

Cassie's back went poker-straight, confirming his suspicions. "Nothing's wrong." She threw him a glance over her shoulder. "Why do you ask? Is this your mom? Has to be. You have her smile."

"It is. And you're lying to me. Why is that? We can go through every picture and book in here 'till you're ready to talk." Angling his head with a rueful smile, Brody waited.

"I'm not..." Catching his bland stare, she sighed. "All right, why is it you see through every damn thing? I swear you're the only one besides Nathan I can't fool."

Brody patted the spot next to him, and Cassie took a deep breath before sitting down and curling up to look at him.

"I warned you I suck at this whole dating thing," she said. "It's your own fault for wanting to keep on. We could have just left it at really amazing sex."

"We could have, but we chose something else. Something better, even though it's a challenge for both of us."

"It's stupid." She shook her head. "I haven't had another person to worry about including in the equation for a while — what they want or prefer. Even when I did, there was always an expectation of what things were supposed to be like when I came home from being away, and it was never good. I'm sorry. I guess I'm just nervous wondering what you expect, and I'm tired on top of it all and don't really know if I'm up for any of it. Even if the sex is really amazing." Brody listened and heard more than what Cassie actually said. He saw the war she had within herself — wanting to please him and battling the scars of the past. Setting down his glass, he leaned forward to trace her face. "He really messed with your head, didn't he?"

Pain crossed her pretty face. "I told you it was stupid."

"It's not stupid. I don't know what I can say to put your mind at ease. Except to show you I'm not him." Laying his lips on hers, Brody savored once more having her home with him. "Cassie, whatever expectations I might have had for tonight, I'm not an idiot. One look at you and I could tell you're damn near exhausted. When did you last sleep more than four lousy hours straight this week?"

Cassie grimaced. "I can't honestly remember."

"Baby, as much as I want to get you naked right now, I want to take care of you even more. So let's take off these heels you didn't have time to change out of yet." After easing them off, Brody pulled her feet across his lap and rubbed the sore arches. "We'll have some dinner when it's ready here soon, then you can curl up with me and watch a show and the fire. If I'm lucky, you'll fall asleep in my arms so I can feel like a hero again and carry you to bed later."

Cassie let out a groan of pleasure from what his hands were doing to her feet. "I don't deserve you. You know you're getting a bad end of this deal right now."

"You know, sometime in the future, you'll have to deal with my schedule crap too. Long days and longer nights sometimes. If we keep going together, there will be times you may not see me for weeks or months, depending on what part of the world I'm filming in. It's all about compromise and making it work." He lifted her onto his lap and helped her undo the jacket and peel it off.

Cassie laid her head against his. "If we keep going together, huh? It's only been a few days."

His fingers tangled in her silky red waves. "A full week. Happy anniversary, baby." Holding her close, Brody loved how perfectly she fit against him, as if Cassie was made only for him. Every single curve.

"I never did thank you for the flowers today. They were a

beautiful surprise."

"You're very welcome. I really like you, Cassie. Awake and energized. Tired and exhausted. Any way I can get you."

"I really like you too. And I did miss you. Especially the way you kiss and hold me."

Brody smiled with wickedness. Taking her wine, he set it aside. "How about you let me kiss you for a while then, till dinner is ready?"

Dinner was pure comfort food and left Cassie a blissed-out mess. Brody had done something clever with lemon, herbs, chicken, artichokes, and spinach that Cassie would never have been able to figure out. Ladled over a bed of pasta, the dish was pure heaven on a fork.

Curled up back on the sofa later, enjoying the fire after being shooed out of the kitchen by Brody telling her to put her feet up and relax, Cassie could only wonder at how lucky she had gotten with such a wonderful man. Watching the flames dance in the stone hearth, she heard him come into the room. A gift-wrapped box settled in her lap before Brody did the same behind her.

"What's this?" she asked, puzzled by the present.

"Open it and find out." Wrapping arms around Cassie, Brody snuggled her up to him.

Teeth tugging on her lip, she looked over her shoulder at him, unsure all of a sudden. "You don't have to buy me stuff, you know."

"This I did. Open it up."

Cassie caught the gleam in green eyes. The one that spelled mischief as only Brody Miller was capable of.

After tugging off the bow, she lifted the lid and cracked

up in relief at what was on top. A bra and panty set in jet black. Lacy, thin, and very, very see-through, it reminded her of their first night together at the holiday party last week.

"Funny." She rolled her eyes and held them up. "How'd you know my size?"

His hands slid up to cup her breasts, making her laugh more, and a low chuckle vibrated next to her ear from Brody.

"I've made a thorough study of you, Cassidy. But I sneaked a peak in your drawer last weekend to make sure." Brody drew the top layer of tissue off the box in a sweeping flourish, and Cassie let out a choked sound of disbelief. "Seemed a good idea to get some extras. In case I want to rip something off you every now and then," he explained.

He took his time exploring her neck with a string of lingering kisses. For once, she worked really hard not to get distracted by the lips and mouth working their way down. It was a battle no woman could win with the skill being applied.

The box was filled with lingerie in every color and style Cassie had ever seen and some she'd never thought to consider looking at. She held up a teddy in sheer fabric of palest pink and another one in deep bronze. Bras and panties followed the same. All of it La Perla, Gilson, and La Bruna. She wasn't sure about the last two, but she knew La Perla was decidedly high end.

Brody stopped long enough to confess without apology, "I might have gotten a little carried away while shopping."

Casey choked out another snort, holding up another handful of colorful strings with not much else between them. "A little? Good God, Brody, you went off the reservation. I didn't think you were serious about bags of underwear."

Eyeing another lacy pair of sapphire blue panties with tiny

crystals scattered across the front, Cassie swallowed hard. She really wasn't the super confident kind of woman who wore most of this stuff. Victoria Secret models were selected for a reason, after all. They were tall and statuesque, something she clearly wasn't.

"Well, I admit I was just going to replace the ones I ruined, but then I thought what the hell and indulged the heck out of myself. Purely selfish reasons were the root cause of my decision." His fingers played with the buttons on Cassie's shirt until his hand slipped inside and her head fell back on a moan.

Struggling to focus, Cassie pulled his hand away and shifted to look at him better. "You can't just buy all this. There has to be a small fortune here. It's too much."

"As I said, purely selfish reasons. Let me spoil us a little bit."

"You can't do this. You have to take some of this back."

It was becoming apparent, very quickly, how well-off Brody Miller was, how different their incomes ratios were. Tonight had been a brief but insightful glimpse into his world, and she hadn't even seen him surrounded by adoring fans yet. Cassie did well and was a successful six-figure earner — Halcyon would show a profit for the third year in a row — but she was nowhere near in the same league as Brody.

Money had always been such a huge thing for Daniel. How much was spent? What it was spent on? Why was that needed in the first place? He'd greatly resented the money it had taken to start Halcyon even though all of it had come from Cassie's personal savings and a gift from her grandparents' inheritance.

All of that twisted viciously now, wrapping in Cassie's head and leaving her feeling guilty that Brody had spent so much on her. She didn't know how to deal with it or with the man looking at her with a mixture of disbelief, confusion and what she hoped wasn't possible annoyance.

"I'm not taking a thing back. Except if it doesn't fit," Brody said, trying to tease her and hoping to bring back the fun of when Cassie was smiling and enjoying his surprise. Exactly the way he'd imagined while shopping online.

The comment only made his woman's face fall in sadness. Brody wasn't sure what the real problem was, but it sure wasn't based around the fact that he'd bought underwear. Granted, he had gone a little crazy and he'd readily acknowledge that point of the discussion, but Cassie would look good in almost anything. What was a man supposed to do when faced with so many sexy choices?

Still, he didn't like seeing her unhappy.

"You spent too much. I don't need all this. Please."

The last word was a plea so softly spoken that Brody almost missed it, as though Cassie didn't really know what to do as she stared at the lingerie still in the box.

"Is this about money?" The thought had occurred to him and was confirmed by the look in Cassie's eyes, making him drag a hand through his hair in frustration. "Cassie, come on? You can't be serious."

Hazel eyes, wide and worried, met his own. "I just never really thought about this difference between us. You're here buying lingerie that costs the earth, more than I would spend in a few years on clothing. You keep houses on both coastlines. I'm… I'm not with you for your money and fame or for you to buy me expensive things."

It was more than just that, he realized. The money wasn't

the only difference standing between them. She was battling the past again. Misery swirled in those deep eyes the way it only did when Daniel snuck his evil way back in to pick at Cassie's confidence.

Taking her hand, Brody brought it to his lips. "Was money a big issue in your marriage?"

At first, it seemed Cassie wasn't going to answer, then she finally nodded. "Yes. Always. Mostly around my business, but it grew. There seemed to be arguments over everything. Furniture, vacations, even clothing. I'm not a huge spender on any of it, but I hated having to justify things like needing a new pair of running shoes because my current ones were worn out." She took a deep breath on a shake of head. "I'm sorry. I'm projecting all this crap again, and it isn't fair to you. It just weirded me out a little to have you buy all of this at once. I didn't mean to sound ungrateful. It just seemed… well… it was kind of a shock. I want money out of the way between us. I don't want you to ever think that about me. I can pay my own way."

"It never crossed my mind. You're too damn independent to ever be comfortable taking a handout."

The look of relief on her face made him hold her closer to give comfort.

"Okay, I'm glad you think that," Cassie said bringing her hand to his face.

If Brody was being honest, the whole situation left him a bit dumbfounded, since he'd never had this happen before with a woman. Most of them wanted his money. Usually they wanted that even more than him, expecting the large and lavish gifts that came with wealth. Cassie, however, was the first to look like she'd be happier if Brody took his gift back.

It was so damn refreshing, it made her even more special to him.

"Look at me." Brody waited for her eyes to meet his. "Understand something about me now. I can't change my net worth. I'm not Bill Gates or Mark Zuckerberg, but I am extremely well-off. I got it through doing something I love, and I've been very lucky over the years. I won't apologize for it."

"I didn't ask you to."

"No, you didn't. I don't want you to. Just understand that a big part of me likes pampering the people I care about. So I might choose to spoil you every now and then with something special. Do extravagant things just because I can. Maybe like I did here. If it makes you feel better, you can count this one as a couples present since I promise to fall on my knees in gratitude when you wear them for me."

Cassie smiled softly and shook her head. "That would make quite a picture."

"And I don't want you to take this the wrong way or cause another argument between us, but you're my woman. There's no way you're paying for a damn thing when you're with me."

"Brody, that's not—"

A single finger to her curvy lips cut her off, then Brody leaned in for a kiss. "How am I supposed to feel like a big manly hero and treat you like a princess if you don't let me?" Taking her lips again, he enjoyed her lovely taste until Cassie was sighing and melting back against him.

"You know that's not the damn point," she murmured.

"Course I do. It's just money. Please, don't let it hold things back between us. I have more of it than I know what to do with. Take every dime you make and do whatever you want with it. Put it all back into your business. I don't care. You're a smart woman who knows what's right for her own life."

Her fingers stroked his face as Cassie looked at him in amazement, and he thought for a moment she might cry with the moisture that glistened. "All right. I love that you feel that way about me, and I'll try to be more open to all of this with you. It's quite an adjustment. Thank you again for the gift."

Laying her head back, she settled in with a contented sigh to watch the fire with him. Brody smiled softly and pressed a kiss to her forehead before he lifted his woman better onto his lap to hold her closer. Cassie had unknowingly given him a gift he hadn't been expecting — someone who didn't care about all the extras he could bring to the table. That she only wanted him gave back a level of pleasure he'd not known was even possible, much less expected to find. She'd surprised him further while she was away by keeping what they were trying to build close to her heart.

He hadn't seen a single rumor or tabloid article about them, and nothing showed on her personal social media pages, which had about a hundred thousand followers – and growing, referring to a magical weekend with a new guy or a hot new something in her life. In doing so, whether she knew it or not, Cassie had given Brody what he needed. That he could trust her to keep those lines of privacy he so desperately needed from the public in order to function and create like he needed to.

Lacing their fingers together, he squeezed them warmly. "We okay then, baby?"

"Yeah, I think we really are. More than I thought we could be."

"Good. Now that we've cleared up this little matter between us, let's go back to when you first opened that box. We call this a retake in acting, by the way," he joked, just to see her smile as he put the lid back on the box. "I've been dabbling in directing, here and there, so I'm in a fine place to coach you through. This time act all happy — lots of smiles and over enthusiasm." He tickled Cassie until she was giggling helplessly for good measure. "And action."

Playing along, Cassie drew off the lid and exclaimed in raptures, "Oh Brody, you shouldn't have!"

When they both stopped laughing, Cassie slanted him a look of interest. The gift had unexpectedly allowed her to talk through another hurdle, and Brody had, once again, been understanding as he listened. She could think of only one way to thank a man in such an instance. And how could she not want to give back a little when he had taken such sweet care of her and made her feel so special all night long? All of his royal treatment had even picked up her flagging energy.

"Which one should I wear first for you tonight?" she asked, cocking her head.

A flare of heat lit his emerald eyes before it was carefully shut down with only a look of caring. "Are you sure? You don't have to do anything. I'd rather you sleep tonight. We've got tomorrow."

"I can sleep when you're done with me." Laying her lips on his, Cassie let them curve against his before sinking her teeth gently into his bottom lip. The slow hiss of response as he shifted to claim her deeper said volumes on what Brody preferred.

"Hmmm… baby, I was sure hoping you would ask me that.

There was one I kept picturing on you, over and over again." Reaching in the box, Brody drew out a confection of deep forest green and his lips curled in a sinful way at Cassie's widened eyes and single "oh."

"Why don't you go upstairs and get comfortable? I'll be up in a minute. It's the last bedroom at the end of the hallway."

Taking her new collection up the winding staircase to the second level, Cassie found a tastefully decorated master suite that held a lake of a bed in the middle of it. The wide-paneled platform-style looked decadent enough to sink into and not want to get out of for at least a solid week. Another huge wall of floor-to-ceiling windows framed the far wall with patio doors that once again opened to outside terraces. The whole house seemed laid out to enjoy Mother Nature.

Entering the bathroom revealed more cleverly designed cabinetry and countertops, just as the kitchen had, with an oval porcelain tub that she couldn't wait to try out someday.

Cassie took a peek in the mirror, after slipping out of her clothes and into the sheer green fabric with wisps of lace and satin that clung, lifted, and molded in a way that was surprisingly comfortable. *Holy moly!* Even she thought she looked great. Brody had amazing taste in undergarments. Having never really explored seductive lingerie — since Daniel's opinion was that she was too flat-chested for anything good — Cassie felt empowered and sexy all in one fell swoop.

Figuring that what Brody wanted was a sex goddess, she hoped this fit the bill and that she would once again measure up in bed. After giving her hair one last fluff and putting on an extra layer of lipstick, she stepped out wearing a look she hoped was pure temptress just as Brody walked into the bedroom.

He stopped dead in his tracks, and Cassie couldn't help but smile. She'd always dreamed of making a man do just that and had the pleasure of seeing his jaw drop before his mouth formed a single reverent "wow." She sent up a silent thanks for all the workouts she'd sweated through that allowed her to pull off the seduction.

"Do you like it?"

"You about stopped my heart." Coming over, Brody assessed every inch of her with eyes that burned. His gaze traveled over her as he trailed a single finger down over her shoulder and arm, grazing the side of her breast before brushing over a nipple that went to a single hard peak at his caress. "Turn around."

His voice had deepened and gone thick and husky, sending a shudder of anticipation racing through her. Cassie did a slow turn. Emerald eyes darkened to almost black raised to meet her own and she reached up to twine her arms around Brody's neck and pull him down for a kiss she hoped would blow his blood pressure through the roof.

The picture on the website he had bought the outfit from hadn't nearly done the piece justice. Cassie in it was a whole other story. The bits of green and silky straps rode exactly where he wanted his lips to follow — over all that soft, creamy skin. Red hair waved like firelight, making her elfin eyes huge, and lips, slick and soft, met his own to ignite a storm that blew straight through every cell in his body. Drowning in his own need, Brody almost missed the hesitation riding in Cassie eyes and cautioned himself not to take her like an animal.

Barely able to control himself, he molded her to him before lifting her to carry to bed. A week without her had been harder than he'd thought possible. Five days had dragged on forever. Feeling as though he had heaven back in his arms, Brody lowered her onto the bed and let his hands and lips roam. With the taste of her skin, however, the desperation changed. He'd thought he would want to tear off the green fantasy with the same desperation of their first time together, but Cassie's floral scent was making his head spin. Something sweet and fragrant mixed with the lush heat of her skin. For some reason, he only wanted to sink in and savor, to indulge them both.

Thinking Brody would want the rush, her fingers flew to the buttons on his shirt. Her words urged him to hurry as she undid his belt and whipped it off and reached for the snap at his jeans. Brody stopped her, and Cassie felt old fears sneak in. She had always been expected to be ready for sex, hot and fast, after being away. Closing her eyes tightly, she waited for the cut-down.

But Brody only pulled her hands off him and guided them over her head where he pinned them in place with one hand. The other continued working over her body with singular skill and focus.

"What's the rush, baby? Slow down."

Mortification mingled with embarrassment. "I... I thought you would want... I've been gone. Let me please."

"Shhh."

Soothing and tender, he calmed her with leisurely, deep, and drugging kisses. Holding her hands above her, all his glorious weight pressed her down until Cassie went soft and dreamy-eyed.

His voice was low and seductive in her ear, as much of a caress as the hand moving over her breast. "I do want that. But not tonight. Sometimes the fire and flash is what's needed, and other times… other times, it's a slow burn. Tonight, it's a slow burn, baby."

Her mind spinning out from what Brody was doing to her, Cassie struggled to remain a full participant. "I don't mind, really. I've been gone. I'm sure you just wa—"

His mouth cut her off again, and their tongues tangled, making her body ache. A low moan escaped her when his hips pressed against her own.

"I do want you. More than anything. Let's relax and enjoy. Just let me explore. I've had all week to miss you. I want to feel you burn, Cassie. The way you burn only for me."

Rolling her over, Brody straddled her, and his hands, strong and warm, went to work massaging the tension and stress out of her neck, shoulders, and back.

Then his lips followed.

Everywhere.

All the knots and tightness bled out like mist under the skill being applied, leaving only the need that pulsed like a slow bass rhythm, steady, deep, and never ending. Unable to believe the tenderness and care in the way Brody was touching her, Cassie gave in and gave over.

Brody was right. She only felt like this with him. The heat and fire. Like a secret lover of old, caressing and stroking, his hands traveled over her, reigniting secrets known only to the two of them. Awakening. Building with each sigh and questing touch, making Cassie groan at each new level that built to an aching pulse. His mouth found her nipple through the fabric and laved before sucking deep. She felt the heat curl through her then pool between her legs. Ones she was only too happy to let fall open to his questing mouth. Hooks slipped and fabric slithered away and off like a warm summer breeze, then his mouth was on her, exploring each fold and silken line before delving deeper to drink the liquid heat that flowed like fire through her veins. Cassie arched up, floating on a sea of pleasure and need. Her hands tangled helplessly in his hair when Brody refused to let her pull him up to her until his name fell from her lips. Then the world simply melted away.

The gilding built as he traveled back up her body, devastatingly thorough until he at last claimed her lips with the taste of her still on them. Both of them groaned at the feel of him pressing and stretching her as he slid inside. Burying his head in her neck, Brody moved. Home at last and delirious, Cassie held him close, absorbing each slow thrust of his powerful body, which built the fire brighter between them. Helplessly caught in his eyes when he laced their fingers together, she met him willingly. They climbed higher and higher until at last their bodies flung them toward the sun, where they hung before falling back to Earth.

She tried to stay awake after, but words from Brody fell soft, low, and deep against her skin. His warm, strong hands held her close, continuing to stroke and massage, pulling her under. Content and satiated to her very soul, Cassie drifted off to sleep.

Brody tucked Cassie into him, holding her tenderly as he traced her face. Her beautiful features were softened in sleep. He brushed a soft kiss across her half-open lips and heard her sigh his name as he smiled down at his sleeping beauty.

Cassidy. His sweet Cassie. She drew from him every ounce of caring and wonder he thought he could hold for someone and then some. Brody didn't think she even knew how much strength she had in her. It had only been a week — more if he counted all the time since they had first met. How many times had he picked up the phone, wanting to call her? Fighting himself since he'd said he would leave her alone, contenting himself instead with a casual friendship he'd hoped one day might evolve into more. He hadn't been able to forget her, and now fate had brought them back together. Cassie didn't know it yet, but he was crazy about her on every level that mattered and already picturing her in his future.

For Brody, it was easy. When you knew someone was right for you, you knew.

In time, he hoped Cassie would feel the same about the connection they had and what might be built out of it.

All it took was two people willing to try.

Chapter 14

Clouds and raindrops were dripping outside the room when Cassie drifted to awareness, curled up against the most incredible warmth she'd ever felt in bed. It was wrapped around her as much as the throw pulled over her, calling like a lover for her to slide back under into dreams of a dark and handsome hero. Opening eyes that were slow to focus, she soon figured out that the golden expanse of what she thought was the sands of a beach was actually a broad male chest. One strong arm was wrapped around, holding her close, so that she was pillowed half on top of Brody with her leg thrown across his in abandon. Shoving back messy hair, she peered around.

He was awake, holding her on one side, reading a bunch of papers on the other. Remembering the last of the night before and pretty sure she had fallen asleep on Brody, Cassie looked up at him. He brushed an absentminded kiss on her head, intent on what he was reading. Content to snuggle in, Cassie lay there and let herself wake up. As was her habit, she always took a few minutes to review the previous day before setting her intentions for the current one.

Everything last night had been incredible. Brody had taken care of her in ways she hadn't known were possible. The only person Cassie could blame for trying to ruin it was herself and her silly hang-ups from the past. As she'd learned the hard way building a business over the last few years, when something wasn't working, it needed a change. Just like a change was needed now. It was time to draw a line in the sand. She could continue letting the past sneak in and ruin all that they could have together, or she could choose to trust, relax, and enjoy connecting with this amazing guy the universe had decided to bless her with. Everything happened for a reason, and Brody was part of her life now for however long that was meant to last.

NO!

That thought was nothing more than self-defeating. Brody had specifically asked her not to think like that of the two of them. She drew that line in the sand once more.

It wasn't fair to either of them to always think things might fail. Even worse — actively looking for ways to make that happen. Maybe part of that was wrapped up in Daniel and how things had all fallen apart, but that was the past. Brody was nothing like her ex in any way, shape, or form. He was content with what he had and who he was as a person. If the most selfish thing he had done so far was buy her a big box of sexy underwear, well, Cassie could let it go. And maybe he was just as cautious about sharing his personal life as she had been, but unlike her ex-husband, Brody seemed happy with whatever she was willing to share with him. So far, he had accepted her just the way she was. Even when she worked nonstop and came home with only half of her brain intact. Outside of Nathan and Anna, Brody was the only one to have ever done that. To accept her as is.

And Cassie could be more for Brody because of that easy simple acceptance.

She *wanted* to be more.

Content with her analysis and decision, Cassie smiled, happy to begin letting go, at last, of the past that had haunted her far too long.

Casting her gaze about the room, she took in the buttery gold color on the walls. Dual reading chairs and plush ottomans draped in dark teal tones sat in the corner. Deeply cushioned, they invited a person to sink in and enjoy the patio view and a book. No TV was present in the bedroom — unusual for a man in Cassie's experience but the painting over the dresser was stunning. Instead of a traditional mirror, there was a landscape, bold yet somehow a relaxing swirl of the forest in the evening light. It seemed to glow from within and under the foliage that had been painted, like fairy lights were hiding inside, drawing the eye into the magic and mystery of a path just barely laid out between the trees. Like a magical Elven forest. It was a painting you could stare at for hours and get lost in. True artistry.

Next to them on the bedside table stood a haphazard collection of books about Abraham Lincoln, and she wondered if it was research for a future role. Cassie's eyes fell on what Brody was reading. She'd never read a script before and found it fascinating. It was completely different from reading an actual book, since it had only the dialogue scattered in with suggestions for overall body motions and facial expressions.

"That's really serious stuff. Is that for your show?"

"It is." Setting the papers aside, Brody pulled Cassie up to him, and she propped herself up on his chest. "I was wondering if I should wake you up. Forgot to ask when you needed to leave today."

"Maybe later this morning or early afternoon. Depends when you need me to leave. I tried to work ahead to free up some time for spending with my guy." She said it shyly, but the label made Brody smile with approval. "What time is it?" When she saw the clock on the bedside table next to him, Cassie's jaw dropped. She never ever slept that late. "Oh my God. How is it ten a.m.?"

"You can stay as long as you want. All weekend, if you like. It's ten a.m. because your body apparently needed it. You passed clean out, sweetheart. Slept like the dead. I'll be a gentleman and not mention that you snore."

"I did not. Did I?" It was out before Cassie caught the teasing light in his eyes. "You rat."

Brody pulled Cassie full on top of him. She loved the feel of her naked breasts against his skin and took an extra moment to enjoy all the lean muscle of his long frame.

"Feel better?" he asked.

"I do. Thank you for relaxing me so well. I was all but purring with that massage you gave me." She slanted a glance down at him. "I feel like I could charge a mountain today. Which I will do next week. Last travel before the holiday." Giving a shimmy of excitement, Cassie caught on quickly to who else was excited.

Even more exciting was how really great it was to start the day with a sexy man in bed. Brody Miller, laying there with a knowing smile and rumpled bed hair, was the definition of sexy.

Pressing a kiss to his lips and enjoying the feel of his two-day-old stubble, she couldn't resist asking, "What exactly are you reading?"

"Last show for filming next week. Working on my lines."

Having Cassie slithering over him was no hardship, but it sure was making it hard for a man to think. Especially when she adjusted and made sure that the core of her could slide better up and down his throbbing cock. Since he could get fully on board with her intentions, Brody reaching into the table next to him and slipped out a condom as Cassie started exploring.

"I watched episode one of your show."

When she traced her tongue over the tight bud of his nipple and sank her teeth into the surrounding muscle, he jerked in response. His hands grabbed hold and lifted her up for a kiss.

"What did you think of it?"

Cassie could only blink, trying to focus through what his fingers were doing. Brody smiled against her lips, loving how he could drive her a little crazy as he traced his hand up her side, savoring the feel of those absolutely perfect curves.

"Of what?" she murmured.

With her gorgeous pink nipples caught between fingers, his woman had no idea what he was asking.

"Of the show?" He teased her lips. "The one you watched."

"Oh… right… Blake is a total jerk." Breathless, she kissed him back and groaned when Brody spread her legs and his fingers played inside her perfect wet heat. "He's… a chess… player."

Cassie practically panted the words, and Brody swore he grew another inch just listening to her.

"Manipulative… devious… always looking for the next play…"

Brody fit himself to her and eased Cassie down on a groan. Slowly.

"He's… nothing… like you."

Her mouth sought out his as he lost himself to the feel of her.

Sprawled out on top of Brody, Cassie stretched, grateful to the soles of her feet that she could actually move. She'd had no idea the things her body was capable of before she met Brody Miller, and she sighed happily with her fingers playing in his dark hair.

"You were right. Mornings in bed are much better."

"Correction, mornings in bed with you are much better." After a fond pat on her bottom, Brody rolled her underneath him. "I need food. Desperately. I'm going down to take care of that little thing for us. Then, fair warning, I might throw you over my shoulder and cart you right back up here to bed." He kissed Cassie lavishly then swung out of bed. "You have anything that's not a suit to put on?"

Admiring Brody's supremely well-formed naked ass while he tugged on sweats, it took Cassie a second to focus on the question. "I do actually. Just need to run out to my car. I have my carry-on."

Thick brows drew together over narrowed green eyes. "You haven't been home yet? Gone all week?"

Wincing at the words and scrutiny, Cassie tugged the sheet up higher. "I had to take a late phone meeting with a client. If I'd gone home, I would have been later than I already was getting here last night."

Leaning down, Brody smoothed back her hair. "I appreciate you coming over, even late and all, but baby, you have a right to at least a change of clothes and to shed the week before you do."

"It wasn't a big deal," she said, sitting up to face him and trying to make him understand and knowing, on some level, she'd upset him.

"Your keys in your purse or coat? I'll go get your bag. You stay here and keep warm for a bit, all right?"

"Coat." She acknowledged his thoughtfulness for her with a kiss. "I don't need you to take care of me. But I'm glad you want to."

"Thanks for letting me."

After grabbing a shirt, Brody strolled through the house until he located the keys then went to Cassie's car. He stared inside the trunk, which held said carry-on and also her checked bag with the barcoded tag still on it from Dallas, and tried to fight the frustration over having a workaholic girlfriend. He'd work on getting Cassie to add in some more relaxation time. If nothing else, Brody was at least going to take care of her as much as he could.

In a kitchen that was about four times the size of hers, boasting top-of-the-line appliances, Cassie sat at the counter on a bar stool, admiring the acres of countertops done in poured concrete and cabinets made out of reclaimed materials. Perfectly designed, she supposed, for someone who loved to cook, and it was as open and airy as the rest of the house now sparkling in the sun that had decided to show up after the rain. The kitchen also held an island that was just that — big enough for a person to sleep on if they wanted.

The job of slicing fruit had been generously delegated to her. She'd offered to cook breakfast, but the chef had said he'd only let her if she did it in just her bra and pant-ies. Laughing herself silly at the idea, she enjoyed the show as Chef Brody whipped up scrambled eggs topped with fresh herbs from the pots from the windowsills. Cassie had chopped those while Brody guided her hands to show her what a chiffonade meant for the basil and a fine dice for the thyme, joking about how he was going to teach her about cooking. She could admit that the chopping lesson hadn't been that bad. If fact, she'd even call the experience a pos-itive one. Brody had been patient, putting her at ease when she was nervous handling the deadly sharp blade.

Brody spoke up while Cassie found plates, cups, and cut-lery to set the table. "I have to pick up some groceries and a couple of other things later. How about I drive you home and you can grab what you need for the weekend? You're welcome to work here today and tomorrow if you like."

Leaning against the wall next to the stove while he cooked, Cassie watched Brody pour the eggs into the hot skillet and swirl the mixture expertly. He let the high heat set them while she thought about his offer.

"If I do stay here again, that of course works to your ad-vantage, right?" She eyed him over her tea cup and got a wag of eyebrows in response.

"I can come to you later too. Either way. I'm flexible. We don't shoot again till early Monday."

"I'll think about it. I guess if you don't mind me working here, tonight wouldn't be a problem."

"Where are you flying off to this week? You leave tomor-row evening again?"

"I do. New York first, then Salt Lake City. Chicago is on the way back. I won't get in till late Friday afternoon, maybe evening. I'm not sure yet. Depends on the after-seminar part. This Chicago company likes to party."

"So... plan on seeing you Friday night, or let you rest up and see you Saturday?"

Biting her lip, Cassie ran the details of next week's schedule quickly in her head. "I don't know for sure. Can we play it by ear? In case I'm tired and useless?"

"We can. There's a cast party that day after wrap up. Depending on how long we run, getting together might have to be Saturday anyway."

"Right, then just a few days till we both leave to go home for the holidays."

"Yep. Spend them with me? Those few days, gorgeous?"

The request caught her off guard until she caught Brody's eye. "You're serious?"

"I am. Think about it. Gives us a chance to get to know each other more. You're gonna miss me over Christmas. I'm half tempted to scoop you up and take you home with me," he said, tickling Cassie and nipping at her neck.

"It's still a bit early to go home to meet the parents. Let's hold off on that for a while."

He switched off the burner on a shake of head at her comment. "This is done. Let's eat."

Chapter 15

"Hi. Hope I'm not catching you at a bad time?"

"Nope, not at all. I'm on break in between set changes. How are you, gorgeous? You're in Salt Lake today, right?" Brody's voice drifted out of the phone and sounded like a little slice of melted dark chocolate, bringing back exactly how it felt to be with him in person.

"Yes. Delayed and stuck in the airport with a storm about to hit. I'm assuming they'll start grounding planes soon. Mine hasn't even arrived yet from wherever it's coming from. If I don't get on something out of here by three, I'll start moving meetings for Chicago."

"I hate when that happens. What time you need to be in Chi-Town by?" Brody asked and got Cassie's answer. "I tell you what, why don't you sit tight? Go get something to drink and let me make a call."

"Okay," she said slowly, a bit confused and feeling like Brody was blowing her off. To think she'd been sitting here thinking about how much she missed him. "I guess I'll just talk to you later. Have a good day."

Fifteen minutes later, an unknown number called her phone. Cassie picked up to a person who introduced herself as Jerry Patville, Brody's personal assistant. She hadn't even known Brody had one. Figured. Jerry started asking questions about Cassie's flight, destination, and time frames, then she asked Cassie to hold.

Jerry came back on a few long minutes later. "Miss Rhone, I have you booked on a private flight at terminal D. Please proceed to the nearest gate there. I'm arranging your luggage to be moved as well. Your flight leaves in forty-five minutes. Have a safe trip."

"But, wait a minute. What are you talking about? I don't have a flight booked. I'm on Delta."

"Mr. Miller said you might protest. He also asked me to pass along the following — 'get going so you can get home sooner.' I would advise you to hurry, Miss Rhone."

After she hung up, Cassie stood there gaping. Her phone rang again with Brody's number.

"Hi. What's going on here?" she asked.

"Just getting you to Chicago. Call me when you land, all right?" The low southern drawl sounded full of himself.

"On a private flight?" Cassie practically hissed and ignored the people starting to watch her pace. "Brody, I won't let you do this. You—'"

Seemingly unconcerned about the bother, Brody chuckled and brushed it off. "Why not? The alternative is to lose the account and have delays. Go catch your flight. You can yell at me when you get home."

"Brody, I can't let you do this!" But she was talking to a dead phone. He'd hung up on her.

Cassie fumed as she tried to figure out what to do. Fate chose to further mock her then, when the gate attendant announced that her plane was delayed until almost seven o'clock, if not even longer with the way the forecast looked. Caught between frustration with her man, the hassle and headaches of rescheduling, and possibly losing an important account, Cassie grabbed her carry-on to make the hike to terminal D. As she stalked through the airport, she muttered out loud to herself about how they were going to have a little talk about extravagant gestures when she next talked to Brody.

Cassidy followed Jerry's instructions and was soon being escorted out into a private jet. One that boasted luxurious everything, including plush leather seats with acres of leg room and private in-flight service. The plane departed in minutes.

Cassie took a few deep breaths, looking around. She laid her head back on the seat and tried to find any semblance of emotion that might be close to gratitude. How did one stay on an even keel with a guy who could buy and sell anything he wanted?

Chapter 16

The rush of December finally done, Cassie stepped off the plane in Atlanta on Friday afternoon and breathed a huge sigh of relief for having made it out before the blizzard hit Chicago that day. The same one which had snowed in Salt Lake City.

Travel was over and done for the year. She was home for the longest stretch off in months and could dial it down until January to being only eighty-five percent productive.

Snagging her bag off the baggage claim, Cassie walked out to the arrival pickup area to meet Nathan and came up short. Brody stood there along the line, leaning against his car. The height was impossible to miss even though he was trying to disguise himself, hunched against the chilly breeze in a Yankee's ball cap and sunglasses. Only in the high fifties, Atlanta felt like a spring balm after the chill of the North.

Cassie took a deep breath and walked up, keeping her face neutral. "Hi. You're not who I was expecting."

Nathan was dead meat. The blood elf traitor. He knew she was pissed at Brody. Now her best friend's insistence on meeting her today, when Cassie usually just found an Uber ride or cab to get home, made perfect sense.

"Funny thing, Nathan called me a couple of hours ago. Asked if I was free to pick you up. He had a thing come up.

Said it was an emergency. Lucky for me the cast party ended early, so it worked out."

Catching her wrist, Brody pulled her close. Didn't ask. Just wrapped his arms around and laid one on her until Cassie was melting with the feel of him that had blown straight through and had barely a coherent thought left in her head. God. How could she be so frustrated with someone and still miss him beyond belief?

"You still mad at me?"

Sighing, she shook her head and stepped back. "More irritated than mad. I'm trying to just be grateful. Once again, you didn't have to do it."

Brody took her bags and lifted the carry-on off her shoulder to stow them in the back of the SUV, then he opened the car door for her to climb in. "I can apologize again for it if you like. Don't really see the point though."

Shutting the door on her before Cassie could respond, she was left staring at the side mirror and the reflection of a swagger of tall man heading around the car. The move only spiked her temper back up like a match to dynamite.

That casual, South-of-the-Mason-Dixon-line, pat-the-little-woman-on-the-head crap. Fuck! She hated that about the men down here. And she'd worked so hard over the last few days to set the incident aside.

After taking several deep breaths to calm down while they drove off, she said, "It's not that I don't appreciate what you did. It's just that I don't need you to ride to the rescue and save the day."

"Cassie, you were going to be stranded in Salt Lake and not get to your next city, then have to move everything around and be more delayed getting home. I made a phone call and got you a damn plane and you've already blistered my ears off for it. Could have worked out just the same that there wouldn't have been a plane available. It's not a big deal, so I don't understand why you're turning it into one."

"Because you didn't just get me a damn plane. It was a private jet, a ridiculous expenditure I didn't ask for. I've been delayed plenty of times and dealt with it."

Brody still didn't see what the big deal was, especially if it brought her home to him, but he would swear on a stack of Bibles he'd never do it again if Cassie would just let it go. She took a deep breath to debate the next point, and he jerked the car over to the side of the road and threw it in park. Unsnapping his seat belt, he leaned over and took her mouth. Hard.

"I swear, I'll never interfere in your business again," he said softly after he had her clinging to him. "I'm sorry, but don't expect me to not want to be your hero and save you every now and then when I can."

"You can't use sex as a weapon either," Cassie said just as softly. "I don't mind you being my hero. Just dial it down a bit. I don't need all the wow factor. I just need you."

He laid his forehead against hers on a sigh, still amazed that this one woman had the power to undo and bring him to his knees. It was something unreal. The only person he'd ever been with didn't care about all the extras he came with. She only wanted him.

Cassie was the shift. She was a such a gift.

He'd just have to get used to her stubborn independence. It was part of what made her so attractive — how she could stand on her own and was only with him because she chose to be. The truth was they both brought something to the other that hadn't been there before.

Brody traced her face. "I'm sorry again for interfering. I promise I'll work on it. Forgive me?"

Cassie nodded.

"Good. I'll let you tie me up later and torture me for payback if you want," he offered, leaving her laughing as he pulled back on the road.

"You really are too much sometimes," Cassie said.

Laughing with her, Brody took her hand and held it the rest of the way to her apartment.

Their first big fight and over something so strange.

She had probably blown it all out of proportion, but getting used to the fact that your guy lived by a completely different set of social rules took a bit of adjusting. Cassie would get there in time — she hoped — but the shock treatment had taken her by surprise. Looking at Brody, she could only wonder why fate had thrown the two of them together and why they enjoyed each other so much. She hadn't been quite so swamped this trip and had actually gotten to spend a few minutes here and there talking with him.

Before the plane incident.

The conversations had never been strained or forced. Intellectual at times and light at others, Brody kept her laughing and in good humor while having a ready ear for the challenges of the day, and she had done the same for him. Having someone to talk with about something other than business before she went to sleep had been really nice. And the flowers he'd surprised her with in her hotel room on Tuesday had been lovely — made even more so by the sweet poem he'd included. Cassie still had the note secretly tucked away in her notebook.

Squeezing his hand, she remembered the words of the poem. "I'm glad I'm home and glad you picked me up. Thanks for riding to the rescue. Nathan wanted us to kiss and make up, I think."

"I guess I can only thank him," Brody said, slanting a grin at Cassie.

"Can I take you out to dinner tonight or try to cook for you?" she asked, offering an apology of sorts.

"You could. But I figured you might be tired, so I took care of it already and picked something up on the way to get you. This way neither of us has to do a thing. I'm glad to wrap up my week too." Brody pulled in to the parking lot of her apartment building then shut off the car. "Your place or mine? Makes no difference to me."

"I'd like to just be home tonight, if you don't mind?"

"Not a problem." Still holding her hand, Brody brought it to his lips. "Cassie, I really hated you being ticked off at me. I'm sure I'll screw it up again in the future trying to take care of you, so be patient with me, all right?"

Cassie laid her head against his. "I will. Be patient with me too. I'm probably just a bit sensitive about the whole hero thing. I've gotten used to being the sole person steering my own little ship and world."

"There we go. All made up and friendly again. Look at us. You weren't kidding though. You have a heck of a temper, but I like it. If you would have been home, we could have kissed and made up sooner." He brushed his knuckles across her face. "When can we make up tonight?"

"Whenever you let me out of this car and drag my bags

upstairs," Cassie said, grinning with anticipation.

Brody's green eyes went large, and he was out the door so fast, Cassie thought he was on fire. She didn't even have time to gather her purse and briefcase before the door was open, Brody waiting there with a hand held out.

She learned exactly how many ways you could actually touch someone while lugging baggage around. Brody locked onto her in the elevator and didn't let go until it opened on the eighth floor. Cassie managed to escape with her purse and carry-on, running ahead as fast as she could, only to be caught at the door, spun, and pressed up against it in a soul-searing kiss. Fighting to get closer and battling coats, they were both laughing and panting madly.

Cassie turned to jam the key in the lock only to drop it when Brody sank his teeth into her neck with a near growl. Saying he would get it, stealthy hands worked a path down her body, leaving her leaning dizzily against the door. Finally getting the door unlocked, they both burst inside.

Tossing her bag aside, Brody hooked an ankle to kick the door close and fixed his gaze on Cassie with nothing but the promise of ravishment ahead.

She backed away.

He stalked her around the living room.

"I thought we were having dinner when we got home," Cassie teased, dancing nimbly aside out of his reach.

"We are."

He feinted left and Cassie fell for it going to the right where Brody spun, caught her, and lifted her over his shoulder on a shriek.

"Later," he said, carrying her down the hallway into the bedroom.

Brody tossed her on the bed before following her down, and Cassie welcomed him with open arms. A week without him had been way too long.

"I really missed you, Cassie."

"I'll say. That was some performance." She lay near co-matose next to him, thankful he had rolled her over so she wouldn't have to suffocate in the pillow.

Brody had launched his attack to make up for lost time and apologize for their argument, and Cassie could only say she was grateful for his extremely thorough nature. She might have to argue with him every time she left town just so she could come back to this. A smile twisted her lips at the idea.

It just kept getting better with him every single time. And it wasn't just the sex. He brought in the fun as well. On some level, Brody actually got her, the core of what made her tick. The fact that he understood that truth, in such a short amount of time, should have scared her. Instead, their rela-tionship only seemed easier, knowing that he got why she lived the way she did and the how of what it would take to meet her goals.

Completely wrung out and so fucking happy to have her home with him, he'd been watching her lying next to him. Cassie had become like a drug in his system. Fire and light. Just the taste of her was so damn addictive, Brody didn't think he'd ever have enough. Already he wanted her again. This had been the first time she'd attacked him right back, no hang-ups or memories coming between them. Cassie had ridden with nothing but pure instinct, just as eager as he had been. His back would show the proof of what a wildcat she'd been in that eagerness.

Now, she was a gorgeous, naked sprawled out mess — tumbled hair, flushed skin, and lips swollen from their kisses. A half smile spread on her lips as her eyes closed. The woman had to be the loudest thinker on Earth.

"What are you thinking about that's making you smile?"

Cassie only smiled a little bigger. "I was just thinking I like fighting with you. Daniel always hated to fight. He preferred discussions. Logical, rational discussions. I love the fact that you let me fight and you yelled right back at me on the phone. And you didn't mind me still bitching about it when I got home. It was all so… normal. You don't fight dirty. You just fight." Hazel eyes, more deep green in the darkening light, opened to look at him. Teeth sneaked out to tug at her lower lip as she grinned. "I could get used to make-up sex by the way."

"Yeah?" Brody rolled over to lay one on her. "I'll try to think up another problem for us to get into. Maybe buy you a car next." He grunted when Cassie hit him square in the chest then rolled out of bed before he could snatch her back. "Get back here. I want to fight with you some more."

Chuckling, Brody grabbed his pants and followed her out of the room. She'd taken his denim shirt and was standing in the kitchen with it on, rolling up the ridiculous length of sleeves while assessing the refrigerator's contents. It might as well have been a dress on her small frame, and Brody couldn't think of a single reason to ask for it back.

She peered at him over the door. "You mentioned taking care of dinner. This is hopeless in here. Are we ordering in?"

"Got it right here," he said, carrying in a bag he'd dropped by the door. "Grab us some plates while I heat it up."

They ate curled up on the couch, watching a movie on what Brody termed a deplorably sad size of a TV with an equally sad sound system. He teasingly offered to buy a whole new setup for her just so they could fight again. That comment earned him another playful punch in the arm, and Cassie dissolved into giggles when he retaliated by tickling her.

The movie lay forgotten, droning in the background, after they ate. Brody pulled her closer, and they spent the night talking, curled up with a bottle of wine between them on the couch, utterly content to have each other home.

Chapter 17

Brody had talked Cassie into moving into his place for the few days they had left together before they went their separate ways for the holidays. Such perks as a sauna, gym, fireplaces, and Jacuzzi were pointed out as bonuses, along with more importantly emphasized details like a fully stocked kitchen and a larger bed to roll around in.

Cassie had fallen for it lock, stock, and barrel, and it was on her first day at his house that Cassie discovered boredom did not suit her.

She had made the initial mistake of saying she had nothing pressing to work on that day, and the man had challenged her to a whole day of being "off the grid." Leaving her computer within Brody Miller's reach was her second mistake. She'd brought her tablet along and it could do most anything she needed done in an emergency, but Brody had confiscated both devices that morning, along with her phone, after his challenge.

Cassie made it about three hours before she felt like climbing the walls and taking Brody's place apart, nail by nail if need be, to hunt them down. However, she had given her word that she wouldn't look at any device connecting her to work until the next morning, and it was that part and only that part holding her back, because if anything was sacred to Cassie, it was her word of honor.

Brody had disappeared into his upstairs office for what he'd referred to as a video audition and to take a few calls, leaving Cassie by herself. She'd had a light breakfast then taken advantage of the gym downstairs that rivaled any professional setup. In it, she ran four miles, did some weight training, and finished with thirty minutes of yoga movement to stretch herself out. That had taken care of the exercise portion of the day.

Exploring all the little nooks and crannies of Brody's house took up more time. She took a walk outside to check out the landscaping and property, fiddled around with his extensive music collection — another thing they had in common — and eventually made a cup of tea to enjoy by the fireplace with a book.

And was bored senseless within twenty minutes.

When had she become so work-horse-oriented that she couldn't even enjoy a simple day off? It was pathetic.

Staring at the book and not really seeing the words, Cassie realized she'd actually become one of those women with, as she always referred to it, rushing woman's syndrome. The ones who lived, ate, and breathed stress along with going, going, going nonstop. Maybe she could try to take a midday nap? The problem was she wasn't remotely tired.

"You look bored," Brody said, leaning against the fireplace wall where he'd caught her staring at the ceiling from the couch.

"I am bored. I've run out of things to do. How was your call? Go all right?"

"It did. Talked to a producer about a play he wants to develop in New York. Sounds like a cool project I might do if the timing works out."

"I didn't know you did theatre."

"Every now and then if it works out. I love the challenge of a live audience." Coming over and sitting down next to her, Brody tipped down the book she held to catch the title. "*Success and Leadership Principles*. Fuck, no wonder you're bored. When do you ever relax, woman?"

"This is relaxing."

The fact that she was bored doing it was irrelevant. This was the next book on her reading list — a list that focused strictly on self-development and business growth. Always improving and finding ways to better lead their team was a point of pride for Cassie.

Walking over to the bookshelves, Brody pulled off a couple. "While I applaud your personal development time — don't get me wrong, it's an important area of life — but you might turn work off better with something fun to read. You said you were taking the day off. When's the last time you took in a good adventure, thriller, or romance novel?"

"Romance?" Cassie cringed at the suggestion. The last time she'd read a romance might have been in college.

"Thought so. Try one of these instead." Dropping the books into her lap, he tapped one of them. "Spy thriller. This one was really good." His phone rang, and Brody pulled it out to check the display. "I need to take this, baby." He dropped a quick kiss on her lips. "Might be a while."

Cassie settled in with the new book. She could try something different. She used to read for fun all the time, instead of just learning. And damn him, Brody had a point. Within the first few pages, the plot sucked her in, and by chapter three, Cassie was buried in another world.

Brody found her in the early afternoon — after his call ran way longer than expected — feet kicked up on the back of the sofa and her head in the book. Pleased to see Cassie actually relaxing, he left her to it and went to go brainstorm a romantic evening for the two of them. Surprising her with a night out and music seemed perfect.

Chapter 18

Sauce simmered on the stove on their last night together until after the holidays, and what a wonderful few days it had been. Last night, Brody had taken Cassie to one of the best restaurants in Atlanta for a private dining experience at the chef's table. Tonight, he was giving her a lesson on how to make red sauce from scratch. Cassie didn't know if she would ever get her head out of the clouds with all the romance Brody had given her, as promised.

He'd even started teaching her to cook. All of a sudden, the kitchen was a fun and interesting place, instead of just another room to clean or someplace to piece together a meal. Food became more than just fuel or an indulgent night out with friends. He brought together all these different textures and smells to play with, showing her new ways to combine ingredients and learn the way flavors could meld and work together to create something unique. For the first time, someone was patient with her, letting Cassie explore and learn without fear of rejection.

Even when she tried to pull off a surprise breakfast one morning while he slept in and wound up burning the eggs, Brody had just smiled, poured a cup of coffee, and ate them anyway. He gave her a wink and said they were, by far, the best burned eggs he'd ever had. The comment had chased away the anxiety that had built inside her and made Cassie laugh instead.

She'd also learned that the downside of staying with Brody was he had a slightly sloppy and lazy side to him. When you were with someone all the time, it was easier to see their imperfections. No disarray lay in the kitchen — there he was almost obsessively organized and as clean as a five-star restaurant — but most days Cassie could trace the path he had taken from the front door to exactly where he'd stopped by the trail of keys, wallet, jacket, shoes, a spare glove, or phone all dropped casually as he went. Brody did eventually pick up and organize at some part of his day but admitted a little sheepishly that when he worked long hours for multiple days in a row, he didn't give a damn about any of it until he got some down time. When Cassie pointed out how he could just put it all away the first time, then his days off could be spent doing more things he enjoyed, Brody shook his head and said he'd try to work on it but since he was closing in on thirty-five, Cassie shouldn't hold out much hope for change. She supposed their differences were what made their relationship interesting.

It was almost sad, she mused as she chopped romaine, how much she was going to miss him. The simple days they had had together had come to mean more than she'd known possible. To be able to share a part of her life with someone in that way was special. Walking with Brody as they held hands, long talks, cooking dinner together, and waking in his arms every morning made her feel content in a new way. They had even trained together one morning in Brody's gym. One of the things she loved the most though was dancing with him. Having only ever really had Nathan as a dance partner, Cassie adored how Brody would pull her into his arms and move them around the room to whatever was playing. To have a partner to celebrate that movement with was a freedom and joy only few understood.

Whatever Cassie might have thought a couple of weeks ago when she first started seeing Brody, part of her – maybe she had a romantic side after all, now wanted to spend the holiday with him. The logical side of her knew, without a shadow of a doubt, how stupid that would be. Going home to meet the parents and family signified something big. Something they weren't ready for yet.

Sure, they had joked about it — Brody had even invited her to come with him again — but Cassie had put on the brakes. He'd shrugged it off, but Cassie knew, in some way, she had hurt him. And she had had to put that aside because she wasn't ready to share them with the rest of the world. There was no way her family would ever understand just how happy he made her. Outside of Nathan and Anna, Cassie hadn't told a soul she was dating a really wonderful man, who just happened to be a famous actor, and was having mad crazy delicious sex with him every night.

That famous actor slid his arms around her from behind. "Salad you're making there looks good. Almost done with it?" Sensual kisses worked their way across her cheek to capture her mouth.

"I am. Will that sauce ever be ready? It's cooked for most of a day. We could have just used a jar," she teased, knowing it would earn a horror-filled response.

Predictably, Brody fell back on the counter, clutching his chest. "Sacrilege, Cassie, sacrilege. Jars are only to be used in extreme emergencies. We'll freeze up the leftovers and have them when we need them. Like those long days you and I put in. That's the point of big batch cooking."

"Yes, so you said with the soup and chili. We're stocked up for a war."

Loving the feel of his arms around her as she worked layering olives and feta cheese on the bed of greens, she pronounced it finished. She may not be able to cook as well as Brody, but Cassie could build a mean salad.

"Come with me. I have a surprise for you." Taking her hand, he led the way to the living room couch.

"What have you done now? More lingerie?"

Brody had already shredded more than a few of the pieces he'd bought her. The last time he'd tossed her ripped panties over his head with a wicked gleam in his eye, he told her he was researching more colors and options.

"No, come here and sit with me." Settling Cassie on his lap, he took a small gift-wrapped box off the table. "Merry Christmas."

Thrown off balance, Cassie stared at the pretty red-and-gold box sealed with a gold satin bow. "I thought we agreed we weren't going to do anything."

They had talked about it the other day, and Cassie had been a little relieved by their decision. What on earth did you get a guy who had everything and could buy anything he could think of?

"No, you agreed. I made a noise which may or may not have been noncommittal." Settling back, Brody gave her a smug grin.

"Dammit, Brody, you are such a rat sometimes. That's not playing fair."

"Well, I thought about going for the extravagant piece of

jewelry that cost a ridiculous amount of money, but my gut instinct told me you'd get really pissed off about something like that. This is a compromise." He framed her face with his hands and drew her in to kiss. "Open it. Please?"

"Just a minute."

Cassie wiggled off his lap, went up to her purse, hesitated a moment, and pulled out a festively wrapped package of her own. She came back chewing on her lip. She'd found something for him the other day but had held off since they'd talked about not exchanging gifts. Giving him such a little thing seemed so silly, and she knew it would no way be close to what Brody probably had for her.

Brody gave her a smile that was slow and easy while he shook his head at her. "So much for agreements, huh?"

"It's not much. I honestly thought about not even giving it to you… I-I didn't know really…what you might like. Anyway… sometimes I find things and they just seem right for someone…"

"You gonna let me open it or keep me guessing until New Year's?" he teased, pulling Cassie back down.

"Yes. All right," she said, handing the package over. His arms wrapped back around her, and Cassie waited while Brody undid the bow and slowly peeled open the edges. "Oh my God, you're one of those people who unwraps an inch at a time?" She couldn't help but roll her eyes at him. "Nathan does the same."

Brody only pulled her closer and stopped to kiss her. "You know, funny thing. People don't usually give me gifts anymore. They think I have anything I could possibly want. So yes, I'm going to enjoy the moment here, baby."

Guilt sneaked in, since that had been exactly her thought,

so Cassie sat quietly while Brody went back to the wrapping paper, revealing at last the journal she had found for him in a boutique store outside of her hotel in Chicago. A silly impulse buy that she felt like cringing over now.

"Wow. Cassie, this is wonderful." Opening it, Brody flipped through the empty lined pages that waited to be filled, admiring the imprinted leather cover, his long fingers tracing the pattern.

"It's sacred geometry," Cassie explained. "Four intertwined circles. They represent the five elements of the universe when they come together: earth, water, sun, air, and fire. The balance of human nature inside us all. Susan could tell you in more detail."

"I've no idea what any of that means, but I love it." Brody shifted to take her lips again. "How'd you know I journal most every day?"

"You mentioned it once. And I might have seen your book on the bedside table."

"This is really special, sweetheart. Thank you so much."

That he seemed so touched by the gift left her ridiculously pleased. "You really like it?" Her fingers traced his handsome face and toyed with the edges of his hair falling every which way, depending on how often he ran a hand through it.

"I do. It's perfect. I've journaled pretty much every day since high school. So yes, I love this. You couldn't have picked anything more perfect. Your turn. Let's see if I did just as good. Although I think I'll get to enjoy your gift a lot longer." Brody set his present for her back in her hands.

Nerves danced through her stomach again. Hoping he hadn't gotten her anything too extravagant, Cassie pulled off the bow, lifted the lid, and let out a relieved smile. Lying inside was a framed picture of a gorgeous sun-filled sandy beach. A stunningly designed house sat in the background up on the cliffs. Pure island style. It looked like the perfect place to dream in.

"Thank you. Did you take this picture? What a beautiful place. Where is it? It'll look great on my wall somewhere."

Brody loved surprising her. Watching her smile at a gift that she thought was just a picture, Brody couldn't wait to show her how to dream bigger and better. His fingers crossed on the hope that she would take the rest of the gift just as well.

"It's in the British Virgin Islands. A friend owns the property. It's a great place to relax and get away from it all."

A smile played on Cassie's lips as she glanced at him. "It really is lovely. Your friend is a very lucky guy."

"It's available over the week through and after New Year, right after Christmas. Anytime we want to go." Brody had the supreme pleasure of watching Cassie's expression turn to shock as her hazel eyes went wide.

"What?"

"I want you to think about going away with me."

"I-I can't… I mean… you can't just…"

"And here you're some sort of professional seminar spokesperson." Snuggling her in closer, Brody tipped her face up to his. "I wanna take you away somewhere special. A week of just you and me. Sun and sand." He could tell she was struggling with it from the way she was worrying her bottom lip again, and he brought her hand to his lips. "Don't make it about the money, Cassie, 'cause I know that's where your brain is trying to go. Let me do this. What do you say?"

Her mind was stuck at the idea of a trip, racing between Brody whisking her off somewhere and guilt over wanting exactly that. To let him do it just so she could spend the time with him before the insanity of her schedule took off again after the start of the new year. That war coupled with how she was going to swing her work schedule if she did, and more guilt over the cost of the trip. Cassie struggled with it. Truly she did. How could she turn down a man who was trying to give her something so special though? All about drowning you with the look in his eyes when he asked you.

"Brody." Laying her lips on his softly, Cassie whispered, "This is so much. You make it so hard to say no."

"Then don't. Say yes and come with me."

Her gaze fell on the picture again. An idyllic getaway. One she had thought about treating herself to a few weeks back, and here it was — the perfect gift waiting to be enjoyed. Nathan and Anna had suggested she let the money thing go and enjoy whatever Brody threw out, since there was no way she could compete anyway. They insisted she could find other ways to thank him for caring enough, so she should enjoy the fact that someone wanted to pamper her for a change, from all the little things Brody did to even the wild, outlandish ones.

And sometimes it was the gifts offered so freely which were the hardest ones to accept. Unless you took a leap, trusted, and gave in. One of the things Cassie was trying to teach herself right now was gratitude. She needed to learn how to be grateful for what life had given her in this man who was slowly and steadily capturing her heart. Sneaking around all her walls, or if that didn't work, Brody simply climbed over or kicked them down.

Cassie slid her arms around his neck. "All right. Take me away to this beautiful place. I'd love to go with you."

His eyebrow rose. "I thought it would be harder to talk you into it."

"I probably should fight you about it, and part of me really wants to, but instead I'll be sweet and grateful that I have such an amazing, thoughtful guy who wants to sweep me away somewhere." Fiddling with his collar, Cassie met his eyes. "See? I'm getting better with you being my hero. Can I buy the plane tickets at least?"

Brody only grinned at her and closed the distance to celebrate with a heated kiss. "Not a chance, baby. Being swept away means you let me do it my way. Merry Christmas, Cassie."

"Merry Christmas, Brody."

It was a very long time before they got back to dinner that night.

Chapter 19

Family.

You either loved them, or you were ready to bash their brains in. Right now, Cassie wanted to bash in Christopher's head. Her brother was nagging, prying, and irritating her as only a brother could do. And Claire was helping him out. They'd managed to figure out, between the two of them, from the way Cassie would go off to take a phone call and come back smiling that she might have someone new in her life.

"Just tell us who he is, and we'll leave you alone about it," Claire bribed.

"Yeah. What's up with this guy? Why are you so secretive about it? Is he some weird, homicidal maniac?" Chris said from in the kitchen down the hall where he was almost certainly sneaking Christmas cookies from off the top of the refrigerator — just as he had every year since he was old enough to figure out their mother stashed them there.

"I'm not saying anything. We've only been casually seeing each other for a few weeks. It's too soon." There was no way she was letting them know how deep it had gotten so fast. "Chris, how's that girl in data processing? Get your spreadsheets to line up together yet?"

"Ha! Ha! That's a total bunch of crap. Don't switch the subject. You turned bright red when I walked in and caught you on the phone with him the other night. Phone sex?" He walked back in with a stack bigger than his hand of oatmeal cherry cookies.

Claire's head reared up in an accusing glare. Sex before marriage was not okay in her world.

"No."

She'd adamantly denied it a little too quickly, and Chris lit up with a knowing look. Clearly, Cassie needed to ask Brody for acting tips to coach her on being a better liar. Brody had been trying to talk her into a phone session and Cassie had been on the verge of slipping a hand up her shirt like he wanted when Chris barged in without warning to tell her that dinner was ready and smelled like heaven. She'd barely held back a snicker when Brody overheard and said he'd give her a heavenly experience when next he got his hands on her before Cassie hung up on him.

"Well, I hope you're not giving it all away for free," Claire said, which was no great surprise.

Cassie bit the inside of her cheek to stay quiet. *Oh heavens.* If Claire only knew the truth of how much she had given away to Brody Miller — frequently and enjoying every single minute. For the first time in her life, Cassie was enjoying sex. She honestly didn't care two figs if that made her a huge slut in her sister's world. In Cassie's, it made perfect sense. Brody Miller was everything and more that a girl could dream up, both in bed and out of it.

He wasn't perfect — who was, after all? And Cassie sure wasn't one to throw stones. But Brody's passionate side was incredible, and he was also sweet, caring, and thoughtful. He managed to put Cassie's well-being first and took care of her in ways she'd never expected or thought she might even enjoy. As he'd promised, he was romancing the hell out of her.

Like the Shelby poem he had emailed that Christmas Eve morning. Cassie had no idea who Shelby was, but the words of the poem made her eyes misty and a tear or two might have sneaked out before she called to thank him. Her heart had fallen a little bit further as he took the time to read it to her over the phone. Brody's deep velvety voice wrapping around her, just as his arms would have if he had been there in person, had been absolute holiday magic.

"And what's the plan for the new year? Will we actually see you more than mostly never?" Chris asked, switching from boyfriends to business.

"Not really. I'm on a lecture series for the first four months for different companies around the country."

More insane travel. She wondered how Brody would handle it, and her teeth came out to toy with her bottom lip at the nervous tension that swept in. Especially since Brody's shooting schedule had wrapped and he was free for most of January before his next movie project started. Her schedule would probably mean disaster once reality set in. Never being home during the week plus being gone for a few weekend seminars would probably be the death sentence of their relationship.

Taking a deep breath, Cassie stomped down her inner critic of fear. She'd promised Brody all in or to not bother. It wasn't fair to herself or him to think of failure. He didn't seem to think the upcoming months would be a big deal, and she needed to trust they would make it work.

Chris shook his head. "You work too much and too hard. Whatever you have going, it better be worth it."

"You sent me the final numbers for the quarter. We're in

the black and business is good, brother dear." Frustrated with her family and herself, Cassie stood. "I'm going for a run before dinner. I'll plan on cleaning up since no one wants me on cooking detail anyway."

"That's not true. You made that dish the other night — the chicken thing. I actually didn't die after, and it tasted good," Claire said.

She'd even wanted the recipe, leaving Cassie feeling pretty good. It was one that Brody had taught her how to make. Cassie was glad she'd remembered anything from that particular lesson, since Brody had had his hands up her shirt for most of it while he whispered instructions in her ear. They had ended the lesson by testing out the kitchen island —naked, with more than a few dishes broken on the floor while dinner baked.

"Glad you liked it. I'm heading out. See you two later."

Both brother and sister left in the room exchanged looks as Cassie left. She was never so tight-lipped about anything.

Christmas day and night passed with lights and ornaments, the flurry of presents and wrappings, last-minute decorations, cooking and baking. All the wonderful traditions that they all insisted on carrying on year after year.

Pajama/game day had left Cassie with her siblings giving her the stink-eye for most of it. She'd lost the Candy Land challenge and Twister but had taken them all in Scrabble and Monopoly. Words were always Cassie's weapon of choice with all opponents, and Monopoly was just another version of chess.

She was dreaming that evening about her upcoming island getaway when she felt her phone buzz and looked down to see the display. A text from Brody.

"*It's mayhem and madness here. Wishing u were a part of it. Call me later.*"

He'd sent a heart emoji with it, making her smile, and everything in Cassie warmed into a golden glow. Tucking her phone closer, she messaged him back. "Missing you, too. Two days till I feel ur arms around me again." Adding her own heart symbol and pressing Send, Cassie laughed gaily before she was sucked back into the magic of her nephew opening up his new Lego Death Star Destroyer, eyes lighting up in glee.

Chapter 20

Doing things his way meant that Brody got to whisk Cassie away in style. He didn't really think of it as showing off, but hell, he liked the fact of having reached the point in his career where he didn't have to deal with congested airports, crowds, crappy food, and annoying delays anymore. More importantly, flying privately meant he didn't have to worry about tripping over paparazzi or fans tweeting out his photo. Not that he didn't love and appreciate his fans but a guy was entitled to a personal life. He gave enough of himself during press tours and other things that he did. Privacy was important. Especially when he had a lady with him, and Cassie was his lady in every definition of the word. She meant the world to him, and by whatever means necessary, Brody would protect her from the insanity other stars purposely put themselves through in the game of self-promotion.

Traveling by private means eliminated all of those hassles and then some.

The plane picked up Cassie first, since she was in St. Louis, then landed in Dallas for him. Brody walked out onto the tarmac and up the stairs toward the most gorgeous set of legs standing there at the top dressed in a pretty green summer dress and wedge sandals that showed off candy-pink painted toenails. The view traveled upward from there and ended with beautiful sparkling eyes, a happy smile, and sexy red waves of hair tossing in the wind. The fact that Cassie practically launched herself at him and almost knocked him back down the stairs only made it better.

Catching and lifting her high, Brody grinned at her smiling face before lowering her to take that gorgeous mouth he'd been forever without. Her taste blew clean up and through him, making everything settle into a pulsing hum of raging need.

"Hey there, handsome. Ready to sweep me away?"

Shifting his arms under Cassie, Brody ducked through the plane door to carry her inside. "Damn right. Thought today would never get here."

He tucked her into a chair and sat next to her. It was a shame they were taking off immediately, according to the steward. He would have loved to have a more thorough greeting.

"Do you know everything in here is amazing? This plane is somehow fancier than the one from Salt Lake City. The captain even let me come up front on the way down." She rubbed her hands in glee over the experience then pulled him back in for another smack on the lips. "I missed you."

"How much?"

"A lot. I even bought you some new things to tear off me."

His appreciative grin was all the answer Cassie needed to see.

Deciding that there was no point in waiting, since he was losing his mind, as soon as they hit flight level, Brody flicked open Cassie's seat belt and his own. Tugging her up to her feet, he started toward the bathroom in the rear of the plane. Unlike commercial planes, this one was larger than your average coffee cup. Pulling open the door, he guided Cassie inside, ignoring her snickering whispered protests. Following her in, he shut the door, and backed her right up against it so he could feast on those incredible lips. Her arms came up to wrap around him like a siren of old, pulling Brody under and into her spell. So much so, he felt as if he were drowning.

"God, I missed you so much, baby."

Her breath was skipping like music in his ears. "So much. I missed you too, Brody. I can't believe how much. Touch me."

She fought to get his shirt off, and it landed in the bathroom sink. Brody's hands slid up to cup and mold around her body before he shoved aside the dress to bare each beautiful mound.

"Sundresses are one of my favorite things about summer heat." He nuzzled one already hardened bud with his lips. "Easy access."

His tongue swirled tighter and tighter around her nipple before he drew it into his mouth. Cassie's moan echoed in the space as she arched to meet him. Impatient to feel more, he let his hands roam freely along her sides and around to cup that fantastic toned ass —

Pulling back in shock, his eyes widened in appreciation. "You're not wearing anything under this dress."

Cassie smiled at him shyly. "I had a feeling you might not be in the mood to wait based on our phone calls."

Need threatened to overrun good sense, and it was a struggle to chain down the ravenous beast inside him.

"Ever been to the mile high club?" Knowing without a doubt that Cassie was going to shake her head, he teased along her neckline when she did exactly that. "That's a shame. We better get that checked off your list, all right?"

Her hands drifted down to his pants to tug open the belt

and undo the snap and zipper. Brody's breath came hot and fast on her skin when her delicate hands found and freed him. Those same sweet hands about almost made him embarrass himself like a first-time kid in high school. Pulling away, he went down on his knees, desperate for the taste of that silken heat. Brody nudged her legs apart and eased her hips forward to take advantage of Cassie in every wicked way he knew of until she was screaming his name and fisting his hair.

Unable to wait any longer, he stood and grabbed her ass to boost her up, pinning her to the door. She was so petite and perfect. Every. Single. Inch. Locking his mouth on hers, Brody knew her moan was from the echo of the taste of herself on his lips. One sure move later, he was buried deep with that slick heat closing around him like a homecoming, and his own groan tore out to match Cassie's.

Beautiful hazel eyes met his, and he fell into them.

Home. God, he was home.

Finally, he had her in his arms again. This beautiful woman. His Cassie, whose light shone bright and clear. A light he drowned in as he moved inside her. Surrounded by that light, consumed by it, they burned so bright until Brody's world burst into flame and he poured himself inside her with a guttural growl of sheer heaven.

Chapter 21

The mile high club. Heavens! It was a wonder she could still walk. Brody had showed her as thoroughly as possible how much he'd missed her, then he'd held her tenderly after that firestorm of passion with endless drugging kisses and secret words whispered into her neck until Cassie had felt as though her world was just like the sparkling sun filtering in through the plane windows.

They landed in a glide of wheels on the tarmac, where Cassie was whisked off the plane and to a car nearby. Their bags were packed efficiently by the airport staff before a guy tossed Brody the keys.

Then they were off, climbing the roads and cruising along toward what would be their own little paradise for the next few days. Seven days of bliss. Cassie had managed to clear her schedule, delegating like a mad woman to make this week possible. Determined to turn over a new leaf in the new year, one of her goals was to focus more on self-care. She wouldn't have much time for it, but she was going to go after it. Accepting something like a vacation from her boyfriend fell into that category. Although she didn't think of Brody as her boyfriend. The term seemed too fluffy and trivial for what she felt for him. More of a word one would apply to a high school relationship. What they had together felt like so much more than anything Cassie had ever experienced, as if a part of her that she'd never known was missing had somehow been found.

As they drove, she could see a village off in the distance, the houses clustered together up on the hillsides, their beautiful red clay tile roofs gleaming and their walls a cheerful mix of colors. Maybe they could explore the village one day. Loving the way Brody took her hand on the drive and squeezed it, Cassie enjoyed the sight of her handsome man with his dark brown hair lifting in the sun and wind of the convertible. One hand on the wheel, the other laced their fingers together, and she felt her heart shift deeper yet again. The look in his warm eyes when he glanced over guaranteed more plans of a sensual nature once they finally got to the house. Brody had promised to take her sailing first chance he got. Something Cassie had never done before.

The car turned up a wide graveled road. A seemingly deceptive slice in the hill, it curved and twisted until, at last, it came out on top, opening up to a view of the sea below and the house in front of them. Cassie got out on a laugh and ran to the edge to take in the breathtaking view. She could see stairs drifting down the hillside to the beach and smelled salt in the air.

"This is incredible. Oh my God." Throwing out her arms, Cassie turned in a circle of delight before breaking into a salsa, twisting her hips and snapping her feet as she made her way back to grab some bags.

"You sure do have some moves. I've got some of my own, gorgeous." Grabbing her hand, Brody spun her into him then back out, executing a hip twist that made Cassie screech in awe.

"I didn't know you knew Latin dance. Holding out on me, Brody Miller?"

Spinning her back to him, Brody caught her and lifted Cassie on a spin before he set her on her feet again and spun her away. "We're still learning all our secrets, baby. Come on. Let me show you this house."

Every room was a stunning meld of island design, color, and comfort blending seamlessly one room into the next. Everywhere Cassie looked were places that invited a person to sink in, lay down and relax the day away. They walked out onto the patio and saw a beautiful fall of rock, sand, and lush plants scattered around the poolside. Cassie strolled around checking it all out. It truly was an incredible place to get away from the rest of the world.

Brody walked up barefoot and took her lips. "Best place, right?"

"It really is. Paradise and magic all in one."

Brody bent and lifted her in his arms. "There's one thing we're missing though."

Sensing his intention, Cassie giggled. "Let me guess?"

"Go ahead." Grinning like an idiot, he took off running with Cassie before she realized what was up.

She had no time to do more than give an earsplitting scream before Brody launched them both off the ledge and into the pool. Water swirled over her head in an instant, and Cassie came up sputtering and cussing like a sailor.

"Whoa. Does your mom know you can talk like that, baby?" Brody circled her like a shark. One second, she had him in her sights, then he was gone, snaking to the other side.

"How are you doing that? Dammit! Hold still," she snapped, trying to splash him.

"Swim team, remember? Kindergarten all the way through high school. Mom needed something for us to do with all our energy. Speaking of which, look what I found in my pool — a pretty little mermaid. Come here, gorgeous."

Swim freaking team. How had she forgotten that detail about Brody? He dived and Cassie had two seconds before Brody grabbed her foot and pulled her under. Warm dominant hands slid up from her foot, and his lips found her. Opening her mouth with his, Brody kissed her underwater before lifting them both back to the air. Tropical heat surrounded them like a cool mist compared to what coursed between them. With the water adding a smoother sensual realm to their play, her dress was peeled off and left to float away. His shirt followed soon after, before he drew Cassie back toward him. Warm and talented hands traveled across wet skin, followed by lips and hungry caresses. With all the time in the world, they reacquainted each other with their bodies and words. Reunited at last, until on a final shudder, Brody caught her as she fell.

Afterward, Cassie floated happily along the pool stairs, her head resting on his naked chest.

"What do you think of this place?"

"What do I think?" She propped up on an arm to look at him, moved beyond anything she could put into words and still had to try. "It's so incredible. I can't believe we get to stay here. I can't believe you made this all happen. That you want me to be here with you."

Thrilled and overwhelmed, her heart felt so full from being back with him. Brody made her feel things she'd never before felt for anyone else, not even the man she had married.

"I'm so glad we gave each other a chance," she whispered. "I feel so much for you. It scares me how happy I am when we're together."

"I feel the same way. There's only you."

Brody's hands helped her drift up higher to his lips where she sank in on a happy sigh before he cupped her face. Brody looked at her, his emerald eyes full of nothing but deep affection, warmth and something else that left Cassie trembling on the edge, ready to fall with him.

"Only with you, Cassie, You make it all worthwhile."

PART 2
Interference and Beats

Storms make trees take
Deeper Roots
- Dolly Parton

Chapter 22

Since arriving in the late mail yesterday, the invitation had lain there on the stainless steel kitchen counter, mocking him with the message inside. Like some sick fucking clown, it sneered and cackled while it tore open wounds better left scabbed over. Brody leaned over the flimsy decorative paper scattered with a faded pattern of hibiscus and glared while the joyful words imbedded themselves into his brain.

Swearing loudly enough to blister and peel the paint, Brody gave serious thought to flying home to Atlanta just to beat the hell out of his best friend. As soon as that thought hit, he swore again and knew his mom would have slapped the back of his head for his disrespect. Brody turned toward the coffee pot behind him and set a cup to brew.

While waiting for the coffee to finish dripping, he took the empty whiskey bottle off the counter and tossed it in the recycling bin and cussed some more just because he could. The bottle had been half empty when he read the damn invitation, and he'd reached for it to drown the pain. This morning, his entire body ached from the stupidity of that decision, and his head felt like a keg of dynamite waiting for someone to strike a match.

It wasn't Chase's fault he had found happiness and was getting married. He and Anna had been locked in tight since the moment they first met. The night Brody had met Cassie. He hadn't told a lie that night either. Brody couldn't be happier for Chase. He and Anna were perfect together.

Cup of coffee ready, Brody took it, straight black, out onto the balcony of the rented space in Iceland, where he was currently on location filming. Not bothering to put a coat over his faded sweats and pullover, he let the frigid cold seep in to numb the aches and rubbed a hand over his face, trying to wake up.

Of course he was happy for the two of them. Chase had called before he even proposed to Anna and asked Brody to be his best man. A no-brainer. Nothing would have kept Brody from standing at his best friend's side. What pissed Brody off was the location of the wedding.

Anna and Chase had chosen The Island. The same one where Brody and Cassie had fallen in love and made so many memories in that incredible week together. The idea of going back there, especially since he knew Cassie would be part of the wedding, was pure fucking hell. It wasn't a huge jump to wonder if he actually had the guts to see her again.

Looking back, that island vacation had been the beginning of the end of the two of them. And God, he still woke up every single fucking day wishing for her back.

Those seven days had been full of sun, sand, and relaxing, just the two of them, including one more than incredible night of rum spiced cocktails, a floaty breeze of barely there dress, dancing, and a night of slow passion so intense, both of them had been rocked straight to their foundations with it — the night they had both admitted how much they loved each other.

That particular night at The Island had also left them with

a broken condom.

They'd laughed about it after. Blown it off as a one-time problem. What were the chances? Cassie was taking birth control, so they hadn't really worried.

Three weeks later, Cassie had come up pregnant.

Scared and in full swing with her travel and lecture series, she'd thought at first that it was just the flu or some bug she had caught and hadn't been able to shake. That was, until Brody had walked in on her retching in the bathroom sink one morning. She'd been clammy and pale as a sheet of paper while he helped her clean up and carried her, limp and worn out, back to bed. She hadn't protested once, even with all the stuff she had to get done. That worried him more than anything, since Cassie stopped for almost nothing. Brody made her some honey tea and, for some reason, left the house while she went back to sleep. At the pharmacy, he stood there like a shell-shock victim in front of the pregnancy tests. Finally, he bought one and brought it home.

She'd said he was insane, that it was just the flu. Glared and shouted at him some more but took the test anyway and sat there in his arms, quiet as a mouse, while they waited for the results. The two pink lines confirmed what Brody had suspected. Cassie had cried, thinking he would be upset, but he hadn't been. The idea of a baby with Cassie had left him crazy happy. Shocked but so crazy happy.

He had already been so in love with her. It still blew his mind how fast and hard he had fallen for Cassie. She'd been the one woman he couldn't get out of his head, and once he finally had the chance for more with her, Brody knew. Cassie was his other half. The baby had just helped move things along a little faster for them. Brody had already been looking for the perfect ring in his spare time anyway. Cassie was it for him, and he knew there would never be another.

Then the worst thing possible had happened.

They lost their baby.

She'd been three and a half months along, and he'd been so worried about her. Her travel schedule was nonstop, which he could have lived with and helped her through. But the entire first trimester had been full on with guns blazing and Cassie had been so damn sick Brody didn't know how she made it through the day sometimes.

For most women, morning sickness hit in the morning and was done for the day. But Cassie had been sick and nauseated every minute of every single day. Nothing the doctor gave her seemed to help. She'd even once been admitted overnight for IV fluids when she'd gotten too dehydrated. Hardly able to eat anything more than crackers and sips of water, she'd dropped weight she hadn't needed to lose and was exhausted all the time. She'd once told him she often felt like she could sleep standing up if someone would just prop her into a corner.

Brody had flown out to meet her on the road as often as his schedule allowed, to take care of her. She'd never once protested his wanting to be with her during that time. Then she'd woken him up one morning in New York — bleeding. Small spots at first that only increased. A few horrible days later, their baby was gone and both of them had broken with the news. He'd cried with her, not realizing how much he'd wanted everything with her until it was gone.

With no small amount of luck, exchange of money, and Simon's help, Brody had managed to keep Cassie safe from any word of their loss leaking out. God only knew what the press would have done to her.

In the weeks that followed, neither of them got over the loss. Brody had buried the pain. His only thought at the time was helping Cassie, who blamed herself, from being eaten up with guilt over, as she put it, "one more thing she had failed at." For her, losing their baby was the worst possible thing for her to fail at.

Brody, for the first time in his life, didn't know how to help, how to fix it, or how to make things better.

They'd started to fight and bicker over petty crap. Both burying themselves in work until one night they'd had a fight of epic proportions and said horrible things to each other. The next day, Cassie moved out, and Brody hadn't done a thing to stop her. What could he have done since she didn't want him there anyway? At that point, she barely let him touch her anymore.

Now he stood looking out over a frozen country of Iceland, just waking up for the day. He was due on set for make-up at five thirty and was grateful for what was supposed to be a grueling day packed with action sequences that would probably need take after take to get perfect. At least his body would be exhausted at the end of the day and hopefully, for a change, his mind would be as well. Brody prayed to be so exhausted that he could pass the fuck out and sleep till dawn.

He hadn't had a decent night's sleep since Cassie left, he'd gotten used to living on less. But things had only gotten worse since Chase called with his happy news. Brody had probably reached too often for a glass or two of whiskey, every now and then, when sleep had proven impossible.

Two months. He had two months until the wedding and he

would have to see her again. Time enough to get his head on straight and figure shit out.

Chapter 23

Anna stood at the living room windows of their home in Atlanta, looking out at the frozen winter wonderland that had settled in with a vengeance. Crystalline frost and a light coating of snow had brought the city to a standstill, as only two inches of snow could do in Atlanta. Melancholy hit her in a smothering wave, and she was enough of a spiritualist to acknowledge the discomfort. Sometimes it was okay to feel sadness. To embrace rather than deny it.

She was wondering if they had made the right choice. The wedding invitations had gone out over a week ago, and responses were already trickling in. She and Chase wanted a fun, intimate — well, maybe not too intimate — celebration, and they had debated long and hard before settling on what they thought of as the perfect place. The place where Chase had whisked Anna off for a weekend — where they had fallen in love – just after she had met him.

"What's on your mind, darlin'?" Chase slipped his arms around her from behind and rested his head on her shoulder. "I can tell your vibes are sad today."

"They are. Just wondering if we made the right decision."

There was no need to elaborate further. The decision had come after a lot of hard conversations and meditating. Even Nathan and Philip had been brought in to consult. In the end, no one wanted to hurt those they cared about, but their wedding needed to be about what was important and special to them, including the location. Plus, everyone agreed that this was a chance to get Brody and Cassie back in the same degrees of longitude and latitude and, if possible, get the two of them talking again.

Both were absolutely miserable without the other, and Anna, Chase, Nathan, and Philip could no longer stand to see their suffering. Even Cassie's family had been in touch with Nathan, worried to death about her, after the last time she'd made it home.

"We're doing the right thing. For us and them. It'll be all right. Have you heard from Cassie yet?" Chase asked.

"No. I think she's in Sydney this week, or it could be Auckland. Who can keep up?" Nathan would know if Anna asked him. "I should talk to her maybe tomorrow morning or the next day with the time difference. Brody?"

"On his way home now. He called and said of course he'll be there. He's confident the film schedule works around it. He made sure before he said yes to being best man a few weeks back, before I asked you."

"How did he sound about it?" Anna asked.

It was one of those questions Chase hated to answer since it meant he had to dig deeper than the usual guy speak. To be more intuitive and sensitive. She loved that he did it for her though.

Chase grunted and went to grab a beer out of the fridge. "He was polite. Stiff. Probably one of the most awkward conversations we've ever had. He'll be there." He tipped his bottle at her in a salute. "He gave his word. Cassie? You think she'll make it?"

"Yes. I talked with her weeks ago to make sure the date was good. It's inked on the calendar. She never goes back on her word once it's given."

"All right then, darlin'. You've got yourself a setup. The main characters will be there. Let's see how the story rolls out."

A-the beer down with a snap and came over to hold her tight.

"I just hope this doesn't make things worse for them. That's not my intention." Her healer's heart broke all over again for what Cassie and Brody had gone through and how neither of them were dealing well with the pain. Anna and Nathan had finally gotten Cassie to wake up and start taking better care of herself physically, but she had so much more emotional healing to do and until that emotional side of a soul healed, the body would always have more of a struggle to find its way to better health.

"Hey, what is it you always tell me? That oracle card stuff? It's already laid out how it's meant to be. The universe guides those who are ready. You know I don't get it, but even I can see it. I've never in my life seen Brody so ripped up. Can't remember the last time I saw him really smile. If ever two people were lost without each other, it's them. Let's at least give them a shot to be happy again."

Anna nodded and held tight to the gift the universe had given her with this wonderful man. Her mate. "You're right. It's why I love you so. Let's give them that chance and wrap it in our love when we do."

Chapter 24

Anna couldn't be serious. Cassie blinked twice then squeezed her eyes shut again and pinched her nose for good measure, praying the screen would change. When she reopened them, she cringed again. Cassie sat somewhere between shock and nausea over the picture of the maid of honor dress that Anna had selected,

It was… white…

Why white? Of all the colors in the universe that Anna felt in alignment with and was drawn to for whatever reason that made sense only to Anna, why on earth had she selected white? There had to be a mistake.

"Do you see it yet? Did it come through?" Anna said excitedly through the phone.

Cassie was currently in Sydney and from there was headed to Melbourne then Paris. The city of lights and romance. As beautiful as Paris was, there was probably no place on Earth she would rather not be going — unless she factored in The Island. The place that Anna and Chase had selected for their wedding venue. God, how she hated that they had chosen that place.

"I do see it. This is your dress, right? You sent me the wrong picture. This is white."

"No, I didn't." Anna laughed happily, in full planning

mode. "You're wearing white. I have the most gorgeous dreamy gown in palest orange."

Cassie barely kept her eyes from welling up when the second picture came through. The "palest orange" gown was a shining confection of flowing fabric and lines that would only complement Anna's golden skin and honey-highlighted hair.

"It's perfect. You're going to look so beautiful. Hair down, right? Little wavy curls worked in here and there, waving in the breeze. That's how you're going to wear it, right? Flowers tucked in?"

"Ohhhh, I can just see it perfectly now. I was thinking up but down… your vision is it, the only way to go."

"Try it out with your stylist first and make sure." Cassie sighed. It was so like Anna to just drift along with whatever came to her, fortunately it always came out right. Just like Chase had. Thinking of Chase brought immediate thoughts of Brody and the knife-edge of pain and memories that always went with him.

"You're thinking of him, aren't you?" Anna asked quietly.

"Yes, dammit. How do you always know?"

"'Cause I'm your friend. It would be the same if it was Nathan."

"I know."

"Are you sure you're okay sharing maid of honor duties with him as the best man? I know—"

"Everything will be fine," Cassie cut Anna off abruptly. "We're both adults. Your day will be perfect. I promise."

She would practically take a blood oath to ensure it if need be. Her friend's day would not be ruined because of the past. Cassie had already played out a number of scenarios in her head and various conversations with small talk to keep it civil between herself and Brody. But she knew seeing him again would be the hardest thing she'd ever done in her life.

"Okay. I love you so much for being my witness on this beautiful day."

Letting out a laugh, or as near to one as she managed these days, Cassie sighed and wished she was there to reassure Anna with a hug. "It will be all your dreams come true, my friend. You have my word. Make sure I have the schedule for that week." The happy couple was planning a full week-long celebration before the wedding on The Island. "Now, are you sure about this dress for me? White is impossible for me to keep clean. You know how I am with white."

"Yes. You will look like an angelic jewel. Which you are anyway. The fitting is set up for when you come home in a couple weeks."

Cassie listened, took meticulous notes, and lined up details about her duties to the bride, which included things such as the bachelorette party and bridal shower. She'd manage and shuffle it all in like she usually did. It was easier these days. Cassie had taken great pains to lighten up her workload. When your body turned traitor on you, you had no choice left but to wake up, smell the coffee, and see the tiny ticking time bomb that represented your body about to implode.

"Did you look at the retreat information I sent you?" Anna asked.

"I have. The idea sounds a little crazy, but the place looks beautiful."

Cassie was still rolling her eyes and shaking her head over Anna's plan for them both to go on a healing yoga retreat to help Cassie get her health back. Apparently, the massive doses of high potency vitamins, supplements, strict nutrient-dense foods, and low-impact exercises weren't already enough. But Anna was vehement that Cassie's soul had to begin to heal and that was why the rest of the treatments were barely helping. Cassie had finally thrown her hands up and given in, letting Anna book the retreat.

A little while later, Cassie hung up, took another call with Nathan back home, and finished her updates for him. Then she reviewed feedback from her latest seminar and the next round of tweets and social media postings that needed approval for all their various forums before she closed her computer down for the day and put it away. Finally making sure everything was packed and her clothes were laid out for her flight to Melbourne in the morning.

The company she had keynoted for today had set her up in luxury in the penthouse, and the spacious hotel bathroom boasted an acre of countertop. Cassie stood there after washing her face, making sure all makeup residue was off, and carefully and meticulously smoothed on her night cream. Looking at herself in the mirror, she gave in, letting her shoulders slump as she admitted to herself what she couldn't say out loud to the bride.

How on earth was she going to face Brody again?

She'd said so many awful things to him the last time they fought — when she'd been hurting so badly that she could barely see straight. Even knowing all he'd wanted to do was help and how much he cared for her, she hadn't been able to stop herself from lashing out at him. They had both said horrible things to each other that night.

And now Anna and Chase had picked the one place in the bloody universe Cassie never wanted to see again.

That beautiful place where Brody had held her and they had watched the sun set across the ocean every evening while it burned, painting colors in the sky. With the beach below and the stars above them, Brody had made love to her on the chaise by the pool. Cassie had fallen for him so hard, she realized that whatever her previous marriage had been was a joke compared to what her heart held for Brody.

He'd healed everything in her that had been broken, then they had been given a beautiful gift. One neither of them had been expecting. And they hadn't survived the loss either.

Tears threatened again, and Cassie had learned in recent months to let them come. Things were worse, physically and emotionally, when she buried her sorrow. Switching off the bathroom light, she climbed into bed and wept for the loss of their baby and even more for the loss of the man she had loved so much and probably still did. As she slid into an uneasy sleep, memories filtered in, as they always did, like a movie reel.

"Dammit, Cassie, you need to take some time off. Some time to heal," Brody argued as they stood in his kitchen.

She flinched at the words as if they were a slap. She knew, deep down, the truth of them, even if she couldn't admit it out loud. "I took time already."

"Baby, three days is not taking time off. Three days was just while your body wa—"

The glare Cassie sent stopped him mid-word. "I can't afford to take time off right now. I've signed contracts that I can't just back out of."

"Then have Nathan lead the seminars, or someone else on your team. Train them to do it. If it's the fucking money, I'll write you a goddamn check to cover it." Frustration evident,

Brody paced, an arm thrown out with every other word to emphasize that frustration.

Cassie's vision went red with fury as she pointed at him. "How dare you toss your money in my face like that's all this is about! I can't just hand off the baton to an unknown. They signed me to keynote and do the trainings. I can't just stop right now. The company is on the next big edge. If we lose momentum—"

"That's a crock of bullshit and you know it. You're using your job as a crutch instead of dealing with what's happened," he yelled. Stopping, Brody looked about to break. He reached to touch her, but she flinched away. "It wasn't your fault."

"Don't tell me it wasn't."

She'd been healthy. She'd always taken care of her body. She still couldn't understand how it had all gone so terribly wrong. God! She couldn't deal with this right now. She needed to leave again the next day. Fighting to keep calm, Cassie reached for the control that had always served her in the past and ignored the part of herself that wanted to do what Brody said — curl up for a week in his arms.

To cry. To breathe. To find a way to feel happy again.

It had been so long since she'd felt happy...

Brody took her hand and leaned down to brush her hair back. "You need time off. We both do. Let's just go away somewhere together and figure this out." Green eyes full of caring pleaded with her.

"I'm sorry that you don't understand, but I can't take the time right now."

Brody whipped away on a growl. "Fuck, you make me so mad, woman. You're so fucking stubborn."

Grabbing the glass of water on the kitchen counter, he hurled it at the wall. It shattered and water dripped down the wall onto the floor. Neither of them moved to clean it up.

"You're just as damn stubborn that you won't leave this be. I'm fine. I'll figure it out."

Everything in Brody went as still as a statue and his face turned to granite. No trace was left of the man who loved her. "You're not doing fine. I'm not gonna sit here and watch you destroy yourself because you won't deal. You need to talk to someone. We both do."

The past curled through her like a viper, hissing and spitting at the ultimatum. Poisoning Cassie's blood to ice.

Therapy — God, how she hated that word. How much time had she wasted in endless sessions, pouring out her heart and soul to a stranger who only pretended to listen and offered nothing in return? She'd spent too much time on that road before.

Turning back to Brody, the rest of what was left of Cassie's heart shattered. "I won't do that. Not even for you."

She knew as she said the words that they meant the end for them.

Chapter 25

"It's so spectacular!" Anna cried in pure delight.

"I truly hate you for this." Cassie threw an annoyed look at the bride-to-be, happily sipping champagne with her brown eyes shining, perched on the ottoman next to where Cassie stood getting fitted in the white dress that was doomed to disaster. Probably within ten minutes after she put it on, knowing her track record with white.

"I don't suppose you would think about extensions for the wedding, would you?" Nathan piped up from next to Anna. "It would just look amazing. All that red hair cascading down with flowers — a little less elaborate than the bride's, of course."

"Not happening. I've grown it past shoulder length for you, Anna. That's it."

Three months had been more than long enough to take Cassie's hair from chin to shoulder length, since it always had grown ridiculously fast. Anna envisioned Cassie's hair swept up on one side with waves of curls falling down the other. Jewelry and earrings had already been selected in copper metallic swirls that went perfectly with the bride's dress and her woven copper jewelry from the same artist.

"You look like a fairy sea goddess," Nathan said with admiration.

Cassie sighed and turned. The dress — strapless, simplistic, yet so much more than just whimsical — wasn't something she ever would have picked out. The bodice ran in a straight line across her chest, gathered right under the breasts in an Empire waist, and fell in a soft straight rain of silk and light gauzy overlay down to her toes. Tiny crystals in the palest orange — to match Anna's dress — were scattered under the high waistline and gathered in the back to tumble down the skirt. It was quite simply stunning.

"The shoes," Anna presented with a flourish.

Open-mouthed Cassie looked in the mirror at the coppery twists of straps that went with the heels that would add inches to her height. "You have to be joking, right? How can I walk on the sand with those?"

"Well, the ceremony is up on the terrace. You'll be fine there, and you take them off for beach pictures later. The skirt will look fabulous draped across the sand. Besides, next to Brody's height, you'll need something extra," Anna pointed out.

The heels weren't exactly the point. She wore them professionally every time she stepped onstage. She was nervous about the man she would be paired up with. Cassie sighed internally at the idea. "What color is Brody wearing? Please, let it be white and humiliating as well."

Anna laughed her off. "No, of course not. He has dove-grey linen pants and vest. Light blue button-down shirt. No ties. We're having the guys leave the top few buttons open and sleeves rolled up for a very casual, laid-back look."

Of course, no white for Brody Miller. Another internal sigh swept through her. He would look amazing in those colors, knowing Anna's eye for fashion.

Brody looked amazing in anything. Especially on those

rare occasions he'd dressed up to take Cassie somewhere special, like the night he'd taken her to the opera in New York. Brody had rocked her world that day when she had finished keynoting to a crowd of five thousand entrepreneurs and walked off stage to see him standing there with a thick growth of stubble, a tailored Fedora, and open arms to surprise her. He had been almost unrecognizable and Cassie had been blown away not only by the surprise but by Brody's look of utter pride when he had told her how incredible she had been onstage.

She stared at the formal-gown-covered woman in the mirror and barely recognized herself from that vibrant, healthy time. Shadows that never quite went away anymore — unless they were carefully covered with makeup — rode under her eyes. Every bit of her still looked too skinny from the lost muscle tone she'd been so proud of. Now, she just looked… well… not as good. Cassie didn't really know how to describe it. Taking another deep breath, she let it go.

Slowly climbing the ladder back to health took time Dr. Lane had said, and it would only be more so in her case since Cassie had allowed herself to get so rundown.

Finished with memory lane, Cassie turned, stepped off the measuring step, and thanked the seamstress. The gown would be incredible any way it was worn.

"You have outdone yourself as usual," she told Anna. "Now it's the bride's turn. Let's see this dress you and Nathan picked out while I was away."

Anna jumped up and nearly bobbled her glass of bubbly. "It's so perfect. Wait until you see it on me." On a laugh, she practically danced into the dressing room.

Cassie sat down next to Nathan. "You could have helped

her pick out something, you know, not this." She accused holding up a handful of white skirt.

He flicked away her comment with an absent shrug. "What can I say, Cassie Bear? It's fantastic on you. Anna has an eye for these things." Nathan tucked a stray piece of hair behind her ear and took her chin to tilt her face right and left while he nailed her with vivid blue eyes. "Still not sleeping well, I see. No worries. We'll have an expert makeup team on hand for the big day. You decide to take anything yet?"

It was an observation that only a best friend could make and one laced with concern. Cassie hadn't slept well in a long time, and her old doctor had, a few months ago, hinted not so kindly during Cassie's check up that she should consider anti-depressants, at least for the short term. That suggestion had been met with a single middle finger followed by her firing her old physician. Nathan and Anna had guided Cassie, in their own pushy and insistent way, to Dr. Lane, who was finally helping Cassie make progress.

"No, I don't need anything. I hate the idea of the side effects, remember?" Never in her life had Cassie been good with medication of any kind.

"That meditative track Anna sent you to help with sleep. Have you tried it?"

"I have. It helps me go to sleep better, so thank you." She was trying lots of things thanks to her two friends, and she was getting better, just slower than she would have liked. "I'm still waking up religiously at three a.m. every night."

Closing her eyes in defeat, she laid her head on Nathan's shoulder. His comfort had been there with her as long as she could remember. Someday she would get used to sleeping alone again. How could such a short time with someone leave you so lonely that even months later, you continued to ache to feel their arms around you? Brody Miller had done that to her.

Nathan wrapped an arm around her shoulders. "It'll all get better soon. I promise. Now, let's put on our happy faces. The bride should be out soon."

As if on cue, Anna stepped out, radiant in her one-of-a-kind gown. The couture design suited her to a T. The bottom mimicked Cassie's gown, though it was a little fuller and more trailing as befitted a bride, but the top... the top was a stunner. The silk overlay went in a square cut across her chest, and straps cannily wrapped and twisted over her shoulders to cross in the back. It exquisitely showcased Anna's beautiful toned physique. And the color of palest orange against her honey-gold skin was *perfect*.

"Well, if Cassie is the fairy sea goddess, you sweetie, are the earth goddess." Nathan saluted Anna with a flourish. "Chase is going to bow down with gratitude when he sees you walk down the aisle."

Anna's radiant smile was all Cassie needed to see, and she knew that she couldn't let her friend down. There had to be a way to get through the wedding week, only a few short weeks away, and come out alive. Seeing Brody again might be for the best, giving them closure and a chance for a final conversation — for Cassie to apologize on her part. She took no pride in the things she had said to Brody that last night.

Wedding details swirled around them for the next several hours as they shopped for accessories, found lingerie for the bride, and spent lunch reviewing all the details of the trip ahead. Cassie just had to finish October, and after a brief trip back home to see her family, she would be flying to Santa Barbara for the yoga retreat. Deciding to table any more fun and bonding with her family for the year, Cassie had agreed to spend Thanksgiving with Nathan and Philip. The Island wedding would follow four weeks after, then she could sweep in the new year.

Chapter 26

Gratitude dropped through her like a stone as soon as the plane touched down outside of Santa Barbara. Surviving the brief visit with her family had been a trial that tested the last of Cassie's patience. Christopher had been supportive, if a bit worried. Claire — well, Cassie had almost punched her at least half a dozen times within the first three hours of being home, then she'd given up and moved in with her brother because staying with her sister was intolerable. Her parents… well, her parents had been quietly worried, as always, though the worst — her mother — was a silent wall of passive-aggressive disapproval.

Good intentions aside, Claire had cornered Cassie with prayers and concerns of love, all misguided and wrapped up in her faith. If ever Cassie was not interested in hearing about her sister's interpretations on how Cassie could better her life, it was right now. To each their own, but no matter how much Cassie had tried to turn to the good book over the last few months, she had found no peace or sanctuary there.

Her family still had no idea that anything had happened with Brody, and the distance provided by living in separate states came as a blessing since they never really had to see how bad she had gotten. Maybe that was part of the problem — that she had never really talked about things. But outside of Anna, Nathan, and Philip, Cassie hadn't felt the need to share. Her family didn't need to know because what had happened was private, and she knew no one in her family would have understood. Especially having a baby out of marriage.

So rather than risk an argument and burn all her bridges with her sister, Cassie had stayed quiet. All she'd told her family was that she was overstressed with work and had plans in place to lighten her load. For the most part, that was true. She was making changes for the better. But even with those changes in place, the human body still took a long time to heal.

The hired driver Anna had sent up to the airport drove Cassie to the yoga retreat center in the heart of Santa Barbara. Anna wanted a combination of best friend bonding and spiritual centering to ready herself for the big day because she felt that a cleansing of the mind, body, and soul was needed before the start of a new union. It was also a chance for Cassie to dive deeper into her healing on the mental and spiritual level. The next few days would focus on mediation, yoga, and something Anna called the Five Stages Dance — whatever that meant. If it involved dancing, Cassie doubted she would be a full participant. Her body seemed to have forgotten how to move to music anymore.

No matter how much the struggle was for Cassie right now though, there was only one priority that mattered; whatever the bride wanted for her special day was what Cassie would make sure that Anna got.

Getting out of the car, she looked around at the location. The facility housed a generous ranch-style, south-western design of white stucco walls and a green tiled roof in a U shape. The courtyard was landscaped to perfection and led inward. Cassie followed the entry path, rolling her bag behind her. A sign at the entrance noted that the path would traverse through a garden back to where guests would check in and that the garden's twisting paths were representative of the journey from the outer world of chaos and distractions to the inner one, where a person could center properly and be present within themselves. Cassie followed along, enjoying the riot of color everywhere she looked off of the graveled pathway, turned a corner, and her breath caught.

In the middle of the courtyard stood a Shanti statue surrounded by a pool with water lotus floating within. The statue was so graceful and feminine in the lines and the expression on her face that Cassie felt something stir and lighten deep within her soul as she stood there, lost in the tranquility and peace represented before her. Minutes, hours could have passed — all she saw was a piece of her missing self. The part that used to know peace. Or at least something close to it.

"She's beautiful, isn't she?" Anna said.

Cassie turned to see her friend through her tears. Anna also represented that centered peace, wearing a flowing blue-and-white wrap dress that fluttered in the breeze. A long strand of mala beads in brown, amber, yellow, and green encircled her neck, draping beautifully downward. With her golden-brown hair twisted up in a bun on top of her head, Anna looked like the embodiment of happiness and welcoming spirit.

"She really is. So beautiful."

Anna enveloped Cassie in a hug that went on forever. She

simply held and supported her friend, knowing as only a true friend could how much Cassie needed that contact. Drawing back, she held Cassie at arm's length. "The next few days will be hard, but they'll help if you're open to letting them."

Nodding, Cassie pulled Anna back in. "I'm ready. I'm ready to find me again. If not me, then something better than what I am right now."

The hug deepened as Anna rocked her. "We'll go on this journey together, sweet sister. I am blessed to witness your journey and that you came to give support and love for me as well. Come on, let's get you settled in."

The next few days were hard, just as Anna had said they would be, but Cassie opened up and let it all in. At least what she was able to let in. Part of her was still so closed off from the world.

The second-to-last night of the retreat featured a candle-light yoga meditation and the Five Stages Dance. Cassie almost didn't go. She still didn't feel like dancing with a body that was so stiff and unyielding. Music rarely played in her home anymore, and when it did, it was only the radio on low in the background.

But she went because of the promise she had made to Anna and, more importantly, to herself. The intention of this night and ritual was to say good-bye and release grief. Grief over any actions or deeds misplaced. Grief in any decisions of the past. Grief over any loss.

Tonight, the mist of the sea wrapped around them on the beach, and something shifted within Cassie while the music played on low. Cassie swayed stiffly to it with the other women present, but her mind was elsewhere. Then the instructor took them through an exercise in envisioning peace and tranquility.

A piece that had been frozen inside her broke and melted like ice, turning into that mist, it traveled upward where the stars became diamonds in the sky. All the while, the rhythm of the beat twined through Cassie's body and mind.

Lifting her up and up into that glittering sky.

Until she saw something in that beautiful, everlasting and endless light.

Something she couldn't believe possible cracked the ice around her heart and soul.

A sparkling light bounced and danced with joy in the heavens — their baby. Their baby was happy and safe where she was now, held by the ones who would care for her in the spiritual realm.

Cassie swayed forward and backward, in and out. She felt something wet on her face and realized it was tears pouring down. Like joyful rain.

Her feet moved and stepped, twisted in and out, and her head flew back on an arching whip sending her hair flying in a circle around her. She leapt, arms wide to twist, tumbled to the earth, rolled and leapt and did it all over again.

The movements of a lifetime of dance came back and vibrated within her body, releasing and relishing the freedom of finally having her chains cut free.

Cassie danced and danced.

Long after the practice had ended and the music stopped, she danced.

All there stood witness and supported her. She moved until her body could no longer respond, then she collapsed, laughing in Anna's arms.

Chapter 27

Hanging up from a call with Nathan, Cassie smiled over his progress report about their new team of speakers. The feedback from this week was encouraging and proved that the new changes were working out just as they wanted. Just as all the other little changes were doing for Cassie. Every day since the retreat had been a little bit better. She felt lighter and freer inside. She'd even begun to laugh again, fully and with complete presence, not just the superficial persona she had maintained so everyone would worry less. Her body wasn't as tight. Sleep still wasn't as good as it could be, but the time that she did get was leaving her more rested and alert. In the past two weeks, she had put on three whole pounds, so she considered that even bigger progress. The rest would come with time.

Chapter 28

Surliness didn't suit Brody Miller. Neither did the constant irritation and low-edge of pissed off anger that had ridden him like a nagging toothache ever since the invitation arrived.

The plane was more than halfway to The Island, where he would join the rest of the wedding party. Swallowing the last of his drink, Brody stood and swayed with the jolt of the plane. At least, he was pretty sure it was turbulence. He walked to the galley, motioning for the steward to stay seated as he did so, and located the bottle there. With wealth came fine privileges to be taken advantage of, he thought, watching the slow pour of liquid into the tumbler. One of those was some of the choicest whiskeys a man could lay his hands on. The Pappy Van Winkle, at twenty-five hundred dollars a bottle, splashed neat over a single ice cube, and for a moment, the liquid caught the sunlight pouring in the window and flashed to red-gold.

Cassie. Hair like flame on fire.

Brody closed his eyes and leaned on the counter as the memory of her walking hand in hand with him, laughing in the sunlight, shot through him.

"That's your fourth one since we took off, you know?" came a low drawl close to him.

Brody turned, winced, and hissed as the move caught

his side, still tender from the fight he had picked with his brother Simon.

Jake was the one who had commented. Three brothers, and every single one of them a bit annoyed at him.

Brody raised the bottle in a twisted salute and made it a double. "It's five o' clock somewhere. Takes a lot to get me drunk." He was a big guy after all, so it was manageable.

"I'd say you're already well there. It's bad form to show up drunk for your best friend's wedding."

That pithy evaluation came from Cooper, who was currently sprawled with legs stretched across the cabin floor, attempting to nap with his hat tipped down, looking like some version of Indiana Jones. He matched Brody in height, if they weren't almost exactly alike in looks. Or they would, if Brody could get rid of extra muscle and beard he had put on for his current film in progress.

"The wedding's still a week away. Saturday," he clarified for all of them, which included his three brothers and parents. Everyone except his dad was awake to witness the conversation.

Simon didn't even glance up from the investment magazine he had open. "Still bad form. You're being a moron. Need us to kick your ass again? Plenty of time before we land, although it's a really nice plane. Hate to see you have to pay for damages, Mr. Hollywood." The most stylish and corporate-looking of the lot of them, Simon hardly ever had a strand of hair out of place, but hell if he couldn't hit hard. The ache in Brody's side proved it.

Brody chose to maintain a sullen silence rather than comment.

It *was* bad form.

Even worse was knowing the woman he still loved would be there and he no idea how to talk to her.

Two months later hadn't left him with any answers except that he wanted Cassie back. Period. Knowing that she probably still hated him only increased his continuous bad mood and irritability. One bad enough that no one had held back on informing him of what an ass he'd been over the holidays. True to brotherly form, the three of them had jumped him one night, and they had all gone down in a mess of limbs until his mom had waded in and smacked heads.

The tiny dynamo who was his mom sat, quietly watching, and patted the seat next to her. Brody walked toward her, tripped over Cooper's legs, caught himself, and gave an internal round of applause for not spilling a single drop of Paddy's before sitting down heavily next to her.

"You need to stop this, Brody. It's not who you are," Jean said, grabbing his hand. "I miss my happy, smiling, teasing boy. It's time to talk to this girl and figure things out."

He knew she was still reserving judgment on Cassie and had a hard time saying anything nice about the person who had broken her oldest son's heart. Brody took another sip. It might have been a big one, since his mom's eyes narrowed as he did.

He laid his head back, enjoying the burn that went all the way from his tongue to low inside, spreading warmth as it went. "Don't even know if she would talk to me, Momma. We didn't leave things good between us."

Jake sat down next to him. The shadow of a bruise across his left temple where Brody had caught him was finally beginning to fade. "Won't get any better till you do. Fate's putting you two together again. You've got plenty of time before the big day. Figure it out. We've known Chase since all of us were kids, and he asked you to stand at his side as his best man. You owe him better than this shit, brother."

Of all of them, Jake got the closest to understanding what Brody had gone through, but even he had his limits. After all, Cassie was still living, Jake had bluntly pointed out as they cleaned out manure one morning. In Jake's opinion, all Brody needed to do was go the hell after her and get her back and he was a jackass if he didn't.

Brody took one more large swallow before they confiscated his drink and replaced it with coffee, straight and black, in a vain attempt to try to sober him up before landing.

Chapter 29

Cassie ran full out, skirts hiked up to the knees, away from the little demons pursuing her down the beach. For six-year-olds — Anna's twin nieces — they were fast. Tearing up the beach stairs to the house, Cassie was breathing hard with the effort and a little frustrated that she couldn't do it as fast as she used to, which would have been in under thirty seconds. Her thighs burned and were protesting heavily by the time she was near the top. She'd get back to her healthy self soon enough. Laughter, shrieks, and more giggles followed Cassie, paired with the patter of little feet on the stairs behind her. Cassie was almost at the top, took that last step, and sneaked a peak behind her to see where the girls were.

Tripped and crashed into a wall of solid male. Arms came around her to steady her, and Cassie knew, in an instant, exactly who held her. Time stopped and everything else faded away as she focused on the deep black T-shirt in front of her face, how it stretched across a broad chest, and she raised eyes to meet those of emerald green.

Brody!

The sight of him whiplashed in like a hurricane to her senses, surrounding Cassie with the scent of fresh mountain air and deep earth, intoxicating as it mixed with the salty air. His hair was cut slightly shorter, the deep brown lifting in the sea breeze, and he wore a shaggy growth of beard she'd never seen him with before. Her hands lay trapped between them, feeling nothing except the heat from his body.

His teeth flashed like a razor in a lopsided half smile, bringing back memory after memory of Brody watching her with pleasure riding his handsome face.

"Cassie." The word was breathed out in a slow drawl, low and deadly to her ears.

She was in his arms again. To Brody, the realization was like heaven and hell all at once as he reeled from the feel of her again.

"Look at you. Aren't you a sight to see." The words were breathed out in worship.

"It's good to see you too," she said carefully, her pretty hazel eyes wide and wary as they looked up at him.

She was pushing. Trying to get away. From him.

"Is it now?" Brody narrowed his eyes at her. Why was she pushing?

A throat cleared nearby. Pointedly.

Remembering where he was, Brody swept out a hand to include his family and had to brace his feet wide to keep from falling as he kept one arm locked tight around his woman. Cassie might try to get away. Like vapor in the wind.

"Introductions," he said a bit loudly, even to his own ears. "Cassie, my parents, Jean and Martin. Two of my brothers, Jake and Simon. Cooper is…" Brody looked around, amused. People were gathering to watch. He knew some of them. Maybe. "Cooper's somewhere. Everyone, this is Cassie! Hello, gorgeous."

Cassie gave him an odd look. "You're drunk."

The accusation hung in the air like a waving flag. Slightly swaying, Brody looked down at her. Her red hair was longer than she usually wore, tumbling madly around her face in pretty waves. So beautiful it was like a fist to the gut. What a lucky catch that Cassie had fallen right into his arms again so he could save her. Just like the night he'd met her so long ago. Beautiful, beautiful Cassie.

Leaning in, Brody said emphatically, "I am not drunk." Why wouldn't everything just stand the fuck still? "As our friends across the pond would say, I'm slightly pissed at" — he double-checked his watch — "2:38 in the afternoon."

"You're drunk. Let me go."

Brody swayed, and somehow Cassie slipped out of his arms, like a pretty mermaid and slippery as an eel in a long blue maxi dress that made her look like a dream. The halter style left her arms and shoulders bare except for the straps that held it all in place. All a man could think about was sinking in to feast.

"I wanna talk to you."

She gave him a look of pure derision before she turned away. "We can talk when you're sober."

Irritation spiked at the rejection. He'd waited so long to see her again and missed her so damned much. Brody snaked out a hand and caught hers, spinning Cassie back to him. "Don't you walk away from me again, woman."

A delicate fist thumped his chest. Brody barely noticed.

"I'm not talking to you like this. Go cool off."

Any happiness Brody had felt at finding her again blew off, and pure temper came out. "Cool off, huh? You're right. It is kinda hot out, Cassie. You should definitely cool off."

He bent, slung her over his shoulder, took the few steps

to the pool, and tossed Cassie in, enjoying her ear-splitting scream before the water closed around her. Standing there waiting for her to come up, Brody was vaguely aware of his brothers and parents yelling at him in the background.

Where the hell was she? It shouldn't take her that long to come up from the bottom.

Finally Jake's voice broke through the fog. "Uh, Brody, she's not ok." He pointed into the water, already toeing off his shoes to go in after her.

Brody's eyes focused. *Shit!* Without a second thought, he dove in and down. The skirt had twisted around Cassie's legs, keeping her from swimming up as she struggled to get them free. Grabbing her under the arms, Brody kicked and pulled her back up to the surface, where she sputtered and clung to him.

"You fucking asshole!" she screamed when she could breathe again, her hands beating madly at his back and shoulders.

Brody drifted along, loving the feeling of Cassie wet and soft against him, even if she was mad as hell. Thinner than he remembered...

Cassie, his pretty little mermaid by the sea. Brody's feet found the bottom and he lifted her to carry her to the pool stairs as she still rained curses down on his head.

"I'm so sorry, baby." Setting her down, Brody knelt next to her. His hands worked, fumbling a bit, to undo the tangled twist of fabric — that refused to cooperate— from around those beautiful legs. He glanced at her face to see the red waves, now a dripping mess of tangles, and pretty eyes spitting sparks at him. Brody couldn't help the snicker that escaped.

Cassie's eyes only fired brighter as she glared at him. Triumphant after freeing the last twist of fabric with a flourish, Brody stood to help Cassie up.

"Look at that, baby. Got to play hero again." The words slurred out of his mouth. Maybe he was still drunk?

Pain blew like lightning across his jaw, snapping his head back, and Brody fell with a splash. He came up for air and was shoved back under again by hands that held him there while he could hear her screaming above him.

Brody was choking when he surfaced, and he saw Cassie stomping up the pool stairs, dripping water and fury like a reigning warrior sea goddess. She stood at the top, looking down at him, her hands fisted and shaking with rage before she stalked off.

"You're a fucking idiot, Brody Miller!"

Laughter hit like a storm, and Brody's mouth spread wide as it rolled out of his whole body, his face stinging with the effort. It had been a helluva long time since he'd found anything so funny. Brody crawled up the pool stairs and flopped over to lay back. The cool water lapped at him while laughs poured out of him, jaw aching like a son of a bitch where Cassie had punched him.

Damn, she was sure something.

Chapter 30

Nathan and Philip took Cassie back to her room. Finished cursing her way through every variation of every foul thing she could think up to call the idiot named Brody Miller, she snapped off the shower and opened the frosted door to Nathan holding a towel for her to wrap up in. Since he'd seen her in every single form of dress over the years, Cassie didn't bat an eyelash.

"That was some performance outside." Still obviously trying not to laugh, he kept pressing his lips together as small snorts kept escaping.

Cassie muttered some more about idiot men in general and took the second towel to wrap her hair in. One of her favorite dresses, one she had loved for years, lay in a sodden heap on the floor. Dammit. The thing better not be beyond repair.

"I'll be fine. Thanks for caring. The stupid ass. What the hell?"

"Oh Cassie Bear, I think he's still very much in love with you, based on all that."

Incredulous, Cassie rounded on Nathan. "And you drew that conclusion from what? The way he just tried to drown me with that Neanderthal caveman routine?"

"No. That was just an accident — from him being a drunken idiot." Nathan handed her the body cream and watched while she toweled her hair dry.

Cassie pointed a finger at him on a hiss. "Don't you dare defend that moron."

"I'm not. Just looking at the facts. Don't worry, I might kill him on principle before he gets a chance to apologize for what he did to you, but it's good to see you mad and fighting for a change."

Philip called from outside the bathroom, "I have a pot of tea for you to warm up with and some island pastries and fruit."

"At least there's one man on this earth worth something," Cassie muttered, walking out to find something to wear.

She yanked on some clothes then grabbed a blanket to wrap up in since she was still shaking from the adrenaline. Her hand smarted from hitting a man who had a face like a rock. Never in her life had she been so terrified. The dress had wrapped around like a maniacal water demon. Every move just made it tighter and tighter, pulling her down, until strong arms had caught her and Cassie's heart had almost stopped, knowing Brody had her. That she was safe.

Until air came back into her lungs and she remembered who had tried to kill her in the first place.

The door to the bedroom slammed open when Anna burst inside, chest heaving. "I just heard. I was down on the beach. My God, are you all right? Chase might kill Brody. He's the maddest I've ever seen him."

"She'll be fine. Brody, on the other hand, might launch himself off this cliff when he sobers up enough to think about what he did," Philip said.

"I'll help push him off," Anna fumed. "His brothers apparently carted him off after they dragged him out of the pool

— still laughing like a loon, my sources say."

"Calling him a loon is insulting to the bird," Cassie said low and tight. "He's a pure idiot."

A cup of tea appeared in front of her eyes from Nathan. "Chamomile, sweetie, to soothe the nerves. Idiot or no, when Brody realized what was happening, he didn't hesitate to save you. And before he went all caveman, the look on his face said he was pure happiness to see you again. Granted, it was drunken happiness. I think he just couldn't figure out why you wouldn't talk to him." At Cassie's furious glare, Nathan added with an indulgent smile. "Cause he was drunk."

Sitting down next to her, he hugged Cassie tightly. Anna joined them on Cassie's other side and curled up to pat her arm.

Philip sat across from them. "You two just need to cool down. You can talk later on, or maybe tomorrow."

Cassie sat there in stony silence, sniffling with it as she sipped her tea and indulged the need for sugar with a bite of the mango pastry Anna put in her hand. "Damn him. I hate that I still care about him. The big stupid idiot."

Nathan only pulled her in tighter. "It'll be okay. You guys will figure it out."

Cassie laid her head on his shoulder and smiled. Her temper was finally easing off enough to find the humor in it all.

"'Got to play hero again,'" she said, quoting the big giant idiot, and sighed. "He always loved playing my hero."

One of her favorite things. Sometimes she used to think he didn't believe her legs worked. The man just loved feeling big and strong and taking care of her. Especially when she was tired and just home from a week of traveling. He would have extra things in place to pamper her, like flowers and dinner to warm up if he was still working late, or Brody himself to cook in person. And because he always took such good care of her, Cassie had never minded accepting those things he needed in return, such as the need to help guard his privacy and protect what they had together from prying eyes.

Sobriety always bought with it a special kind of something on the rare times Brody went too far. This time it brought a splitting headache, an aching jaw, and the humiliation of what he'd done to the woman he loved. What had he been thinking? Tossing Cassie in the pool? All a man could claim was stupidity — amplified by drink.

Cooper handed over an ice pack, which Brody gratefully accepted from where he lay stripped down to his shorts on the couch. He applied the ice pack, wincing at the tenderness from where Cassie had cold cocked him. Who knew she could hit so hard for such a little thing?

Simon and Cooper had dragged him out of the pool as he had been delirious and talking nonsense about slippery redheaded mermaids. Jake had taken his legs, and the three of them had tossed Brody in the shower in his room, still fully clothed. Simon had grabbed the shower wand and turned on the water.

Cold.

Straight in Brody's face.

The frigid blast had done what the coffee hadn't — sobered him up fast.

Simon hadn't offered an apology, and Brody couldn't say he was expecting one any time soon.

Jake stood above him, glaring down. "You owe me one for this. Mom and Dad are fit to tan your hide. I got them to go take a walk on the beach and cool off."

"I owe you, man. Anything. Anytime." Brody groaned. Shit. His mom and dad would only add to the embarrassment, and God above, he'd like to at least be able to stand up straight when they chewed him out. "You sure Cassie's all right?"

"She's fine. Still mad and cursing up a storm, last I heard. I just checked with that honey-colored girl Chase is marrying. She got a sister, cousin, anything?" Simon grinned.

Brody sighed. "No, Anna is one of a kind." *Just like Cassie.*

"Hmmm. Damn shame. Anna is, however, and I am directly quoting the bride here, 'Ready to kill you dead.' She says not to show your face until you're clean and sober."

Chase strode in and blew out a tired breath. "Okay, I have the women and men settled down. Finally. Brody, what the fuck? Nathan is set to take your balls off with manicure scissors."

Every man in the room visibly cringed.

"Am I going to have to send you the hell home? What was all that?" Chase asked.

"That was our brother demonstrating his fine, albeit very strange, courtship skills," Cooper said, legs stretched out where he lay on the floor due to the lack of extra chairs. "Just so you know, we've decided Cassie is under our protection from here on out. You try anything like that again, and we will defend her honor. Beat the holy hell out of you if we have to. No one here cares when you have to be seen on camera next."

Grunts and nods came from all present, and Brody closed his eyes. "I'll be fine. Swear to God, I won't drink that much again." He stood, head still spinning like crazy, to face Chase.

Brody owed him that much. "I'm sorry. I was out of line, and it won't happen again. You have my word. But I understand if you don't want me here to stand next to you. I'll personally apologize to Anna. Make it right."

Chase shook his head. "Shit, how could I get married without you here? You're my best friend." He took the hand Brody offered and pulled him into a one-armed hug. "I know it's Cassie and all, but get it pulled together and get things fixed with her." Taking Brody's chin, Chase angled his face to see the vivid purple rapidly spreading and grinned. "Maybe let her cool off first though. She's got a hell of a right hook. Haven't seen anyone take you down like that since that bar fight in Brooklyn."

Both of them laughed at the memory, but Brody winced and groaned as pain shot through his jaw. For the time being, it would be better to lay back down with the ice.

Seeing Cassie again had made one thing crystal clear though — Brody was still in love with her. He didn't know how just yet, but he was going to win his woman back. Just like he'd won Cassie the first time around.

PART 3
Harmony

I was lost
Until I found a Home in your Heart
- A.A. Ream

Chapter 31

For the next two days, Cassie didn't see Brody, but she would have sworn with everything she owned she could feel him watching her. She'd have a glimpse out of the corner of her eye of a tall shadow standing one minute in the window and gone the next, or maybe she'd be on the beach below and look up and see him at the top of the hill. Watching and waiting, making her glad that neither of them had run into one another in person. Cassie honestly didn't know if she was ready to face him again. She still alternated between being mad enough to hit him with a shovel and wanting so badly to speak to him and clear things between them.

The wedding was in five days. According to Anna and Chase's preferences, the only ones sharing the house were them, their parents, the best man and maid of honor, and a select few guests. Everyone else came and went from the village below as they saw fit, enjoying the island activities of sailing, beaching, shopping, and exploring. An ever-ready kitchen staff had an array of assorted foods and beverages on hand to welcome any who stopped in. There was an air of celebration and joy all around.

Tonight, they were having a pre-wedding celebration and couples shower for the happy duo. Tonight, there was no way Cassie would be able avoid Brody anymore.

"Are you sure you're ready for this?" Anna asked as the makeup artist buffed up her face with a few final strokes of bronzer before moving to put the finishing touches on Cassie.

"I'll be fine, I promise. Why do I need professional make-up done tonight? It's not the wedding day."

"Because Chase's mom wants photo documentation of everything and she would like us all to look our best." Anna rolled her eyes. "Don't worry, I've sneaked behind her back and told the photographer no staged or formal shots. Chase and I want to just enjoy the party, so it's candids the whole evening." She was obviously thrilled by her canny plot.

Chase's parents were more formal old-fashioned Southerners and driving free-spirited Anna insane with requests to guide the wedding to their preferences — or more specifically, his mother's preferences. So far, Cassie had never seen the woman with a single strand of hair out of place, making her such a contrast to Anna, whose favorite look was flowing clothes in soft fabrics and no makeup. It was a mystery to Cassie how Anna always still managed to look like a runway model.

Tonight's light sea green off-the-shoulder Grecian-style dress suited Anna perfectly. Her honey-gold-and-brown hair was twisted up in a bun like she usually wore it, but a few flowers were woven in around the top, giving it an elegant edge.

"I bow to your stealthy methods. She doesn't stand a chance against you. By the way, you do look amazing. I don't know how you do it, but you're always right on the mark." Cassie saluted her with the champagne they had opened for them as they got ready.

"It's all how you put yourself out there. Own your own

strength. Now, you my dear, need to stand a little straighter and throw those gorgeous shoulders back. Strapless should be worn with confidence."

Not having had time to shop, Cassie had let Anna direct the fashion for the week — it was her strength anyway and she loved to get Cassie out of her box of professional business clothes. Doing a turn, Cassie had to admit, her friend had struck gold yet again — except for the fact that tonight's pants were white.

What was it with Anna and white?

The linen and silk white pants flowed to pair with a strapless triangular top that went to mid-thigh. What made Cassie stand out was that the top was painted in a vibrant floral pattern. The greens, reds, and oranges created an uplifting tone and set off the light kiss of sun Cassie's skin had acquired since they'd arrived. Heels with thin silver straps encased her ankles and ensured Cassie would be able to dance if she chose to later. A long chain of thin gold that ended in a small coin stamped with sacred geometry completed the look. Cassie felt chic and posh and like an island girl all at the same time. The stylist had boosted her natural waves and added some depth to her eyes, making them a deeper green than their normal hazel.

"It's ridiculous how you do this every time." Cassie twisted to see in the mirror better. "You nailed it. Somehow I don't look like a wraith."

Seven more pounds to go until she regained the full fifteen she'd lost over the past year. When you were already petite, losing that much weight didn't make you look thinner. It just made you look sick. Cassie missed her athletic muscle tone and what her body used to be able to do physically — like charge up the beach steps without even breathing hard. Or do one single stupid pull-up.

It would come back. Already she had put on more weight since the retreat before Thanksgiving. A sure sign that her body had finally started to heal.

What Cassie didn't know yet was how to handle tonight and being near Brody again. Rather than worry about it, she decided, for a change, to go with the flow and let things happen as they were meant to. That was one of the things her new counselor had been working with her on — not everything needed to be planned out, organized, highlighted, and color-coded for the day to be perfect and productive.

When she stepped out into the living room with Anna, both men were there, and her heart did a silly erratic beat when she saw Brody.

He wore casual island style the same way he wore faded jeans — easy and relaxed. Lightweight tan pants and the tailored T-shirt suited him perfectly. He'd shaved down the beard some so it was more of a trimmed-up four-day growth than pure shagginess. So much handsomer and more rugged-looking than Cassie remembered, even sporting a fading purple-and-blue bruise on his jaw which failed at hiding behind the scruff.

"Ladies! Don't you both look amazing." Chase walked over to take their hands, and Cassie smiled internally at how Chase only had eyes for Anna and she for him.

He offered both arms to escort them over to the bar, where Brody stood watching Cassie and no one else. Piercing in intensity, his eyes left a stroke of warmth everywhere they landed on her. Their green was only marred by a sadness that rivaled Cassie's own.

"Hi, Brody."

One corner of his lips lifted in a wry acknowledgement. "Cassie."

Brody reached behind him toward the bartender and grabbed one of the fruity rum drinks that Cassie loved, passing it over to her. Their fingers brushed as she took it, and a lash of heat curled in her belly, settling deep and throbbing inside. Cassie's eyes widened in surprise that her body could even remember how to feel desire. She'd felt nothing for any man since the two of them had separated. Not that she had been interested in dating again, but Cassie had simply assumed that that part of her was dead. Like everything else had been until a few weeks back.

Brody's face showed that he felt the fission of heat as well. His emerald-green eyes narrowed slightly in response.

Chase cleared his throat. "A toast to the four of us. Two good friends who met two other good friends. Now, two of those are getting married and the other two better figure out a way to get along the next few days."

The warning was said lightheartedly but clear as a bell.

Brody nodded and raised his glass before taking a sip of his drink. "We'll be fine. Maybe you two could give us a minute before we go outside to all the fun?" He didn't bother to take his eyes off Cassie's.

"Sure thing. Have fun you two," Chase said, turning to his fiancée. "Let's sneak off so you can show me how to get you out of this dress later."

Anna's giggles met Cassie's ears and she couldn't help rolling her eyes while Chase pulled her friend off to the other side of the room.

A smile broke out over Brody's face. "They sure are cute

together, aren't they?"

Cassie sighed. "They really are. Did I do that?" Her hand was touching his face before she thought about it, and she drew back hastily, not knowing what to do. "Sorry."

"Nah." His hand caught hers and brought it to his lips. The rough and silky texture of beard brushed her skin. "I deserved it. Probably a whole lot more. I was way out of line, and I'm really sorry."

"Does it hurt?"

"Not that bad anymore, and only when I smile. Christopher teach you to punch like that?"

"He did. After I had a high school date who had trouble taking no for an answer."

"He's a good brother." Brody's hand still held hers and squeezed it gently. "We need to talk."

Cassie shook her head. "Not now. Please." Taking her hand out of his, she tipped her glass toward Anna and Chase. "Tonight is their night. For Chase and Anna."

"You can't avoid me forever."

"I'm not trying to. Just… not right now, okay? Please?"

Penetrating and assessing eyes held her own. At last, Brody slowly nodded. "All right. When you're ready, we'll talk."

Cassie made it through the socializing, the dinner, and the speeches. She even managed a conversation or two with Brody's brothers and parents. Of them all, his parents surprised her the most. His mom and dad both pulled her into a hug and apologized profusely for their son's behavior by the poolside. Cassie tried to assure them that it was all fine, and she thanked heaven when Jake — at least she thought it was Jake — stepped in to distract his parents. Two of the bothers looked exactly alike, while the third one simply looked like a blonder, more serious version of Brody. All had variations of green eyes and the height they'd gotten from their dad.

Beyond that single conversation at the bar, Brody didn't speak to Cassie except when necessary. He almost made it a point to not touch her when they sat together during dinner, while Cassie tried to focus on anything other than the man next to her who still made her heart race.

The music started up after the sun set, blazing like a gold-and-purple mirage across the end of the earth, before the stars came out. Reggae and salsa music pumped the party full of island flavor, and the energy kicked into full swing, loud enough to drown out the ocean below. Nathan pulled Cassie out to where a section had been cleared for dancing and cut loose to showcase his skills around her.

Caught up in the fun, Cassie's feet and hips moved as Nathan twirled her in a complicated spin to the cheers of the crowd that had stopped to watch. Nathan spun her out and into him again before dancing side by side in a series of salsa steps that left Cassie breathless. Her head snapped back and forth to the rhythm as she smiled at the freedom of dancing again. She gave thanks for that and for Anna's help in finding a way to heal — and a fabulous outfit that stayed put even with its strapless design.

Cassie caught Brody watching her during one spin. A warm crooked smile twisted his lips as his eyes lit with pleasure, and her smile faltered. Nathan spun her back to him and twisted to send her out again. On the outward spin, her foot caught and twisted. Letting go of Nathan's hand, she stumbled and—

Arms encircled her, saving Cassie from the fall by pulling her against a chest she remembered all too well.

"Need a rescue, gorgeous?"

How on earth had Brody moved so fast? Her breath slammed in her chest. As she was pinned there, time simply fell away so that all she wanted to do was dance with Brody again. To feel him hold her and how the two of them would move together so seamlessly.

Instead, she stepped back. "Thanks."

"It's good to see you dance again. It's so good to see you period."

"It's good to be dancing again… and to see you as well," she admitted.

They stared at each other and the crowd faded away.

"I'm sorry," they said at once then smiled together.

Brody held out a hand. "Take a walk with me?"

All of a sudden, the crowd was too loud, too overwhelming, and Cassie wanted nothing more than to be away from them.

"Yes." Her hand slipped into his as if they had never been apart. The warmth and security she felt from a single touch made her heart ache for what they'd lost with each other. What they could never have again because of how badly they had hurt each other.

Brody didn't say a word as he walked with Cassie's hand tucked into his. Part of the misery inside him eased from just having that small thing again. After guiding her through the festivities to the beach stairs, he went first, leading the way down. Landscape lighting scattered here and there along the stairs cast a cheery glow all the way to the beach. Reaching the bottom, he turned and paused, taking in Cassie's outfit. The one that had driven him crazy with her beautiful curves, bare shoulders and arms all night. Brody's heart had almost broken when he saw Cassie dance again. She'd stopped dancing with him and even for herself after their baby.

"Let's take these shoes off, how about? So you can walk." He bent to help her out of the heels. The flowered scent she wore wrapped into his brain bringing back so many memories of being close to her. Of being twined together, wet and sandy, kissing and drowning in each other on that very beach.

"Thanks," Cassie said.

His hand tightened for a second on her hip, and Brody fought to not pull her into his arms. Reminding himself to behave, he kicked off his sandals and left them beside hers. "Come on. Let's take that walk. If you want to talk, we can do that too."

They walked for a long time along the damp sand, soft and gritty underfoot, and through the foamy surf that melted along playing against their feet until they were far from the noise of the party above, where the beach quieted and the sands opened up with the evening tide. An almost-full moon rode high overhead, casting its light over the ocean that moved in and out in a rhythm established before time itself.

Brody took a deep breath and started to speak, but Cassie beat him to it. "I, um… I wanted to say I'm sorry. For the way things ended between us."

"Me too, Cassie. I'm sorry. For so much of it."

"Don't." Cassie stopped to stand in front of him. She forced herself to meet his eyes and speak the truth. They both needed the truth so they could begin fresh and move forward. "You… you didn't deserve any of that. You were only trying to help me. I'm the one who used everything I knew to shove you away."

Brody shoved his hands into his pockets. "I didn't know how to help. I was so lost."

"I know. We both were, but you were trying at least, when all I wanted to do was give up. I hated you sometimes."

He looked away as pain washed over his face. "I know you did."

Cassie closed her eyes tightly to fight off her own agony. God above, it hurt to know that Brody knew that about her. That at times she had almost hated him. Taking a deep breath, she continued. "I hated you for shoving green smoothies under my nose, making me eat when I didn't want to, forcing me to go on walks. For making me live again when all I wanted to do was give up. But instead of doing either, I shut you out and buried myself in work to cope."

Brody only stood there, shaking his head in frustration. "You weren't a quitter. I couldn't let you be."

"I know that. Now. I'm sorry I didn't then, but I know it now. It's taken me a long time to begin to heal and see clearly again."

"I'm sorry too. For giving up and letting you walk away from me. It was never what I wanted. I just couldn't figure out how to make it better anymore. You were so mad at me all the time."

Cassie stepped closer to him and laid a hand on his handsome face filled with so much torment. Wrapped up in her own misery during that time, she had missed Brody's because he'd hid it so well while trying to help her. "You didn't deserve that anger. *Nothing* you did was worth what I did to you. I was so mad at myself. For not taking better care and being so sick. For the fact that I couldn't stop working — or worse, wouldn't at that point. I took it all out on you."

Defeated, Brody sat on the sand and pulled Cassie down next to him. He held her hand as he stared across the water and dragged a hand through his hair. "You did nothing wrong, baby. The doctor… you know the statistics he said."

"I know," Cassie's voice broke. "It didn't help or change anything in my heart. I'm so sorry for what I did to you. To us."

The water rolled toward them, calming in its steady rhythm. Brody's arm came up to wrap around her shoulders and hold her closer.

Cassie knew it was just as Brody said. The doctors had laid out in black and white for them that one in four pregnancies would spontaneously terminate during the first trimester, sometimes even after for whatever reason. Women lost babies all the time. Those facts hadn't made it any easier to bear, just as Cassie knew they had probably brought no comfort to any woman who had ever lost a child.

That time had been so horrible. From the moment the spotting started and she'd woken Brody up in New York to all the days they had waited afterward while Cassie stayed on bedrest per doctor's orders. The two of them trying to stay positive and work through the boredom of having to rest. But Cassie had known through it all that her body was losing, failing to save their baby. The proof had been there every time she had gone to the bathroom and the bleeding had been worse.

They sat in silence, watching the water while Brody held her. Every now and then, a tear would slip down her face for the missing pieces of her life — for this man who had done everything for her and their child lost to heaven.

Brody had been one to help Cassie heal from a broken past. He'd supported her and shown her in the best way possible that it was okay to be a strong woman with a big dream – to even be able to open up and share that with someone else while it was just them, and he had looked so excitedly toward their future together when life blessed them with a baby. And when it had all been lost, Brody had only tried to do what he did best — care for Cassie to help her heal again. Now her heart broke all over again when she thought about how he had suffered just as much.

Brody broke the silence. "Part of me hates them for picking this place to get married."

"I do too. I'm happy for them, I really am, but at the same time, I hate that it's here. When you brought me here… it meant so much." *It's where I knew I loved you.* Cassie couldn't bring herself to say those words.

Guiding her head to rest on his shoulder, Brody leaned his head against hers and laid back, taking Cassie with him. "I always pictured us getting married here."

"Here? You never said anything." About *marriage.* How had she never known that he had been that serious? They had only talked about it casually, like something they might do much further in the future, since both of them were swamped with work.

"I was going to ask you to marry me."

"You were?" She tried to sit up to see him, but Brody held her still.

The deep breath he took more of a shudder. "I kept waiting. Wanted to have you feeling better and not be so sick with the baby. I should have asked you. Maybe if I had, we wouldn't have broken."

There was nothing she could say. All the pain that was still there coursed through her and left her shattered. Keeping her arms tight around, Cassie held him back.

"Stay with me here for a bit. Let me hold you. Just hold you." Brody sounded so exhausted.

Exhausted herself from the past and the confession of facing her truth, Cassie let Brody hold her. The simple fact was that it mirrored Cassie's own feelings —she needed him just as much. The stars floating above them, the cushion of the sand below, and the sound of the ocean drifted in and out surrounded them with its own special healing. Like dissolving into the mist.

Chapter 32

Without even having to roll over to see the clock, Cassie knew that it was around three in the morning. No matter where she was in the world or how tired her body was, three o'clock was the magic number. Or the witching hour, if you wanted to look at it as such. Cassie would wake up then and be unable to get back to sleep.

She'd once heard someone say that waking up between three and four in the morning was due to the mind and body dealing with old regrets. She supposed that was true in her case.

If the mood was right, trying to meditate was an option, or she might read for a while until her brain shut down and put her to back sleep. Sometimes she would try a cup of warm milk or tea instead. So far, no foolproof method had been that magic key. Mostly, she just lay in bed or got up and wandered. Tonight, she lay there staring at the ceiling, remembering the night's walk with Brody.

The two of them had lain on the beach in silence before they talked a little more about wedding duties, then Brody had taken her hand and walked Cassie back to the house with no more words said between them. By unspoken agreement, neither of them wanted to rejoin the festivities, and Brody had taken Cassie to her room. At the door, he pulled her into a tight hug before pressing a kiss to her forehead and walking off. Cassie almost called him back, aching for the feel of his arms holding her again.

The loneliness after the door closed had been unbearable.

Recognizing the signs, Cassie knew there was no way her mind would shut off anytime soon, which made wandering aimlessly better than anything else. Getting up, she pulled on some clothes and grabbed a wrap. At the patio off her room, she followed the path down and around the house to the pretty side garden lounge area Cassie had discovered during the time Brody had brought her here. Semi-enclosed from the rest of the house yet still open and shaded to the sea below and starry sky above, it had been Cassie's favorite place to curl up and relax. Brody would invariably find her, and they would talk for hours or he would seduce her yet again.

The night breeze was cooler than she'd expected and made her glad for the wrap. Cassie rounded the corner and found Brody lying on one of the cushioned outdoor couches. It seemed more than one person in the house had trouble sleeping.

He looked… awful. Clothes twisted as though he'd gone to bed without bothering to change. Haggard. Exhausted. And when she truly looked, he seemed… haunted.

The tumbler of drink in his hand spoke volumes.

Brody had sworn he wouldn't drink that heavy again. At least, not so much that he made a jackass out of himself again. The party had been good. He'd stuck to a single drink and water the rest of the night. But talking with Cassie had done him in. The entire night had done him in.

He might be a bit warm from the drink right now, but he'd

kept his promise. He wasn't anywhere close to drunk yet and damn if he didn't wish that were less of a fact. At least when he was drunk, he had the illusion that everything was all right. But he knew that in the past couple of months — longer if he admitted the truth — since that fucking invitation had arrived, and with it the realization that he would have to see Cassie again, he'd been turning to that comfort more than he should have to fight how much he wanted her back.

Flowers and light.

Bringing the glass to his lips for another swallow, Brody cussed low and vicious, swearing he could smell the faint scent of Cassie on the wind. For the most part, he'd gotten through talking to her again. The pain of ripping out all his feelings and letting them bleed fresh had been needed. They had needed to talk but God, holding her again had left a gaping wound inside him. Maybe a better solution would be to just throw himself into the Hollywood party scene and drown out the pain with other women like some in his business did?

The problem was, there wasn't another woman he wanted to touch. The added irony of that problem was that he was surrounded by beautiful women all the time. Ones who made no secret of wanting to get to know him better. But Cassie had been the only one who hadn't wanted what his money or his fame could buy. All she had wanted was him.

Any time another woman had crossed his mind, all he saw was Cassie. No woman out there could compare to the way she used to light up and smile when she saw him, her red hair lifting in the wind, or her face soft and blissful after they made love. The way Brody could sit with her and talk for hours.

The way she moved when she walked toward him.

Brody blinked, focused his bleary eyes, and shook his head with a smile, taking another drink. Hallucinations were the first part of madness. Followed by... what next? He couldn't remember. Then the hallucination sat next to him on the chaise and leaned down to smooth his hair back. So beautiful in the moonlight.

"Is that you, Cassie, baby?"

A sad smile slid over her face. "It is. What are you doing, Brody Miller?"

"Trying to sleep. Sometimes if I drink enough..." He watched as sadness made her pretty elfin eyes fill. "Don't cry, gorgeous. Please don't cry." Brody couldn't bear to see her cry. "I haven't slept well since... well since."

A liquid diamond fell. Lit by the moon, it trailed in a silver streak down her cheek, followed by another. He raised a thumb to brush them away. Cassie leaned in and took the glass from his hand — it had been about to fall — and set it on the table next to them.

"Brody, you don't need this. You're stronger than this." Soft fingers traced his face like a cool cloth for the turmoil fighting inside him. Words soft and pleading, Cassie said, "I need you to be that strong man again."

"I don't know if I can. It's so hard. I miss holding you so much..." Brody closed his eyes on the fresh wave of pain that the whiskey hadn't covered up. "So much... I miss you." He was so damn tired of fighting it, worn down to the bone from it.

Cassie shifted and lay down next to him, pulling his arms around her to snuggle with her head on his shoulder. Her feminine curves pressed gently down the length of him, and part of the ache let go. Just the feel of her next to him was like a balm to his soul. Closing his eyes, Brody held on, never wanting to let her go.

"I saw our baby," Cassie said quietly. Her fingers had come up to tangle in the hair at his neck and trace the edge of his beard.

The words rocked him to the core. "What?"

"It sounds crazy, I know. But I did — on this yoga retreat a few weeks ago that Anna made me go on. A healing retreat for those who have experienced loss. During the one meditation, I saw this light. This tiny little bright light. It was dancing, and I knew somehow it was our baby. Back and forth, bouncing and twisting, turning and giggling between these four shadows around her."

It sounded so beautiful — the simple idea of it. Brody's pain, that had lingered within him for so long he didn't know how to live without it, lightened a bit and eased away to something different.

Acceptance of knowing that their little one was happy.

"Four shadows, huh? Maybe our grandparents. What do you think?" He was so tired… just wanted to sleep.

"That feels right." Cassie sighed and snuggled closer. Her hand continued to stroke his hair like it used to. Comforting. Soothing. "They were so happy to have her."

Brody lay silent for a moment with the vision wrapping happily around him. Then Cassie's words hit, and a surreal smile came out. "Her? You sure? A girl?"

"Yes." He could feel Cassie smile too with it. "It was definitely girl energy."

"Huh… I'll be damned. A girl…" Letting out a breath, he said, "I'd love a girl. Three brothers are a pain in the ass."

Exhaustion was pulling him under, and the rest murmured out. "Red hair… pretty eyes like her momma."

Cassie propped up her head on a hand to look down at him with a soft smile. It was like a light in the darkness to see that smile truly reach her eyes. "You didn't want a son?"

She was so beautiful in the moonlight and so full of caring. Drowsy to the point that he could barely think, Brody touched her face and his eyes closed as his hand fell away. "Just wanted you. Whatever we had would have been enough. Boy or girl. We lost our baby… I lost you… lost everything."

Sleep took him as Cassie leaned in to brush a kiss to his lips, soft as a feather and just as sweet.

"We're going to be okay. We found each other again. Go to sleep, I'm here. This time, I'm going to heal you."

Laying her head down again, everything drifted away. Content to be with Brody, her body finally gave over to sleep knowing they had each other. Because she had begun to heal, she knew Brody could too. This time, she wouldn't let him down.

Chapter 33

Sun peeked through the swaying palms, the scent of ocean filled the air, and he knew Cassie was with him. It was a dream and a knowing all at once. Brody lay with his eyes closed, savoring the feeling of her there. For the first time in so long, his mind woke clear of missing her and feeling rested for a change. Like he had slept the whole night and then some. For once, Brody felt ready to face the day and whatever came at him without having to force himself out of bed to do so. Breathing in deep the morning sea air and the flower essence that was only Cassie, he imprinted every bit of the sensation of her.

His arm wrapped around with her head on his shoulder, and one leg was thrown between his own. Her hand rested at his neck, fingers buried in his hair, and his other hand was doing the same with hers. The soft silk of that red-gold was so like he remembered. If he turned his head, Brody could feel it brush his lips. Yes, soft silk. He'd loved feeling it against his skin.

This was how they had always lain together. His other favorite way had been when Cassie curled into him, letting him spoon her. A smile tugged at his lips as he remembered the way his hands could play however they wanted. His body stirred at the memory off how she would respond, warm and wet, calling his name as he slid inside her to wake her up in the best way possible.

Shifting so he could see her face, Brody lay next to her, keeping her close, pillowed on his arm.

His pretty little Cassie. Lashes long, dark, and thick were closed in sleep over those hazel depths he used to think were bewitched from the way they would change color depending on what she wore — sometimes a deeper green, or grey, or sometimes tinged blue. All of it was simply fascinating.

His fingers traced the side of her face and down to full pink lips, soft and relaxed in sleep, tempting him beyond belief. Unable to resist, Brody brushed his lips to hers.

Cassie. His little mermaid beauty in his arms by the sea. She'd stayed with him last night. Even seeing him at his worst, she'd stayed.

That choice had to mean something for them — maybe a chance to have a future again.

When he brushed her lips again, she whispered his name and Brody gave in. Over and over he gave her the faintest of kisses, feather brushes and caresses to her eyes, cheeks, nose, and back to those lips that called him like nothing else in the world. Cassie woke dreamy-eyed and murmuring his name as she pressed closer.

Lost, he took her lips and sank into their warmth. Cassie opened to him, and the last was intoxicating. Dream and reality in one.

He was kissing her...
Brody was kissing her...
Over and over.
Calling to her with his touch, the fantasy eased to seduc-

tive kisses that pulled her further and further under and out to sea, where she drifted along to the song of the ocean waves. Wanting more, Cassie let Brody take and take what he wanted. His tongue tangled with hers, deep and possessive, and her body met his, reveling in his touch. So long they had been without the other, but no step was fumbled. Every movement was cherished and spoke of nothing but tenderness and caring. His body pressed against hers like an inferno, and his mouth burned away all the dark, the regret, the pain. All of it turned to ash until there was only Brody.

Sliding away to hover above her, Cassie made a sound of loss, but his lips stayed tantalizingly close to her own.

"Morning, gorgeous," Brody whispered.

Her lips curled in a smile under his and she opened her eyes to meet the green ones she so loved, full of warmth and tenderness. Better looking this morning and less haunted without the demons that had pulled at him last night.

"Morning, handsome. Feel better?"

When she traced the side of his face, Brody captured her hand and pressed a kiss to her palm before lacing their fingers together. "I do. Can't remember when I last slept so well. Why did you stay?"

"You needed me. I never knew you were so…" His finger pressed to her lips, but Cassie pulled it away. "No. Don't stop me. I never knew you were so torn up inside. I should have known."

"How could you? I never told you. I didn't want to make things worse. You were already too heartbroken. You didn't need me adding to it."

"Don't," she whispered. "Don't act like none of this was my fault."

"No one is at fault. It's over. No more blame or guilt. Let it be over so we can move on." Brody slid a hand to her face and lifted to take her lips in a kiss of caring and need all in one. When he let go, Cassie was trembling from the force of it.

"What now?" She searched his face.

The question left the field wide open and the ball of uncertainty bouncing between them. Neither of them wanted to misstep in this new dance.

"I'm not sure... maybe we can just lay here for a bit?" Brody smiled down at her. "Then if my luck continues, you'll spend the day with me doing mostly little or nothing in general."

"Hmmm... I'd like that. I have no wedding duties until later on."

"Yeah?" His face broke out in a smile that lit up Cassie as well.

"Yes."

Brody lowered his lips to hers for a kiss just as soft as the ones that had awakened her. All of a sudden, he pulled back looking completely serious. "Cassie, will you let me try to win your heart again?"

She shook her head, crushing any happiness that had shown on his face before.

"No. This time we both try together," she said. "I think we both need each other. I... I just don't know if we can get our trust back."

"I don't know either." Brody laid his forehead against hers. "All I know is I don't want to lose you again. What do you want?"

"Do you think... no, that's not right... I want a second chance for us. I just don't know... I don't know where to start… or i-if you would even—"

His kiss cut her off, hard, fierce, and passionate, leaving her dazed.

"Does that answer your question, woman? Yes, dammit, I want a second chance with you. We both try. Together."

"Okay."

"Good." His hand roamed over her shoulder and down her side, brushing over her hip and thigh, trailing heat where it went and making her ache. Easing Cassie's leg up, Brody settled more firmly against her, sliding his own leg between hers. "Now that that's settled, I just have one question, baby. Why are you so damn thin?"

A shaky laugh sneaked out, and Cassie peered sheepishly up at Brody. "It's a long story."

"Mmmm…" Another tease of heat crossed her lips from his wicked mouth. "Good thing you're laying here, doing little or nothing with me today. We've got nothing but time."

Chapter 34

Brody lifted his head to look back and check on Cassie. The fun and simple pleasures in life were coming back for them both. Laughter came easier and easier the more time he and Cassie spent together, tentative and careful like a slow first dance between almost strangers. But the way Brody saw it, they were courting each other this time in an oddly poetic way the past few days.

He'd leave her flowers here and there, sometimes with a note or romantic saying, or sometimes he'd be lucky enough to whisper it in her ear in person. Then she would slip a note in his pocket later when no one was watching. They'd taken walks together on the paths around the house or along the beach, talking and sharing with each other what they'd missed in their months apart.

And Brody slept with Cassie.

Not in the way he so desperately wanted. They weren't ready for that, but they'd stolen small naps on their secret patio, and once late in the night, she'd fallen asleep in his arms while they were talking. Rather than move her, Brody had just gotten a blanket out of his room and made them both comfortable. The patio sofa was more than big enough for two and positioned for privacy. He'd gotten to wake up to Cassie pressing kisses down his neck as his body throbbed for her.

This morning, Brody found a note under his door asking if she could take him sailing today. She'd added a heart symbol and drawn a smiling sun in lieu of a signature. How could a man resist that? So here they were, out on the blue sparkling water together.

Motoring far enough out of the marina and cove to be able to set the sail, Brody left Cassie manning the helm, sunglasses on against the dazzling glare and head tilted up to the sun above. She'd tied a pretty blue scarf over her hair, but the edges of its length fluttered in the wind. It had been too long since he was last out on the water, and Cassie had picked a perfect day to make up for it. Arms straining against the brisk wind, Brody winched down the line and locked it into place. Taut, the fabric snapped and filled and he heard Cassie's cry of surprise when the boat responded, leaping forward to skim over the waves. She'd never been sailing before he'd brought her to The Island before last year, and Brody had had a wonderful time giving her that first pleasure.

There was nothing like your first time. He grinned, making his way back to the pretty picture she made standing at the captain's wheel dressed in a cute striped tank top, shorts, and boat shoes, neat as a pin as always. He had to seriously work to stomp down the urge to mess her up a bit. Preferably with his hands under her clothes.

"Doing okay?" Resting his hands at Cassie's hips, Brody braced himself behind her, legs wide to roll with the motion of the ship.

"I'm good. A few more minutes maybe, then you can take over."

Her smile was sweet as candy, one that no man with a pulse could resist, and he leaned down for a taste. "All right.

Don't overdo it, baby."

"I won't. I promise."

Not having the stamina she used to, Cassie tired faster these days, and the wind today was a bit wild and fast, making holding the wheel steady a drain on the muscles. Brody had been so fucking mad when he learned how sick Cassie had been — that she'd let herself get that run down. He could feel the bones at her hips, and her ribs were way more prominent than they should have been. He blamed no one but himself. Guilt racked him at how his pride had gotten the better of him over the last few months and how many times he had refused to talk or even stay in the room if Cassie's name came up. He'd always left rather than deal with the hell of trying to talk about her. If he'd known... well, Brody didn't know what he would have done. Probably something stupid like hunt her down, toss her over his shoulder, and drag her off somewhere to get better.

Wrapping his arms around her, Brody held Cassie tightly. It was time for both of them to let go of the guilt and regrets in order to be able to focus on finding each other again. That didn't mean, however, that a man couldn't take care of his woman in the little ways. A surprise lunch was packed with all sorts of high-calorie foods he'd sweet-talked out of the house chefs. They'd even put in an extra few special treats Brody was hoping Cassie would let him kiss off her lips later.

Her head angled up to him again. "Thank you for doing this. Taking me sailing. I know we have a long night ahead."

"We do? Which one is it? Rehearsal dinner or family only party?" Brody couldn't remember, but he was looking forward to it since it meant more time with Cassie and seeing her dressed up again. None of the parties seemed the hell they had been a few days ago — something to endure and knuckle through.

Three days till the wedding. Three days to win Cassie's heart again or courting her would have to take place long distance once he was back in Iceland to resume filming. For what might be the first time in his career, Brody regretted having to be so far away.

"It's the family party tonight."

His hands closed over hers at the wheel to take some of the strain off her as he held the boat into the wind. "I was wondering, gorgeous, anyone ask you to go with them tonight?"

Cassie's head fell back, and giggles, bright and infectious, fell out. His laugh joined hers.

He held her tighter with one arm around her waist to add to the persuasion. "I'm serious here. You're a gorgeous woman. Someone might have asked you out while I was distracted."

"No." She was still giggling as his beard now tickled her neck. "No one's asked me."

"Good. Wanna go with me?" he whispered in her ear. "Be my official date."

Cassie's breath hitched, and she looked up at him. Uncertain. "Officially?"

The question asked so much more. They hadn't bothered to hide their rekindled relationship, but they also had yet to say anything to their family and friends. They had only shared secret kisses in the dark or stolen moments here and there. A lot of questioning eyebrows were being raised at their renewed friendliness, but so far, everyone had been kind enough not to ask, letting the two of them work it out.

"Yes. Officially. Be my date."

Her look was one of shyness, sweet and endearing. "I'd

really love that."

"All right. Now, where was I...?" Unable to resist, he went back to work on Cassie's neck.

Giggling met his ears as he traveled the distance up to her mouth. Deciding the hell with it, Brody lifted her up and settled her in his lap on the captain's chair. One hand on the wheel and Cassie in his arms made the day fucking perfect with the boat flying over crystal blue water carrying them along.

"What's all this?" Cassie stared down, a bit dumbfounded.

"This is lunch." Brody tugged her hand so she would sit with him on the blanket.

At least a half acre of food was laid out at the forward section of the boat. They were currently anchored off the coast of some small island Brody had navigated them to. Sheltered from the wind on this side, he had laid out a picnic complete with champagne, surprising Cassie. They ate with the tropical island and palm trees swaying on one side, the view of the ocean on the other. The day a brilliant blend of warm sea air and bright sun overhead. Brody lifted another sample of cheese-and-fig-stuffed pastry to her mouth.

"This is not lunch, you know." Cassie felt the need to point it out. "Lunch is usually a little smaller. This is way more food than we need for two people."

"Maybe I'm hoping we'll get stranded out here," Brody said with a wink.

The idea of it made her laugh, head thrown back at his mischief. "No, you don't. Are you taking care of me again?"

"What if I was? Are you okay with that?"

Leaning in, she pressed a kiss to his cheek and fed him a

bite of shrimp ceviche on a pita chip. "Yes. I like it when you take care of me. No one really does, outside of Nathan or Anna. So yes, I like it when you take the time to do all these special things —like try to fatten me back up because you still feel guilty." The wry smile she gave him said she was on to his game.

There was an angled look at her followed by a short and pithy muttered, "Shit," showing Cassie she had struck a nerve.

"Brody?" She touched his shoulder so he looked at her. "No more guilt, remember? We promised each other. It means so much that you would do something like this for me, but I'm okay. Better every day, all right? I gained another pound this week. Today was check-in day with my doctor."

"Look at you. Almost out of the featherweight division and into the lightweight."

"You, on the other hand? I have to say I like the new look, by the way. Graduated to the really buffed up zone. Your female fans must be in heaven," Cassie said in appreciation trailing a finger down a well-defined bicep.

Brody had clearly put on some extra muscle and done some special training for the movie he was working on, playing a hero in an invasion plot. His body had always been incredible, but it now showed something else — a more primitive edge that had been sculpted to leave a raw sexiness that Cassie imagined went perfectly with the ragged beard he had shown up with.

Brody gave her a grin and curled an arm to show off. "Ready to carry my girl anywhere. And I only care what one female fan thinks, and that's you."

The comment set off another stream of laughter. "You always carried me anyway, and I never fully appreciated all that you did before to take care of me. I was too busy feeling weird about money or other silly things in the beginning."

"Cassie, come on." Brody shook his head. "We moved past the money thing, right?"

"We did, for the most part. I just want you to know that all the little things mean as much as the big extravagant things. Like today. So thank you."

"Like bags of underwear?" His grin was sure and sneaky, trying to lighten the mood. Brody toyed with a piece of her hair that had escaped the wrap. "It always made me smile to make you happy and hear you say you were. How am I doing with you now? How's this all feel between us?"

"I think we're doing pretty good. It feels good, doesn't it?"

"It really does."

"All right then, let's enjoy it all."

Brody leaned in to take her lips, leaving her aching for more than just the gentle caresses of the last two days. "How about, since we're finished eating, you come take a swim with me around the boat?"

"I don't have a suit with me. You planning on tossing me in again?" Cassie saw the spark flare in emerald eyes and knew instantly she had just made a huge error.

"Hmmm. A fatal flaw in my otherwise perfect plan. I like your idea better." Standing, Brody bent and scooped Cassie up before she could gather herself to run.

Walking to the side of the boat, he blatantly ignored her screams of protest. He pulled her shoes off with one hand while he balanced her on the rail and toed off his own as she continued to struggle in arms of steel. It was a losing battle, given the difference in size between them.

"Dammit, Brody, I'm warning you. Don't you dare." Her

fists beat uselessly on his back. "You can't manhandle me like this."

Laughing like a loon, Brody lifted Cassie over the edge with him. "Don't worry, we've got plenty of time to dry off, baby." And he jumped.

They broke back to the surface with Cassie cursing and Brody laughing like an idiot.

"You stupid ass. What is it with you and trying to drown me?"

"Don't know. But it sure as hell is good fun."

Brody stopped laughing long enough to dive. The water went eerily quiet with only the waves lapping around her. Waiting, Cassie madly turned, treading water, trying to see or feel anything, knowing he was down there — somewhere.

Plotting his next move.

Even knowing that particular detail didn't help matters when something skimmed past her thigh. Cassie screamed and felt it cruise past her on the other side, giving her another jolt.

Hands gripped her waist, and Brody came up in front of her. "Gotcha."

Not sure whether to trust him or not, Cassie pushed away only to be caught and tugged back on gentle hands as Brody brought her to his waiting lips tasting of sun and salt water.

"Look at that. My pretty little mermaid in the sea. I sure am a lucky guy."

Cassie grinned despite herself. Brody was back with all the fun and mischief she had fallen in love with. Knowing that she had had a part in it, happiness swamped her like a wave.

"You're still an idiot." She laughed shoving his head under the water.

Unfazed, Brody dragged her down with him.

Since she couldn't reach the ladder to climb back on the boat, Brody boosted Cassie up until she could grab hold. Then he waited for her to climb up before following.

"A good swim, huh?"

Meeting him at the top, Cassie tugged him closer for a kiss. "It was."

Swimming with Brody had left her feeling warm and fluid, completely turned on and slightly disappointed that he hadn't tried anything else other than swimming.

Brody patted her backside fondly. "I'm going to dig up towels for us. Be right back."

He headed off and came back with huge terry cloth wraps. After tossing one to Cassie, he stripped off his shirt and wrung it out to lay it across the deck to dry in the sun before toweling off. Teeth tugging at her lower lip, Cassie made no attempt to hide her admiration of the view standing before her. A dark handsome Sea God with wet jeans riding low.

"What's got you smiling like that?" Brody asked when he caught her.

"You and your very superior form."

"Is that so?"

"Yes. Guess it's only fair that I let you look too." Cassie shot him a smile before stripping off her shirt, leaving just her bra, and dropped it beside Brody's.

The look of shock on his face was completely worth it. Brody stood still for a moment before he came over. Cassie's skin burned where his eyes fell, tracing over her before coming back to lock onto her own. Mesmerized by those depths gone dark with desire, Cassie laid a hand on his bare chest. Her breath caught when she touched him again, the feel of him so strong and firm underneath her fingers. So warm in the sun pouring down.

Hands reached to touch her, and Brody's head lowered to hers. Cassie waited for the moment, her hand curling on his chest. The waiting turned to disbelief when Brody took the towel and wrapped it over her shoulders instead.

"Wind's a little fast. Don't want you to catch a chill, sweetheart." His voice was low and husky while his hands rested on her. Brody pressed a swift kiss to her forehead.

Cassie turned away, embarrassed by the rejection, and wrapped the towel tighter. She grabbed her shirt and folded herself up on the built-in bench at the back of the boat, all of a sudden feeling like crying and wishing to be anywhere else.

Even though they were back together, he hadn't done anything beyond kiss her. They had slept together out on the patio, but he hadn't once slipped his hands anywhere under her clothes or even tried to. She missed the physical part of their relationship more than she wanted to admit out loud.

Staring out over the water, Cassie reminded herself that the two of them had only been back together for a few short days. Expecting things to be just as they were before was silly. She had to be realistic about where they were for right now – at the beginning, starting over. But she still felt as if a part of her was so empty. The situation wouldn't have bothered her so much except that Brody had always been such a physical guy with her. Not just the sex but the casual touches and caresses just because he could. One of his favorite things had been being skin to skin with her, and his teasing charm had gotten Cassie's clothes off on many occasions.

She sat there watching the afternoon sun edge its way toward the water, not understanding why Brody refused to touch her.

He'd hurt Cassie somehow and kicked himself for being all kinds of a fool for doing so. She'd whipped off that shirt and the need had hit him so hard and fast, it had almost taken him to his knees. Brody had been so careful to not let his hands stray where they shouldn't or pressure Cassie in any way, but God, the urge to toss her on the deck and strip the rest of her clothes off was a fight he'd barely won. Covering her up was the only sane thing he could think of, and the hurt look she'd given had cut him to the bone.

Now, she was curled up with her back to him, and he was left standing alone, feeling like some kind of martyred jackass. Swearing under his breath, Brody flung down the rope he was about to raise for the sail, went to sit next to her, and swore inside again when he tried to put an arm around Cassie and she stiffened like a board.

Solving the matter, he pulled her back and wrapped her in his arms.

"I'm warm enough now. You can let me go," she said stiffly, trying to get his arms off.

"I'm cold. Stay put." That was a blatant lie. He could probably power a small third world country with the heat being generated by pure lust. Only Cassie could make him burn this hot. "Come here. I'm sorry. Think I went a little crazy seeing you again, without a shirt on."

"Too skinny, huh?" Even though Cassie tried to make light of it, Brody could hear the hurt rejection in her voice. Her hands picked nervously at the edges of her towel as she stared out, unseeing. "Sorry. I know I don't look like I used to."

He only held her tighter and laid his head against hers, praying for strength. "God, no, that's not it. Not it at all." Only with Cassie could he fuck up so badly. Tilting her face up to his, Brody waited until she looked at him. "You take my breath away. You're beautiful."

"Then why won't you touch me?"

The question left him looking at her like a deer blinking in the headlights. He hadn't pressed her for anything beyond simple kisses since they got back together and had deliberately kept it that way between them for a couple of reasons. One of which was obvious — Cassie wasn't one hundred percent healthy yet. Frankly, the physical need was so bad, Brody worried about hurting her when that moment finally happened between them again.

The other… well. That one was going to be a lot harder to talk about, and he wasn't sure they were ready to face it yet.

"I do touch you," he said, trying to reassure her. "Don't think I've stopped touching you since we kissed that morning."

"No, you don't. Not like you used to." Unable to meet his eyes, Cassie shook her head. The look on her face showed nothing except nerves and uneasiness with him, something Brody never wanted his woman to feel. "It's nothing. Forget it."

"Baby, it's not nothing. Come on. You just said earlier things between us feel good. We're not good, not if you feel you need to ask me that."

"Damn it. You still see through everything," Cassie whispered.

"It's a gift. Talk to me so we can be more than good together. Please?"

"I-I just… you seem to not want to touch me… you know…

everywhere. Like you used to. When we kiss... I can feel it. I can feel how much you want to, but then... you don't. You always stop. As much as I love kissing you, it's not the same as before... when you wanted me." Cassie whipped a tear away.

Brody forced her eyes back to him, and the hurt in those pretty hazel eyes undid him. "Look who else sees through things." Tenderly smoothing back red hair still tangled from the sea, he brushed a soft kiss against those perfect pink lips. "Course I do. I always want you, sweetheart. Since the moment you first fell into my arms and I almost did something crazy like kiss you right then and there. I've always wanted you. Even when we were apart, I wanted you. There was no other woman I could bring myself to touch. They were never you."

"Then how come, now... why won't you?"

Brody closed his eyes for a second. Whatever he thought about this new time between them, he was somehow making her hurt again, so he took a deep breath. It was time to come clean so they could both move forward.

He dragged a hand through his hair in frustration. "Cassie, I want to. You have no idea how much I do. I just... dammit, somehow I got it in my head that it seemed better to wait, to take this thing slower between us this time." He brushed his knuckles down the side of Cassie's face then across her shoulder. "We rushed things so fast the first time around. And after..." He stopped. The pain was less than it had been but still there nonetheless. "Afterward... it was so hard for you to let me touch you and we fought so much. God, I needed you so much. Not for sex — I just needed you to want me again in that way. To want me near you at all. Every time I thought things were better and tried... you barely let me hold your hand at times."

Cassie took his hand and pressed a kiss to the palm. "I'm sorry. For after our baby. It was so hard." Her beautiful eyes filled and spilled over. "I should have let you touch me. Part of me needed you to touch me, and I just couldn't with all the pain. Instead, I turned you away. Hurt you more by doing so."

Unable to bear seeing her cry, Brody smoothed them away. Took her lips with his and spoke between kisses, seducing her deeper and deeper with each one. "Shhh… we agreed, remember? No more guilt. No more regrets, baby. We have each other again. That's all that matters, okay?"

Cassie nodded and smiled at him, shy and sweet. "I understand now. Why you would want to be so careful. With me. With us. I'm glad that you want that for us." Laying her head on his shoulder, she snuggled in. "I know we have to go back soon, but will you hold me, just for a little while?"

"Course I will. My favorite thing in the world — holding you. I'm sorry if I gave you the wrong idea. We have another chance with each other. I'm just trying not to screw it up."

Long minutes passed as he held her before Cassie gave in fully and relaxed like rain water melting over him. The boat rocked lightly in the waves as Brody gave thanks for the gift of having her back. They were back at the start, and with time, they would work it back to what they had — maybe this time, they would be something even better.

Taking a deep breath, Brody shifted and pulled back to look at her. "Cassie, you mean everything to me. I didn't want you to feel pressured to be with me that way. I should have said something to you about it."

His hand went farther down to pull the towel off her shoulder, continuing until the back of his hand moved over a curve of breast and cupped her fully. Brody smiled at Cassie's sharply indrawn breath. Her nipple tightened when a seeking thumb moved in a slow circle around it, imprinting like a brand through the thin material of her bra.

Leaning in, he said low and deep in her ear, "Don't *ever* feel like I don't want you. I promise you, baby, when we're both ready, I definitely want to rip your clothes off and have you wrapped around me like magic, calling out my name while I have my wicked way with you."

Cassie gasped, her mouth falling open as his thumb wandered again, seeking and testing just to see her eyes darken in response. His own response was just as fast and dark.

Breathless words fell from pretty pink lips. "Maybe you could put your hands on me a little bit more? I promise I won't mind."

"Yeah? Come here then, and let me get my hands on you."

Brody lowered his mouth to hers as he pressed Cassie back on the bench, giving into the madness of his need for her, letting his mouth dive deep before traveling over beautiful skin, and he tugged aside her damp bra to feast. Close to a year's worth of longing went into that moment when his mouth closed on perfection, and Cassie raised up higher to meet him, back arching like a bow. She melted with her fingers tangling in his hair, her moan of pleasure music to his ears.

Chapter 35

Brody drove them back to the house, later than expected due to the lesson in erotic sensation.

On the boat cushions, Cassie had lost her mind, pressed up against him while Brody kissed the daylights out of her. Those warm and oh so competent hands and mouth had made a lovely exploration of her breasts. Her brains had been all but smoking out of her ears when he mumbled that they really needed to go — and dragged her back to him again. Cassie could only blame herself — she'd asked him to, after all.

He held her hand, leading the way around the house. They were sneaking in like teenagers after curfew, leaning around corners to make sure they weren't caught.

"You said we would have time to dry." She snickered.

"Well, I'd hoped the wind would take care of that detail on the sail back." Her sweet idiot was shaking with laughter.

Cassie was still damp, sticky with sea water, and her hair was going every which way. They were due for dinner with the bride, groom, and family in forty-five minutes. She need-ed to shower quickly, get ready, fix her hair and makeup, and drive back down to the restaurant in the village.

Safe outside Cassie's bedroom patio, Brody slid open the door and handed her inside, stopping her to tilt her back in his arms for a kiss good-bye. "See you in a bit, gorgeous."

Then he was gone, heading up the back pathway to his own bedroom. Cassie took a few more seconds to enjoy the view as he went, wet jeans holding firm to his superior ass.

The best thing about being the bride was, quite frankly, being the bride. Anna was trying to enjoy every single minute of her once-in-a-lifetime experience. Sadly, even though her mother-in-law-to-be was a jewel and Anna adored her dearly, she would be overjoyed when wedding week was over. Said mother-in-law was driving her crazy with wedding details. Their seemingly easy island getaway for a small intimate wedding was being corrupted here and there by loving suggestions to make it more. More glamour, more pizzazz, more anything. Everything that Anna wasn't.

Knocking on the door to Cassie's room, Anna was met with an astounding silence. She knocked again before opening the door and hearing the shower going. She stuck her head in the bathroom just in time to see Cassie's leg disappearing behind the wall of the shower.

Her mouth fell open. "You're just now showering?"

"Sorry, I'm running late."

"How are you late? You're never late. Where have you been all day? I haven't seen you anywhere. You promised to help me with *her*."

"I know. I'm super sorry. I didn't expect to be gone so long. Forgive me? I'll be there this evening. You have my word." Cassie peeked her head out while shampooing her hair, bubbles dripping everywhere, and flashed a happy smile. "Brody took me sailing."

"He what?"

"Sailing," came the answer from inside the shower.

"Sailing… with Brody. All day?" Anna stuck her head into the shower with Cassie. "Are you serious?"

"Yes. It was so much fun. And I'm sorry for the mother-in-law and being late." Cassie finished furiously scrubbing her hair clean, grabbed the bar of soap and moved on to her skin.

How could she be mad while seeing Cassie happy and shining again? Whatever had happened on the boat, Anna owed Brody a big favor.

Done, Cassie shut off the water and took the towel Anna handed over. "The fool carried me over the side of the boat to swim. I wasn't planning on having to shower when we got back. I can't even be mad, it was such a great day."

Quickly drying off, Cassie wrapped the towel in place, rubbed mousse in her hair, and grabbed the hair dryer.

Anna did what any great friend would do — sat down to dig out details. "Yes, I can see that. You're practically glowing. What else happened on this epic day, beside Brody looking for mermaids again?"

"A fabulous sail out to some island, then lunch picnic-style on the boat with champagne. We talked and just had a really good time." The blush that flew over Cassie's cheeks said something more about the "time."

"Yes… I can see how much of a 'good time' you had." She added finger quotes to emphasize her words. "Sounds like a beautiful day. I guess I can let you have that and not complain. I'll be happy for you instead. You look really happy, my friend."

"I am. It's taken us so long to get back to being good

together." When her hair was dry, Cassie twisted locks into place to emphasize her natural waves, added a few pins to sweep it a bit off her face, and started on makeup. She stopped just before brushing on mascara to look over at Anna. "Is it wrong that I want to sleep with him again? So soon? After everything that's happened."

"Why would it be wrong? You two obviously still care about each other very much."

"I do. I think he does too. It's just that…"

"What is it?"

"He's worried. We talked. He's being the gentleman and not wanting to rush things between us. That would be wonderful if I could just get past wanting him so much. I didn't realize how much I missed that part of myself until it all came back from being with him again. It — you know, desire — was gone for so long, I honestly thought that part of me was dead. That I… couldn't anymore. It's crazy," Cassie muttered, turning back to work on her eyes and refusing to meet Anna's questioning look.

"What makes you think that's such a crazy thing? Our sexual selves are a huge part of our physical, mental and spiritual chakras. To ignore that is ridiculous."

"It just is. I know Brody's being sweet, but I don't know how to get him past it."

Since Cassie sounded really frustrated, Anna snickered. Brody had a wonderful old-world southern boy sense of charm and caring for a woman, but with Cassie, he'd always been full of mischief and fun, especially in the bedroom. It was one of the things her friend had always said made him so wonderful. And he'd apparently used every bit of his fun and mischievous charm to help Cassie find herself again as a woman.

"I wish I could offer some input here, but this sounds like a conversation you and Brody need to have together."

"We did. I mean, it helped, at least, to know why he was holding back."

Dashing on eye shadow and moving on, Cassie filled in the remaining shadows under her eyes with a bit of concealer. Anna was amazed at how much better they looked after just a few short days of Brody and Cassie getting back together — even if they hadn't really told anyone yet. The looks the two lovebirds were giving each other was more than enough to give it away, and Brody had been especially attentive, his eyes casually following Cassie no matter where she was in a room, along with doing subtle things like saying the bartender had happened to make an extra smoothie that he set down in front of her as he'd pass by.

"Maybe you should just jump him? Role switch. He always was the more dominant one in that area."

Cassie paused to give the suggestion some thought. "Interesting idea. I'll have to think about that. I'm worried I'll ruin things somehow. Most of the time, it feels really easy with us. Then there might be a comment or something, and it all feels strange and tight again."

"Hey, sister, deep breaths," she said, seeing Cassie was on the verge of working herself up. "In and out."

Taking the makeup brush out of Cassie's hand, Anna tucked a stray curl back in place then smoothed the rest of the blush over Cassie's cheeks. Dabbed some more of the light bronzer across Cassie's shoulders so her skin would glow in the candlelight at dinner. After all, a woman needed every advantage she could get when seducing a man.

"It will all be fine. The strangeness, I think, is normal after everything. How could it not be? You two went through something terrible together, but this is Brody, okay? You two will figure things out, and it'll work out as it's meant to when the time is right."

"I know." Cassie closed her eyes and focused on a few more deep breaths.

"Great. Now go get dressed. We have twenty minutes till we're due down in town. Is Brody driving you, or are you coming with Chase and me? We can drive together."

As if on cue, Cassie's door rang with a knock and Chase called through it, "Anna, come on. Mom and Dad want to go down a little early. Well, it's mostly Mom. She wants to make sure the restaurant is all set up. Brody or Nathan and Philip can bring along Cassie. We need to go."

"Coming," Anna called to her love and snarled quietly so Chase couldn't hear, "That woman! I've told her it's all handled — that's what wedding planners are for. If I survive the two and a half days left, it will be a miracle."

"Deep breaths, sister. In and out. Go on, I'll be fine," Cassie teased from across the room, tugging her festive gold-and-green sundress into place.

Anna paused with her hand on the doorknob then raced back to hug Cassie tightly. "I'm really happy for you. It's so good to see you happy again."

Chapter 36

Nathan and Philip had already left, so Cassie and Brody went together to the restaurant. Cassie's full maid of honor duties would kick in on Saturday, and she knew her friend was on the countdown to the moment she could finally walk down the aisle and start the next phase of her life with Chase. It was especially nice that Cassie had her own special thing to celebrate.

When Brody stopped her outside the restaurant to pull her into his arms and ask if she was completely sure, a special little thrill raced inside. Her answer of yes caused a look of happiness on his face that she knew she'd never forget.

Holding hands, Cassie and Brody walked into the restaurant the wedding party had taken over, and conversations died instantly. More than a few mouths hung lax and wide-eyed friends and family blinked. No one seemed to know what to say as they all stood there. Cassie hadn't expected quite so strange a reaction and stood frozen with them.

In typical Brody Miller style, he broke the tension by slinging an arm around Cassie and flashing that megawatt leading-man smile. "What's wrong? Y'all didn't know we were back together? She took pity on my sad drunk ass." He turned Cassie into him, and all she could do was look at him, wide-eyed herself, as he framed her face tenderly. Brody smiled at her with nothing but deep affection. "Outside of Chase, that makes me just about the luckiest man in the world."

"It's about damn time!" Chase shouted, standing at the head of the table to clap.

After a pause, the entire restaurant broke out in cheers and Cassie buried her head in Brody's chest, completely overwhelmed with emotion. Chase called for drinks, and soon they were surrounded by friends and family giving them congratulations. Brody's brothers and parents even pulled Cassie in to hug her and welcome her to the family.

Cassie looked at Brody over Simon's shoulder as he hugged her again. Her official man raised his glass with a wink. Brody's announcement had tossed her a curve ball. When he'd said official, she had no idea he meant it so passionately. Raising her own glass, Cassie toasted him back on a smile.

Across the room, Brody watched his woman being passed around and congratulated while he sipped his drink. The halter-style dress in deep green set off her creamy skin and flaming red hair while leaving a long tease of leg that a man couldn't help but be grateful to look at. The fact that Cassie was all but glowing with happiness made it clearer that whatever they had together, they were each helping to heal the other.

Nathan stepped in front of him — blocking the view. Deliberately.

"I'd like a word with you, Brody Miller."

Since the glint in Nathan's eyes spoke of nothing but fixed intent, Brody knew there was no way to escape gracefully.

"Sure thing. What's on your mind, Nathan?"

"Cassie for one. Your intentions would be the second." One eyebrow raised in a finely shaped arch of derision. "Consider me filling in for her dad and brother."

"Protecting her, is that it?"

"Damn straight. Start talking, and if I don't like what you say in the next thirty seconds, I'll be kicking your supremely fine ass."

Even knowing Cassie and Nathan had been friends forever and that Nathan was just looking out for her didn't make his threat any easier for Brody to swallow. "I feel the need to point out that this is between Cassie and myself." Nathan's knuckles whitened as his grip tightened on his glass. Brody sighed and looked Cassie's defender dead in the eye. He understood the need if nothing else that Nathan wanted only to protect Cassie. "My intentions are real. She means everything to me in this world."

"You said that before. It still fell apart."

Brody's temper spiked up, sharp as a razor. "What we went through was personal and tore both of us apart. None of it is your fucking business. For what it's worth, I screwed up then and let her walk away from me. I'm telling you the solid truth — I'll fight for her no matter what."

"You could have just about any woman you want, being who you are. I know why Cassie is special. Are you sure you do?"

"She's more than special. She's the only one worth fighting for. I don't want any other woman. I want Cassie. None of what I've gotten or done is worth having without her by my side. I'll fight for her no matter what, but I'd much rather have your blessing." Brody held out his hand to Nathan in a gesture of friendship.

After a long minute as the two men stared each other down, Nathan extended his own hand and accepted. "I'm trusting you with one of the most precious people in my life. Don't you dare let me down again. I'm a master at anything I choose to do. I promise – they will never find your body."

Brody had to admit that as threats went, it was a good one, and he somehow had no doubt that the thin, elegant man in front of him would see it done.

"This looks awful serious over here. What are my two favorite men talking about?" Cassie stepped between Brody and Nathan, wrapping an arm around each of them, and saw Brody nod at Nathan.

Her friend looked at her with a smooth smile she recognized instantly as his cover-up look. "A difference in opinion, darling, on the merits of the Cardinals versus the Braves."

"Liar. Nathan, you hate baseball with a passion. What's going on here?"

Both men remained a couple of stone statues.

"Fine. They want us all to sit down. Dinner should be coming out soon and toasts are needed."

Nathan gave Cassie a quick squeeze and said he was happy for her before moving off.

She turned to the man by her side and cocked a hand on one hip. "Explain."

"Man talk, gorgeous. I'd be breaking a code of honor if I told you."

"Bullshit."

Brody sighed and offered a sheepish expression, which looked ridiculous on such a big man, before he shoved a hand in his pocket, and hung his head. "Nathan was just being a good friend and making sure my intentions are good."

"That's ridiculous. He doesn—"

Brody cut her off with a finger to her lips. "It's okay. He absolutely does, and I would have done the same if the situation was reversed. Come on, a whole night's ahead of us. Let's celebrate. What are you drinking?" Smiling, Brody walked her to their table and helped her to sit.

Cassie floated thought the night. She felt just like she had while lying on the boat with Brody, except her shoes were dangling in one hand, which was looped around Brody's neck, and the other was busy with the buttons on his shirt while he carried her. She certainly wasn't drunk, but she was happily buzzed enough off a couple of cocktails to think that Anna's suggestion of jumping the very sexy Brody Miller — who just happened to be her man — was an idea of profound excellence that should be acted on immediately.

Since he'd taken the moral high road — there was simply no other choice.

Cassie thought it had been a stroke of brilliance when she'd sweetly mentioned to Brody after dessert that she felt a little tired from the day. He'd whisked her out of the restaurant so fast, she'd barely gotten to say good-bye to anyone.

Then she'd launched her attack while Brody was helping her into the car down in the village while the party was still going strong inside. Catching him in a kiss that made him momentarily lose that precious control he was so intent on maintaining. He'd crushed her to him. Those glorious hands had found her bottom, boosting her up to pin her against the side of the car. Legs locked around Brody, she'd taken advantage of the angle to whisper all sorts of interesting suggestions in his ear while his lips and teeth assaulted her neck. The full heated arousal that pressed between her legs left no doubt what Brody thought about those ideas.

Brody had finally peeled Cassie off him and tucked her in the car, muttering something about long ice cold showers. She let him, figuring it was okay — there was the entire drive back to the house to work on him some more, and she had no intention of losing the debate.

Convertibles had certain... advantages. Letting the wind lift her skirt higher, Cassie didn't even bother trying to keep it down. She lifted first one leg straight up to ease off her heeled sandal, then the other. Winding her hand over the back of his seat, she let it play with his dark hair as she stretched to make sure he had a good view of her chest. It was a miracle the car stayed on the road, since Brody's eyes were barely looking at it.

Brody rounded the side of the house with her and Cassie saw the pool laid out in front of them.

"If you jump in again, I will never forgive you," she teased along his neck.

"You sure? It's awful hot work carrying you around. Especially since your hands keep wandering." He shot her a pointed look. "You need to behave."

That comment was easy to ignore. "I thought I was just a featherweight."

Success, at last, garnered the fourth button open on his shirt and Cassie slipped her hand inside to splay out in appreciation of the amazing muscles there and explored to her heart's content. Her low hum of pleasure said it all — Brody felt unbelievable.

"Cassie, stop."

The warning sounded closer to begging. She was winning.

"Why? I want you." Lips on his neck, she shifted to dance her tongue around a handily placed earlobe.

Distracted as hell and on the edge of his last known sanity, Brody tripped and almost dropped her, cursing when Cassie's teeth found his ear, sending a lightning bolt of lust down with it. Only a laugh, low and seductive, tumbled from her as she held on.

"Careful," she whispered in a sultry voice meant to bring a man to his knees. "If you damage me, you won't be able to have your *wicked way* with me."

That same low, seductive laugh had drifted out when her hand found its way between his legs in the car, and he'd almost wrecked it trying to get Cassie off him. She was trying to destroy him — and she knew it.

"Fuck, woman. If you don't stop..." Brody could barely walk as it was, his cock rock hard and throbbing like a bass drum. To hell with foreplay, he was ready right now. Any handy surface would do. Hell, he was creative and strong enough. Standing up would work fine as well.

Brody wished instead for a rock-hard surface to slam his head into. He simply couldn't take her.

They weren't ready yet.

Cassie needed to heal more.

He could hurt her.

It was too soon.

They should wait longer.

They only just got back together.

Reason after reason rolled through his head. Each one sounded weaker and weaker every time she touched him.

As if reading his thoughts, Cassie, who he was now certain was part mythical siren and part mermaid, shifted to lift her chest closer to his face. She was only trying to reach his ear to whisper more suggestions about what he could do to her, but Brody had to agree that her two main points of argument were winning out over his good sense right now.

Those two main points were beautiful, perfectly round, and so very, very soft. Lifted and perfectly shown off in that green dress. He knew how absolutely wonderful they felt and tasted, since he'd gotten reacquainted with them earlier. That had clearly been a stupid move on his part, since it only made him want her more.

When he stopped to take a breath and steady himself, Cassie twined her fingers into his hair and brought her lips to his. Soft and slick, they moved, and her tongue slid in, seeking his own. When she let go of him, Brody was pretty damn sure he might be cross-eyed. Every remaining drop of blood in his body had drained to his dick, and he could barely focus on her beautiful eyes sparkling in the moonlight. The look on Cassie's face was pure seduction with a smile that was slow and sure. To think she'd been shy in bed, once upon a time. He was now in the hands of a temptress and losing the battle.

"I'm tired of waiting. I want you, Brody Miller. Take me to bed."

Fighting himself, Brody prayed for strength as he leaned his head weakly against hers. "Cassie, I'm begging you, baby, please stop. I'm no fucking saint."

The pleading must have finally gotten through because Cassie's expression turned serious as she traced down the side of his face. "I'm not asking you to be. I'm asking you to make me yours again. I want to be with you." She touched his lips with hers, as soft as a feather. "*I need you*, Brody. Please."

She needed him.

Those four softly whispered words sent Brody straight over the edge like a madman racing to his doom. The straightforward fact that she needed him undid him. Just as much as he'd always needed her.

Somehow, he found the side of the house. Both of their rooms too damn far away, but their secret patio was handy. When he laid her on the cushioned sofa, Cassie pulled him on top of her. The skirt of her dress was already pooling at her hips. Hands shaky when he shoved it up, Brody settled between legs that were already curling around him like a dream.

He made one last valiant attempt at sanity, bracing above her. "There's no going back from this. Are you sure?"

"You always take care of me. Just like you're trying to do now." Her hands framed his face, drawing him down to share a kiss of tenderness that calmed and reassured him. "Yes, I'm sure. Of you. Of us. Be with me again — all the way."

Brody searched her face and knew without a doubt that Cassie meant every word. He knew beyond a shadow of a doubt that what he felt for this one woman could be felt with no one else. Only she made his world everything it could be and more with a sense of rightness that comes just once in a lifetime.

Knowing he was lost to nothing but Cassie, Brody sank in. Taking her lips, he completely let go.

She knew the moment he kissed her that Brody had given in all the way. Every cell in her body flashed to a bright flame then settled into a blazing hum of throbbing need. Unable to think, all Cassie could do was feel. And there was nothing to feel except her lover and what he was doing to her body.

Strong hands. God, how she'd missed his hands. So competent and oh so incredible, they slid up her legs and underneath the dress. When it refused to come off, Brody rolled until Cassie was on top of him, never once breaking his hold on her mouth while he ravished her. Cassie could only appreciate his fine technique. The zipper on her dress caught halfway down, and she felt him hesitate, trying to work it loose and realized he was still holding back, his muscles a little too tight and tense under her hands.

Cassie eased up a little to tug at his bottom lip with her teeth. "What are you waiting for, handsome? Tear the damn thing already."

Brody paused briefly before a low chuckle rumbled through that huge body and he relaxed so that she knew he was about to destroy her. She felt the tension melt away as Brody's expression transformed to one of pure mischief. One that assured Cassie her man was well and truly back, at last.

"Never let it be said that I didn't work hard to keep my woman happy."

His hands molded across her bare shoulders then slid down her back and underneath the dress to where it couldn't part any farther. As they curled around the fabric, Cassie felt Brody's smile underneath her lips before a rending sound split the air and her dress tore straight past the hemline, leaving her entire backside bare. Brody's hands were on her a split second later, flipping Cassie back underneath him. He raised up to look down at what remained. Hooking one finger in the material, he tossed it away where it floated like tissue paper to the ground.

"Mmmm…I have to say here how much I've always appreciated your technique."

"Let's see if I can think up some new ones, baby." Reaching under, nimble fingers flicked open her bra, and Brody took his time easing off the lace, giving a slow smile of appreciation at what lay underneath. He hooked his fingers into her panties and slid those off on a hard exhale of breath. "You're so beautiful, Cassie. So beautiful."

His mouth lowered, and Cassie arched with a hiss of pleasure when his tongue swept over and under her nipple. He pulled the tightened bud and breast into the warm heat of his mouth, searing and branding her straight through until she thought she might shatter right then and there. Then he let go and made sure to give equal pleasure to the other side.

Her moans filled the air, mixing with the sounds of the sea below. Fighting his shirt on another wave of need, she finally got it open and pulled off, giving her the freedom to touch the incredible planes and ridges of his broad shoulders, strong arms, and a chest that rubbed so wantonly against her skin.

As Brody explored, pleasure built and built, like a cresting wave that beat against the shore with the rising tide, until he found the center of her, slick with damp heat, and slid a finger within to explore. Cassie sank her nails into Brody's back as her pleasure spiked tenfold, so much, all at once, she couldn't handle it. Like a hurricane, the waves took over and threatened to drown her. It had been so long since she felt this way that she tensed against it, fought to control it.

"Look at me," he whispered above her as her breath changed in rhythm to jagged shards. "Look at me, Cassie."

His hand never stopped moving. Caught and fighting the peak of the wave that was overcoming her, Cassie opened her eyes only to be fixed in place by the intensity of passionate green.

Breath short and choppy, she could only cling to him. "Brody. Oh, oh, my God."

"Look at me."

Caught in the center of that emerald storm, Cassie knew she was safe. Brody had her.

"That's it, gorgeous. Just for me. Let me feel you come apart."

His lips and teeth nipped at her own before locking on in a kiss that declared nothing but sheer possession and Cassie came in a thousand bursts of color as the orgasm ripped through leaving her dazed.

She was so wet, so hot underneath his hands. Blood raged inside him like an inferno, twisting and on fire so that all it wanted was to feed on Cassie. Brody left her only long enough to strip off the rest of his clothes. Foil ripped and he barely got the condom in place before coming back to her. Cassie was sprawled out, naked and open. Dropping his head, he pressed a kiss to the curve of her hip. The scent of her sweet arousal mixed with the sea air and flowers planted everywhere on the patio, sending his head spinning. Brody sank his teeth into the soft skin there before he worked his way back up, faster than he should but unable to hold back anymore. All he wanted was Cassie, who called to him like no other.

Eyes that reflected dreams and the moonlight above smiled at him. Cassie wrapped her arms around his neck while he smoothed the hair off her face. His Cassie lay there — his heart. She opened to draw him in, and he braced himself at the entrance of that sweet heat to kiss her tenderly before easing inside, careful to be as gentle as he could.

His name fell on a sob against his lips as she stretched and opened to him, tight, hot and scorching. Desperate and completely lost to that fire, Brody surged forward to bury himself deep. Nails dug into his back, and Cassie arched beneath him like a bow. Eyes wide, she stared up at him, breathless while her body adjusted. Brody fought to hang on to the last ounce of control he had.

Then she smiled. His temptress. His love. Cassie.

"All mine." She drew him down to kiss him. Lips whispered against his own, slow and sweet. "We're home again."

The desperate edge in him eased and settled into a knowing. "Home. You're all mine, Cassie. Always."

Tongue tangling with hers, he began to move. Home. Only Cassie. Only the two of them. Brody knew nothing else but her wrapped around him. Of being buried inside the one woman he needed. The only one who made him complete.

Her name fell like worship, and silken legs wrapped around him tightly, encouraging, begging, fighting for more. Lost in each other, their passion raged, spiraling higher and higher until it burst and they crashed together on the shore.

The perfect storm.

Sounds of the surf washed up from below in a rhythm as old as time. Cassie lay pillowed on the shoulder of the most incredible man in the world, their bodies still entwined. He'd shifted to take the heavy weight off her but hadn't remotely let go of her either. They couldn't seem to stop kissing or touching each other. Overwhelmed by all she felt for him, a tear slipped out. Brody kissed it away, his lips lingering on the spot.

When he spoke, his voice was deep and filled with tenderness. "I said earlier tonight that I was the luckiest guy in the world. That was a lie. I'm the luckiest man in the universe." His kiss left her aching. "I love you, Cassie. So very, very much."

Her breath hitched — not because what he said was a surprise but because it so perfectly mirrored her own feelings. Undone, another tear sparkled down her face "Brody, I love you too. You make me so happy."

Brushing away the wetness, Brody brought his lips back to hers. His eyes crinkled in the moonlight, creasing at the corners. "If you're so happy, why are you crying?"

Knowing he was teasing, the words made her smile as she stroked the silky roughness of his beard. "Tears of happiness. I'm so glad we found each other again."

"I would have come for you. No matter what, I was coming for you. Chase and Anna… when I heard they got engaged, I knew. You were the only one I could see myself being with."

The idea of it made Cassie smile and tighten her leg over his hip, drawing him closer. "You were coming for me. I like the sound of that. Did you have an actual plan in place?"

"I did. It was simple. Find Cassie. Toss Cassie over shoulder. Kidnap to remote location." Brody grinned and nipped at her chin. "Have to admit, after that, the plan gets a little thin. Mostly I figured I could just seduce you back to my bed."

Cassie couldn't help the giggle that escaped. "Mmmm… I have to agree your plan has some merits. Very primitive caveman."

"It was. It would have worked. But let me say, your way of seduction was cosmic, baby. You fucking destroyed me."

"Did I?" Loving the compliment and loving how his hands were playing again across her skin, Cassie knew exactly what her lover had in mind. She arched into his touch like a cat seeking comfort and hoped with everything in her that Brody would keep her up all night — just as he used to do.

"You did. Without a doubt. Destroyed me with this sexy body of yours." His lips found her neck. "Those hands that wouldn't stop." Another seductive caress burned across her backside. "Lips a man dreams of kissing."

Proving the point, he did just that until Cassie was clinging to him, breathless again and laying on top of him with her hair tumbled down to create a secret space for them.

Brody cupped her and eased Cassie's legs up on either side of him, the heavy pulsing length of him like velvet fire between them. "Ready for round two, baby?"

Cassie's kiss was all the answer he needed.

They wound up in Brody's bed that night. Twined together, Brody finally fell asleep with Cassie curled around him, safe and sound, just where he wanted her to be. Both of them were so sexed into a coma, he didn't know which of them was which anymore. All he knew was Cassie, being close to her, and how every part of his soul felt complete again.

There was no telling how the future would unfold for him, but she would be in it. Of that, Brody was more than certain. As much as he valued his privacy, he knew it would be a special moment when he announced to the world that she was his forever. As he drifted off, he wondered how soon would be too soon to ask Cassie to marry him.

Unlike before, this time, there was no way he was waiting.

Chapter 37

Low appreciative laughter echoed in Cassie's ear when the orgasm washed over her in a wave of pleasure, and she woke gasping and breathless to find her arm wrapped up behind Brody's head while his hands had apparently been enjoying their free rein over her body. A body that clearly knew it belonged to Brody and only Brody.

"Good morning, gorgeous."

Since Cassie could barely speak, just a small hum of agreement was all that escaped.

"Hope you don't mind, sweetness. Couldn't help myself. You felt like magic laying here in my arms."

Fingers still buried deep inside her were slowly stroking her back to oblivion. Cassie couldn't see anything, and all she could feel was Brody. His hand left only to let the strength and power of him press deep, filling, stretching, awakening her until he was buried within. Whispering words of love, Brody rocked them both to oblivion.

Midday outside and you would never know it. Cassie lay dreamy-eyed in Brody's arms. Both of them were soft, pleasured, and oh so overly sensitive that every time Brody stroked a slow caress over her skin, the contact felt like another mini burst of pleasure to feel that perfect silk against his own. They spoke in low tones and soft laughter, cocooned in their little world while the unexpected gift of rain wrapped the house and the beach below in a thick curtain of mist, canceling the wedding activities for the day and allowing all of the house's occupants to hibernate — perfect for two lovers who had spent too long apart.

Cassie reached over and traced the spine of the book that lay on the table next to the bed, the leather-bound journal she had given him last Christmas. "You kept it."

Catching her trembling hand, he brought it to his lips before lacing their fingers together. Brody could tell visions of their past were creeping in on a wave of sadness. "Of course. Did you think I would get rid of it?"

"I guess a part of me did, with all that happened."

Brody shook his head. Traced one slant of her eyebrow and found the sheen of moisture that formed at the corner, brushing it gently away. "Never. It was from you, baby. One of the best times of my life is written in those pages — when I fell in love with you."

"And the worst?" Cassie whispered.

Only he knew the heartache he had written during that dark time. Cupping her chin, Brody kissed her tenderly. To comfort her, he held her close, vowing to never lose her again. "Yes. Even that. It's part of life. The bad times that almost drag you under and the light and brightness that fight them off. You're that light for me. We survived it. Maybe we even love each other more now because of it."

"You're right. What I feel for you now is so much more than before. It scared me before. It was so much and seemed so fast. I never in my life felt so much for someone. And even that — it's *nothing* compared to now."

"We have each other again. That's all that matters. I have to believe we're meant to be." He laid his forehead against hers. "How else would you have taken me back after a drunken idiot tossed you in a pool?"

A shaky smile came out, and tears fell as she whispered to his lips, "Because that same drunken idiot jumped in and saved me. Just like the hero he always was."

"I only want to be your hero. Come back to Atlanta with me? Move in with me again?" A corner of his lips lifted in a smile.

She bit her lip. The idea of it clearly took her off guard, and Cassie hesitated. "I thought you were in Iceland right now? Filming."

"I am. About three more weeks for some reshoots and extras. Then I'll be back to start the next season of filming again for the series. I want… I'd love you to be there when I come back?"

Being Cassie, she would have to look at all the angles and weigh the pros and cons, possibly compile a spreadsheet as well. It was one of the many things Brody loved about her. He brought the spontaneity and fun while Cassie brought the practicality. To him, it was a good balance.

"It seems so soon. Are we rushing again?" she asked.

Brody traced her face, shook his head slightly, and with nothing but tenderness soothed those small fears she still held. "It's not too soon. We belong together. We love each other. What more is there? Be with me. We've spent too much time apart already."

"I still travel, you know."

"I know, and I still act, but you also said you changed things with work, cut back a lot of your schedule. I can make changes too."

"I have made them. Needed to in order to get better. Still, it's such a big leap to consider…"

He'd shocked her with the offer to adjust as well. Brody loved to work just as much as she did, although he'd always balanced the scales better, incorporating downtime between his projects and weekly to-dos, but he was still offering concessions to make things work for the better…

Concessions, letting go, and adapting had been hard things to learn and implement, but she'd adjusted. To cut back at work, she'd developed a mentoring program for those on their team she and Nathan knew had the skills to step up and lead the seminars. Cassie only personally ran about three speaking engagements a month these days, and to have that personal CEO appearance came with an increased keynote speaker fee, something Nathan had insisted she work into the contracts. Cassie had been worried it was too soon to take that step, but Nathan had, once again, proven her wrong. The companies they worked with hadn't so much as batted an eyelash at the additional cost to have the best, and knowing they had created something so in demand made her proud.

"I'm glad you're taking care of yourself. I'm so proud of what you've built. We both work crazy hours. You got a taste of my life before too. But with the right changes, this time we can make each other a priority. You know I'll always support you whatever you build. Come home so I can be there to help with the rest." Brody offered a smile of understanding.

"It goes both ways, sweetheart. I want to know while I'm away that you're safe and warm in my bed."

"You sure it's just not so you can wake me up like you did this morning?" Cassie teased.

"Well, I have to admit, there are certain advantages to having you handy. Like that little bit ago and your mouth on me in the shower." Brody grinned at her like the sexy devil he was.

Cassie blushed from her toes all the way to her hair as she remembered exactly how wanton he made her, how Brody had braced himself on the wall and shuddered above her while she worshiped him on her knees. Then he'd buried his hand in her hair and dragged her up to finish the job at hand.

"I love how you still blush for me, gorgeous. Don't think I'll ever get tired of it," his lips murmured against her own. "What do you say? Come live with me. If you don't want that house, I'll buy us another. Anywhere you want to live. As long as you're with me, it will be home."

"Brody…"

His heartfelt statement left her falling over the edge, realizing just how much she wanted to be there with him. To be welcomed home at the end of the day and wake knowing he was with her always. All the uncertainty seemed trivial. What did she really need to think about? They had a future if they wanted it badly enough. Brody was right — as long as they were together, no matter where they were, it would be home.

"No, I don't want you to sell that beautiful place. It's so you. Wild and unique. I loved being there with you. I loved when you took care of me there. It was the one place where I could relax and turn it all off."

"Is that a yes?"

Cassie pressed a kiss of happiness and smiles to his lips. "It's a yes. What about the rest?"

"We'll figure it all out together."

Chapter 38

Wedding Rehearsal Day.

It was hard to be surly on such a sunny day, but Brody felt he could justify the five minutes to be just that while he tried to drown himself in the shower.

Anna had knocked on the door of his room that morning and walked right on in, proving what a jackass he'd been to not make sure the door was locked. A mistake Brody would never make again. The eager and exceptionally bubbly bride-to-be had all but tossed him out on his ass, saying he needed to keep Chase occupied in the village below and reminding him that she and Cassie had the whole day together, as well as tomorrow before the ceremony. And most importantly, she stressed, the groom could not — absolutely could not — see her before the wedding tomorrow.

No testosterone allowed in the house, but apparently Nathan and Philip didn't count. They were allowed to stay, which only made Brody feel a bit more surly.

Number one at being rudely woke up and number two — banishment.

Not once in his life had Brody ever claimed to be a morning person. His preferred method of greeting the day was Cassie next to him in bed. Naked was even more preferable, if he had to provide a more exact opinion on it. Just like she'd been a few short minutes ago, before said bride-to-be had barged in. Right when his gorgeous sleepy-eyed sweetheart had been about to slip her hands lower under the sheets.

With all that taken into the equation, a man had a right to take a few minutes to be surly and wish like hell for a fucking cup of coffee to help clear the fog out of what passed for his brain this early in the morning with the sun barely past the eight o'clock hour. It was selfish, wanting Cassie as much to himself as he could, but hell, they'd been without each other for so long that Brody couldn't help it. Especially when he was due back in the fucking cold of Iceland in a few days, where there would be no beautiful, warm, willing Cassie in his bed to thaw him out at the end of the day.

Which reminded him — at some point, he needed to ask about the chances of her coming for a visit. Three weeks would be a helluva long time apart.

The scent of coffee hit his nose, and Brody opened bleary eyes that still had trouble focusing. When they did, he saw his naked, grinning woman holding a cup of nirvana and a condom. Or was it reverse — a cup of coffee with nirvana holding it?

"Hi, handsome. Need some help waking up?"

"Praise the sweet heavens above."

He took the mug and drained half without even stopping. Relishing the snap of his brain cells reconnecting again, Brody set the cup on the handy shower ledge and reached out for his next gift. *Cassie.* So wet and warm.

Brody sank into a morning kiss that woke up the rest of his body like a forest fire. After turning her backside to him and pouring soap into his hands, he bent toward a much more pleasurable task than getting thrown out of bed.

Leaning down to explore the line of Cassie's neck, he said, "I do adore your friend, but, baby, her timing sucked."

Cassie moaned at the hands pretending to clean her and reached up to wrap her arms around Brody's neck so she could arch into him better. The soap slithered and slid over her front while the hard planes of his chest and arms rubbed at her backside, surrounding her. His arousal brushed heavy and thick against her, resulting in a sound of complete agreement with Brody's comment. But a girl couldn't complain. Not on such a beautiful day full of love and magic. Magic that may not have included sex in bed, but now looked as if shower sex was a given.

Brody's fingers dove deeper and his mouth found hers. An echoing groan vibrated out of his tall form when he felt how the inside was as soft and wet as the outside. Turning her to face him, his hands cupped her backside and lifted her high. More than eager, Cassie wrapped around him, locked her lips on his, and gasped when he didn't bother to tease — he just slid inside in one earth-shattering thrust. So huge, hard and so very, very deep. Her head lolled weakly at the wave of pleasure as Brody held her before his movements began. Lifting her hands above her head, he pinned them there with one hand. Braced against the wall, he thrust into her slowly. The feel of him sliding all the way out and back in pulled a deep hiss of pleasure from both of them with each move.

"Heaven, Cassie." He panted against her mouth before his tongue met hers. "You're pure heaven, baby. When I'm back in Iceland, this… this is what I'm thinking of."

Cassie was short of breath too. Flickers of her upcoming

trip to Toronto sneaked in. Yes! She would use this moment to stay warm. So hot, she all but turned the water hitting her skin to steam. She didn't know how the bathroom wasn't already a sauna with how Brody felt against her, branding her outside and in. Building and building until he let go of her hands so she could hold on as he took her over the edge.

"Brody!"

All she saw was him. The look of pleasure on his face matched hers as he watched her go over that edge, then a primal groan ripped out of him. Brody buried his head in her neck and poured everything he had inside her.

Music, along with the scents of lavender and eucalyptus, filled the air. Cassie was a blissed out mess, except this time it wasn't because of the hands of her lover but a masseuse named Trina, whose lovely lilting Filipino accent was just as healing as her hands. Trina and her partner, whom Anna had flown in special from Atlanta, were here to make sure the bride was well and truly relaxed for the day of her wedding. After they were done with this, they were moving on to hydrating facial masks, manicures, and pedicures. Lunch would be followed by more relaxation/girl time, and this evening, Anna was leading the women who had traveled to The Island to celebrate their special day in a night of spiritual centering and yoga.

All Cassie had to do on the day of the wedding was keep Chase's mom a bit distracted, get herself dressed, and assist her friend in doing the same.

Cassie drifted along with the hands smoothing away all

the knots from her body. Not that there were many left. Over the past day or two, Brody's nurturing side had kept Cassie pampered and relaxed. He was just as good at massages as Trina, but Brody's idea of a massage included the use of his mouth, hands, and body. She sighed and welcomed the wave of desire as she remembered what he loved massaging most with his tongue. She couldn't wait to see him again tomorrow.

"I heard that. You're not relaxing," Anna murmured on the table next to her.

"Am too. Was thinking of having Brody do this to me soon. I feel amazing, Trina."

"You're very welcome. The tightness is much better than a few weeks ago when I worked on you."

Anna, ever helpful, supplied the answer. "That's because she found her love again. They're so happy together, the two of them are all but glowing with it."

"So says the bride," Cassie said with a giggle. "Could have lit up a third world country this morning the way you looked when you walked in and kicked Brody out." She blew a stray strand of hair out of her face. "Did we really have to throw him out?"

Truly, she had no complaints as she'd felt the need to make it up to him. Every bit of her still felt loose and joyous from their shower play. Even if Brody had had to hurry off afterward instead of snuggling her close as they both loved.

"Yes! He's to keep Chase occupied down in the village. Man day of sailing and fishing or whatever they've come up with. Then tomorrow, they're getting ready with the rest of the family. Doing their pictures before coming up for the ceremony."

Cassie knew all these details by heart but also knew it gave Anna pleasure to talk about it all. Trina asked Cassie to flip over and lay on her back then tucked the sheet around her so the muscles of her neck and shoulders could be worked on next. That section of her body was always the worst. Stress made its personal mission to lodge there and create boulders of rock-hard tightness.

Trina spoke low for Cassie to hear. "Much better this area too. Love is good for you. It's good to know you have your other half. The one you can be with truly."

Cassie's lips twisted in a smile. How could she not be better? Every bit of her felt like a piece of cotton floating in the wind after being reunited with her other half. They had spent the time between physical escapades, both deeply grateful for the rain, just talking and reconnecting in other ways.

It was absolutely true what Trina said about that sense of knowing.

The joy that came from Brody's hand holding hers or the warmth of his emerald eyes lingering on Cassie when she was in a room with him.

The rightness of simply being held and knowing that no matter what, Brody would keep her safe and shielded when she wanted to be and, more importantly, was still strong enough to walk at her side. That he wasn't intimidated by her strength and what Cassie chose to do but was proud of it as well.

Their future might be a little unplanned, but for once, she could just let it be. The details didn't need to be laid out to the tenth degree of knowing. At some point, Cassie figured the rest would fall into place. She had no doubt Brody was serious about being with her, and she hoped with all her heart that sometime in the future, they would talk about maybe having a baby again. Someday, her body would be healed enough to try again.

More than anything, Cassie, who had never seen another man in her future after her divorce much less children there in it, knew with every cell of her being that she wanted that future with Brody. They could have it all together — marriage, kids, career — but most of all, they would have each other. As Brody had said, they would figure it out together.

Chapter 39

Anna twisted to look in the mirror and surveyed what the hair and makeup wizards had accomplished. The duo had been recommended by Chase — they worked on one of the series he produced. Cassie stood behind her, fastening the last of the hooks on Anna's wedding dress, then she stepped aside and fluffed out the small flare of train. It was fitting that only Cassie and she were there for the final steps, except for the photographer capturing the moments. Every perfect beautiful moment Anna would try to remember always, just like the words in the letter Chase had slipped under her door early that day. She'd wept as she read it.

"You're all done, my sister," Cassie said. "And may I say, you're a complete vision. This color on you is surreal and the rest… I can't even find the words. You're just so beautiful."

Anna felt beautiful. Cassie's idea for her hair had turned out to be perfect. Small native flowers were woven into the wavy texture, which was similar to Anna's natural everyday look but bumped up a few notches. Her dress fit like a dream, and the woven copper jewelry glistening at her wrists and neck matched the shoes that graced her feet. The ones that would carry her down the aisle to the man she loved.

And Cassie was another vision. Anna gave herself an imaginary pat on the back. The white was an absolute showstopper, especially with the way the island sun had turned Cassie's natural creamy skin into the faintest of golden tans enhanced by the radiant glow of completeness Brody had brought back to her. Cassie hadn't needed makeup to cover up any fatigue after all. Love, it turned out, created its own special blend of magic, light, and most especially, healing.

The makeup team had swept Cassie's red hair to the side so it could tumble over her shoulder in soft curls, making her hazel eyes even more huge and mysterious. Copper wrist bangles jingled in a musical feast of sound every time she moved, and a pendant of amber calcite dangled on a slim copper chain.

Cassie picked up the bride's bouquet and brought it back to Anna. "Now the bride is ready."

"She's more than ready. How about you?"

"I am." Cassie hesitated and took Anna's hand. "Thank you."

"For what? I should be thanking you for all you've done."

"For giving Brody and me a chance to find each other again. I never did thank you for that. I was so mad at you and Chase for picking this place to get married. But if you hadn't, the two of us would have never had a chance to be together again."

"I don't believe that. Not for a minute. You two were always meant to be," Anna argued sincerely. "To think we met them both at the same time. A chance twist of fate."

"It was. The best twist of all." Cassie carefully held her close. "Thank you, most of all, for helping me heal when I couldn't find a way. I would still be lost without you and Nathan. Brody and I would still be lost. You both helped me to start the path back."

Anna held her tightly right back in the kind of embrace

that only comes from long years of friendship and sister-hood. Who cared if they weren't related by blood? When you had a sister of the heart, that was as real as it got. The photographer captured the moment for all time.

"You're so very welcome." Moisture welled up in Anna's eyes, threatening to ruin her perfect makeup. "Now stop. You're going to make me cry, and I'll be crying soon enough during my vows."

"I'm gonna ask Cassie to marry me," Brody said, button-ing up the vest before he rolled up the sleeves of his shirt.

Chase stopped finger combing and checking his hair in the mirror. One eyebrow lifted in surprise at the state-ment. "You're doing what, man?"

"Cassie." Brody tossed him a nod and a grin. "I'm gonna marry her. Soon as she says yes, that is."

"Seriously? That's awesome. When you going to ask her?"

"Haven't decided yet. I'll know when it's right. You gonna stand beside me for the big day? You're the only man I can think of for the job," Brody asked.

"You don't even have to ask. Good to see you back and in charge again. You're happy. That's all that was needed."

"I am. Cassie makes it all worthwhile. She's at the heart of it."

"Just like Anna is for me. Thanks for being here. Goes ditto, you know. No one else I can imagine being here while I take the biggest step of my life." Chase pulled him into a one-armed hug. "Let's get up to the house. I'm ready to go get my bride."

Brody followed Chase out to the car. When the hell was

he going to ask Cassie? Now that that question had been asked, it was stuck in his head. The ring was already set — he'd found one for Cassie before everything had fallen apart for them. It had traveled everywhere he had, stashed in a secret pocket of his carry-on. Brody had never been able to part with it, for whatever reason, and every time he'd pulled it out to get rid of it, Cassie's face would come back to him, along with all the memories of her — good and bad.

The only part he did know was that he wanted to propose soon, and he wanted it to be perfect. If he didn't do it in the few days left before he returned to Iceland, asking Cassie would have to wait until the retakes were done.

The thought of waiting a month to ask seemed way too damn long.

Chapter 40

Truly a scene from a Hollywood movie made especially for a happy ending, Nathan thought, looking outside at the ceremony setup. It was absolutely perfect for someone marrying a producer. Chase and Anna's dream wedding had come to life and lay before them.

Flowers that were simple but full of elegant whimsy graced the patio, spilling out of decorative urns. They had appeared over the day, brought in by a magical team of wedding assistant fairies. White chairs for the lucky few guests were set up in short rows. On either side of where the couple would get married sat two gigantic planters filled with more of the same whimsical flowers. Tall clear glass hurricanes with vibrant orange pillar candles were already lit and glowing softly in the late afternoon light. The surrounding view said it all in the pristine sparkling blue water which undulated with the whisper of a caress from the wind. Even the late-day sun shone perfectly to bless the day. Music drifted through the air while guests entered and found their seats.

After kissing his own love good-bye, Nathan went to find the two other women that held his heart.

"Are we ready yet? Where's my bride-to-be?" Sticking his head inside the dressing room/bedroom, Nathan caught his reflection. He was pleased with the creamy linen suit and light blue shirt he and Anna had agreed upon. That perfect shade of blue matched his eyes. After all, you only got to escort the bride once.

Anna eagerly came around the corner. "I'm right here. Is he here yet?"

"Oh my God." Nathan took a moment to blow out a breath. Was there anything more perfect than a bride waiting for her moment? "Sweetie pie, you look so wonderful. I'm still overwhelmed you asked me to walk you down the aisle. You have no idea how much it means. Yes, to answer your question. Just saw the groom. Chase looks wonderful as well. His mom is fixing his boutonniere and trying not to fall into hysterics. Never have I seen a more emotional woman in my life. Feel like I need to follow her around with a mop." Then Nathan turned and saw Cassie. A hand flew to his heart with an equally overwhelmed expression. "Cassie, my word! You are a jewel too."

He'd have given anything at that moment to have Philip there to hold him. His best friend from forever was back, and Nathan could tell that every bit of her sunny light and sparkle had returned, healthy and whole. The maid of honor packaging was incredible, but the look in Cassie's eyes said it all. She was happy all the way to her soul. First chance he got, Nathan was going to plant a huge one on Brody Miller.

Walking over, he took Cassie's hands and kissed them in friendship. "I couldn't be more happy for you." A bit more loudly, he said, "Anna, you outdid yourself once again. This is a stunner. And yes, before you ask, Brody is out there too. Twice as handsome, if that's at all possible and looking just as nervous as Chase for some reason."

The idea of that left Cassie amused. She couldn't remember ever seeing her wonderful man nervous over anything. Brody was fun, self-assured, confident, and a really sloppy, goofy drunk on the rare times he went that far. He leaned toward arrogant, overbearing, and certainly overprotective, but that was only when he was making sure he took care of her. He was more caring and gentle than probably even he realized.

Brody had become her hero in every way that mattered, but she couldn't remember him ever being nervous about anything.

Cassie peeked out of the bedroom window one more time. Not just to look for Brody, she told herself, but to check out the whole scene that was unfolding and enjoy the fact that she was here and whole enough to enjoy every single exquisite minute of it.

"Maybe he was making sure he had the ring," she teased.

Just then, there was a knock at the door. The wedding planner poked her head in to announce it was time. Anna squealed and quickly fanned her face before she came over to take Cassie's hand. For a moment, the two of them just stood there looking at each other, a mixture of smiles, tenderness, and both blinking back tears. Anna shifted to loop an arm around Nathan, and the three of them stood there in a hug of love and friendship.

Nathan straightened with a deep breath. "I refuse to cry until after the ceremony or during. Right now, it's just going to ruin your makeup."

He held out an arm to the bride, and Anna practically dragged him out the door, Cassie giggling behind them as they walked down the hallway that opened into the living room where Cassie, Anna, and Nathan took their places by the patio doors. Cassie could hear the faint change of the music to what Anna had picked out for them to walk down the aisle, and the guests all shifted to look backward.

Anna's twin nieces stepped out, carrying their baskets, to the *ohs* and *awws* of the small crowd. Cassie saw Brody standing a head above Chase, so tall and handsome, and the crazy notion erupted that she wished she was walking, in this moment, to him and only him — to say I do. Then the wedding planner gave the signal and Cassie stepped out.

Brody stood next to Chase as he'd been directed, wishing fervently that he'd been able to get past the Nazi disguised as a wedding planner who had barred him from sneaking in to see Cassie. Not that he hadn't enjoyed spending time with his best friend, brothers, and a few friends, but he'd really wanted to see her before everything got started.

He laughed at the antics of the little girls hamming it up as they tossed their petals down the aisle, then he heard the crowd sigh as one. When he lifted his gaze, his heart literally stopped for one breathless moment then kicked up and raced as if he'd run a marathon.

Cassie. She walked toward him, and the world simply fell away. Brody had never seen her in formal attire or had the chance to take her to a red carpet premiere. She was, in a word, extraordinary. Some strapless gauzy breeze of a dress floated around her all the way to the floor, encasing her petite form. That firestorm of hair fell in teasing curls around her face. Whoever had done their makeup should win an award, because all he could see was elfin eyes played up in shimmery copper and golden highlights.

Brody knew he was smiling from ear to ear like a fool in love and didn't even bother to try to hide it.

Cassie's eyes found his, and her smile bloomed a bit bigger and warmer so that Brody knew that she was smiling only at him. That's when it hit like a sledgehammer, out of the blue.

Today. Right now. This instant. This was the right time to ask her. No other time would be more perfect.

His smile and look of appreciation in return said it all as Cassie stepped to the side to wait for the bride.

Chapter 41

Anna practically floated down the walkway on Nathan's arm before she was handed off to Chase. The groom looked as if he could be knocked over with a feather, he was so enraptured with his bride. They turned as one to the minister to take their vows.

Cassie stood witness as the wind of the island and sea teased and lifted the edges of Anna's hair, making it float like magic. The pulsing rhythm of the water below mingled with the soft romantic tones played by the acoustic guitarist who had taken over from the band. Words were spoken by the minister of love, hope, new beginnings, and commitment.

Cassie took her eyes off the bride and groom only to find herself caught in Brody's emerald green gaze, and her breath hitched at the intensity in his eyes. Then Brody gave her the kind of smile that lifted at one corner and left it a bit lopsided. Those handsome eyes crinkled at the edges as he looked at her — the two of them seeing no one else as the words flowed around them and Cassie realized Brody was thinking of her and him together, with those words of love and forever being their own.

In that single moment, love swelled and swirled inside Cassie, blooming like the flowers around them, vibrant and strong.

Hands tightening on the bouquet she held, Cassie's smile bloomed in return. A silent yes between them. A yes to forever with Brody.

Chase nudged Brody's arm, breaking the spell and pulling him back to the ceremony. Brody chuckled and shook his head as an apology before reaching into his pocket for the rings. Anna handed off her bouquet to Cassie.

Chase turned back to Anna and, with the words of forever, slipped the ring over her finger to the sighs of everyone present. Then the moment was repeated as Anna did the same for Chase. The minister announced them as officially husband and wife, and Chase's smile reminded Cassie of a kid's in a candy shop before he pulled his bride to him and took her in a kiss that ended in a dip. When he stood Anna back on her feet, she was blushing and staggering to the applause of everyone present before they walked down the aisle.

Cassie stepped forward, and Brody met her, grinning ear to ear.

"Hello, gorgeous." Brody held out his arm for her to take and bent closer to her ear. "You're a vision in white. My heart stopped when I saw you."

Beaming, Cassie looped her arm around his and kissed him on the cheek. "Hello yourself, handsome. You look pretty amazing as well."

He did. The crisp light blue shirt was the perfect contrast to the light grey of his pants and vest. He looked relaxed and casual.

Brody walked her down the aisle to where the bride and groom stood, ready to celebrate with their friends and family. Before the onslaught of well-wishers could catch up, Brody took a moment to slide an arm around her waist and pull her into a tender kiss.

"I missed you, baby. Sleep well without me?" Brody cupped her chin and brushed his lips to hers again.

Cassie stroked the silk of his beard. "I did. I wore one of your shirts that smelled like you so I could feel your arms around me all night."

Brody looked about to say something more when the photographer appeared to do some formal shots with the wedding party and family.

From then on, Cassie was kept busy entertaining guests and family and making sure to keep up with the coordinator's schedule for the evening ahead. At some point, she lost sight of Brody in the crowd and wondered where he had disappeared to.

Tables were brought out and chairs moved around for dinner. Brody reappeared right before they were due to sit down at Cassie's side, his eyes holding nothing but mischief.

She tugged at his vest to bring him down for a kiss. "Where have you been?"

"Taking care of something." His wink let Cassie know his lips were sealed.

"Fine, keep your secrets. I'll get them out of you eventually."

She certainly would, Brody thought. He'd set the stage, and all he had to do was bring in the two main characters — himself and Cassie. First though, he had a speech to give. After leading her to the head table, Brody pulled out her chair and helped her sit. The scent of his woman drifted up in the night. That perfect scent of flowers mixed in with the sea air made him pause to take a deep breath before picking up the glass of champagne that rested at his place setting.

Tapping a fork to it, he waited until the gathering of family and friends fell silent.

"Everyone, on behalf of Chase and Anna, I want to welcome you tonight and thank you for coming. Let's take a moment here to congratulate this beautiful couple."

Applause broke out, and Brody waited for it to calm down.

"Chase and I, we've known each other longer than..." He shook his head and laughed. "Well, if you really want to know how long, just ask our moms. I'm sure they would be happy to whip out some pictures of us. I have three official brothers, but Chase"—Brody tipped his head toward his best friend—"you are the fourth one. Without a doubt, we've shared every single thing in this world together over the years, from toys, bikes, and video games to cars and all sorts of mischief. Even went off to the Big Apple together and wound up working together."

Chase looked at him as their unbreakable bond passed between them in silent understanding.

"I have to say all of that was great, but the best thing we've shared together so far was meeting these two incredible women on the same night. Who would have ever known that you and Anna would walk out of that and come to be married." He looked at the woman next to him and brought her hand to his lips. "And Cassie here, taking a chance with me, to fall in love as well."

The love of his life took a shaky deep breath and brought a hand to her mouth at the unexpected declaration.

"You and Anna are amazing together. She's an incredible woman in every way that matters. She grounds you and brings you out of all the chaos of our creative world, and I think, if I'm not mistaken, you do the same for her." Anna and Chase looked at each other with love, and Brody knew he'd found the right thing to say. "Brother, I wish you and Anna many, many years of happiness and blessings, and I'm looking forward to sharing them all with you."

Raising his glass, Brody toasted them both to the cheers that followed, and Chase stood up to hug him.

"Jeez, brother, that was one hell of a speech," Chase said.

Anna cut in to pull Brody in for a smacking kiss of happiness, all but gushing in her enthusiasm. "You are the sweetest man in the world. Every word of that was so beautiful. I'm a wreck thanks to you." After kissing him again, Anna waved a hand in front of her face before sitting down again.

Brody took his seat next to Cassie, enjoying one of the best rewards of his life when she wrapped him in a hug and a kiss of her own.

"That was so beautiful. I love you so much," she said.

"I love you too. Think I nailed it, huh?" He grinned, sharing the moment with her.

"It was perfect. I hope it was all filmed so I can watch it again later."

Dinner plates were set down before them, and Brody speared a bite off his plate to lift to Cassie's lips. "Let's eat. Then I want to dance with my baby all night long."

"That's a deal if I ever heard one." Cassie laughed, mirroring the gesture from her own plate.

Dinner lasted forever, it seemed, especially when a man had to follow a speech with probably the most important one of his life. Even so, Brody took the time to savor the moment and the buildup, the taste of the food, their friends celebrating their own fortune, family surrounding them, and relaxing in the joy of the evening. Brody savored the light in

Cassie and the sparkle in her eyes. Most of all, he enjoyed how healthy and happy she looked and knowing he had helped get her there.

Turning back from something said to Anna, Cassie caught his collar and drew him in for a slow, sweet kiss that tasted of champagne and smelled of flowers. All he could do was hold her, his light and gift in this world. The moment hit him like a ton of bricks, and Brody knew he couldn't wait any longer.

Standing, he drew her to her feet. "Come with me?"

"Where are we going? Dinner isn't over yet."

She giggled as he tugged her around the tables and away from the crowd. Brody wanted Cassie all to himself for just a few minutes.

Chase and Anna watched them go. The groom leaned over to whisper something in her ear, and Anna's face went flat with shock then bloomed in wide-eyed astonishment.

Chapter 42

Brody was pulling her along with secrets in his eyes and mischief written all over him. Cassie knew her man well, and he was definitely up to something — in the middle of the reception. Plus he'd been nervous, as Nathan had said, off and on throughout the whole night.

Her hand curled into his, letting the strength engulf her. Brody walked with her close to his side, their bodies brushing, until they rounded the corner to their special place and Cassie stopped in disbelief. Her jaw dropped open in amazement, and her hands flew to her mouth on a gasp at the surprise waiting.

The patio had been scattered with glass hurricanes filled with candles, and flowers were scattered at random across the sofas and ground. Pitchers of the same flowers had been added to all of the tables. Their delicate fragrance mixed with the sea air.

Cassie turned toward him. "Brody, what's all this?"

Brody only took her hand and kept moving until they stood in the center. He took another second to look around before drawing her closer, looking at her with a love that was wide and open.

"This? This is our special place. Our secret sanctuary, where we came in the beginning to relax and be alone together. We fell in love here once, and it's where we found each other again, after all that time apart, and began to heal. We fell in love here again."

She couldn't think, she was so overwhelmed with his words and the heartfelt meaning behind them. Everything Brody said was the truth, and Cassie could only try not to cry as he gave her that magic smile that brought joy to so many onscreen.

"I thought I'd be really nervous about this, but I'm not," he said.

Her hand in his, the entire world shifted on its axis when Brody kissed her, a soft caress meant only for Cassie, then he bent down on one knee and lifted a box out of his pocket. She couldn't stop the tears that started to flow when she saw the look on Brody's face as he opened that small box to the promise laying within.

"Cassidy, my sweet Cassie, I've only been in love once in this lifetime, and that's with you. You are the only one in the world for me. You're my light and my home. The one who makes everything magic in so many ways. Marry me? Let me be that same light and home for you too. Spend forever with me?"

Her voice stuck for a moment through the tears, caught on that same love that flowed through her — higher and brighter than ever before.

This man. Her everything in every way.

They'd lost it all together and had found each other again. Their love had brought her back to her true north home again. A home that was Brody.

All Cassie could do was nod, tears of happiness sliding out.

Brody smiled at her. "Is that a yes, baby?"

"Yes," she choked. "Yes, I'll marry you, Brody Miller. You wonderful, incredible man."

"Let's get this on you, sweetheart. I've been holding onto it for a very long time."

Cassie didn't think she could take another shock, but that revelation shook her. Brody had wanted forever with her — even from the start.

"This represents the light you are to me," he said, sliding the symbol of his promise onto her finger.

A ring of miraculous gold twists locked into an antique setting for a channel-cut amber topaz. Tiny diamonds were scattered along the edges of the setting like sunbursts, unique and exquisitely crafted.

Bending, Cassie brought her lips to his. Everything in her melted at the way he held her close to cherish the moment. "It's incredible. So beautiful and perfect, but wanting me to be with you forever is the most precious gift you've ever given me."

Brody rose to his feet and held her close as he traced her face as if memorizing this moment. "I love you so much. We're going to make a helluva life together."

Wrapping an arm around her waist, Brody drew her up higher to lay his lips on hers. A kiss of forever that held nothing but magic mixed with the moonlight sparkling above them.

Bending, he lifted Cassie into his arms. "Is a month from now too soon? I've waited forever to be with you, gorgeous."

So soon! The joyous insanity of it wrapped around her wild and free. There was only one right answer.

"A month sounds perfect. I can't wait!"

Brody spun her around so she was left clinging to him and laughing.

"We'd better get back to the celebration. They might be missing us by now," she said.

"We probably should." Reluctance was written all over Brody's face, and Cassie giggled as he carried her back. "We can tell everyone tomorrow about our big news. Tonight is for Chase and Anna."

"Agreed." She sighed happily.

"You know, I'm gonna buy this house for us."

"You are not!"

Brody stopped. His eyes, dead certain, met hers as he gave her a confident grin that said he would not be denied. "I sure enough am. Then I can bring my sweet little mermaid here to swim. How about we get married here, Cassie? In our place?"

She gasped at the idea. The loveliness of it bloomed inside her, taking root deep, strong, and sure. There was no other place that would be right for them. Smiling wide at the idea, Cassie pressed her lips to his and traced the face that was hers forever. "I say that sounds just about perfect. You're my home. Wherever we are together in this world and the next is perfect, as long as I'm with you."

"Let's go celebrate then."

Carrying her back to the party, Brody and Cassie walked into a crowd that stood waiting for them with glasses held high.

Epilogue

ONE AND A HALF YEARS LATER

Brody Miller, award-winning actor and award winner on both film, TV and stage stood shaking and as unsteady as he'd ever been in his life. A tiny bundle was handed first into one arm, then another second tiny bundle was placed in the other by the nurse. A mile-wide smile of epically shocked amazement split his face. Brody thought he might burst with pride and joy.

Twins! Who would have ever thought?

His two sons lay in his arms, chubby-faced, angelic, and swaddled with blankets. Little caps covered heads already crowned with a bit of dark hair to match his own. Both looked at him as though he held the answers to the universe and beyond. He could already tell they were the smartest things about to take over the planet.

"You're keeping them all to yourself already," Cassie teased from the bed.

Brody looked at her, still smiling like an idiot. His beautiful Cassie, her hair tied in a messy ponytail and looking tired but happy, smiling back at him. A miracle of a woman if there ever was one. She'd sailed through this pregnancy, after the first trimester of sickness, like a champ, amazing even the doctor by carrying the boys to full term. A rare thing with twins, he'd been told. Brody had almost passed out after the delivery the day before.

Two boys — they had waited to be surprised by their genders.

"Can't help it, gorgeous. They sure are something." Carrying them to the bed, Brody set one wide-eyed boy in Cassie's waiting arms, lay down next to her with the other, and put an arm around her to snuggle her close. His head was close to hers so he could kiss the light of his life. "I love you. We made something beautiful together here, baby."

"We sure did." Her hand took his and laced their fingers together. "Our home is a little bigger now."

His thumb rubbed the ring on her finger. His promise to her for forever. Brody pressed a tender kiss to her lips. "It is. My perfect home, always, with you by my side."

The End

Acknowledgements

It takes a soul searching journey to arrive at the point in your life where you are ready to stand in your truth and pursue a dream that you held secret all your life — to finally put words to paper. I am beyond blessed to have and hold onto a life that surrounds me with fellow light bringers (my word for creatives, healers, and, overall, inspiring people).

For my Mom, Sister and Dad — I love all of you so much and am so glad that we are family together and especially my mom, whose grace, strength and giving heart is always there for us and everyone whose life she touches.

For Amy - What would a girl do without her best friend in the world. You always stand with a ready ear and are strong enough to call me out when I start to slip. If ever there was a sister of the heart, you are it.

For Gina — my dear friend and creative sister. My life truly started to change the day we connected.

For Angela, Nicole, Debbie and my entire MORWA family. You are my writing tribe and critique partners. Thank you for embracing a newbie to this wonderful world, having my back and helping with endless questions. You all are amazing and I wish you huge huge success.

For Joy Editing and Cassie Cox, my editor, who took a story full of love and healing and polished it like a diamond. You challenged me to go deeper and make this all it could be. My writing is better because of you.

Lastly, it may sound self-indulgent but I also have to give thanks and honor myself for, at long last, taking a stand to chase a dream and acknowledging what my inner soul, inner spirit and inner child what being called to do — to write romance stories of heart, heroes and, of course, heat. Outside of being a mom, I've never been happier than when I am channeling the next amazing character, scene, or idea into words.

About the Author

Mia Silverton is a St. Louis born, contemporary women's fiction and romance author. As a writer, she feels called to help change lives in a different way — by crafting dynamic stories. She promises to bring worlds full of strong characters, witty fun dialogue filled with heroes and heat.

She strongly believes that we can all find happiness, sanctuary and even healing in a beautifully written book. Many times in the past, a well crafted phrase, word or story created a shift in her when the time was needed and she feels called to pay that forward.

Mia loves to interact with her readers and you can connect with her on FB, Instagram, Twitter or visit at www.miasilverton.com. Make sure to stay up to date with the latest and greatest news by joining Mia's Silver Pen Tribe on her website.

Twitter & Instagram: @miamsilverton
Facebook: /mia.silverton.5

Coming Soon October 2017

THE REBOUND PROJECT

After being left in tears weeks before her wedding, Kelsey Channing's only goal was survival. Survival meant paying her debts—by working multiple jobs if necessary—and keeping her professional dream alive. Kelsey was not—repeat not—looking for a rebound to mend her broken heart, no matter how often her friends said that was a solid plan.

Screenwriter Cade Grinner's new farm came with a home to rehab, peace and quiet from his ex from hell, and a chance to get over his damaged pride. Unfortunately, since saying yes to hiring Dr. Kelsey Channing, it also came with a hot housekeeper who flipped his world upside down every time he saw her.

Then one joking comment sparked a new kind of interest, the start of a journey to heal themselves, and a crazy project outline that may or may not get them in trouble

∽